PRAIRIE FIRE

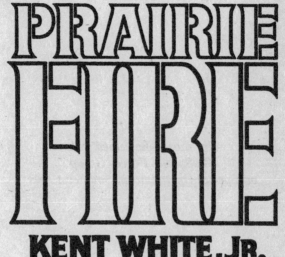

PRAIRIE FIRE

KENT WHITE, Jr.

BART

NEW YORK

For those who served with
5th Special Forces Group
on Special Operations in Southeast Asia

Copyright © 1983 by Kent White, Jr.

Reprinted by arrangement with Daring Books

ISBN: 1-55785-062-3

First Bart Books edition: October 1988

Bart Books
155 E. 34th Street
New York, New York 10016

Manufactured in the United States of America

I

Fifteen kilometers outside town, the pilot of the Huey UH-1B suddenly banked the helicopter hard to the north to follow three Vietnamese peasants running ankle deep in rice paddy muck. He swooped down within fifty meters of the men and followed them to a tree line.

Caught up in the chase, the pilot failed to notice the bright flash from the window of a small, ramshackle hut to the left of the peasants. An inexpertly fired RPG-7 rocket spun erratically toward the helicopter, missing the cockpit by less than two hundred meters.

Instinctively, the door gunner snapped back the slide bolt on the M-60 machine gun. He quickly released it and fired on the men who had cunningly tried to lure the chopper and the crew into their destructive trap. The two nearest the trees struggled to stay on their feet as chunks of flesh and bone tore from their skinny limbs.

Sergeant Steve McShane curiously poked his head out of the open doorway of the Huey to watch. The third Vietnamese was performing an imperfect swan dive as a score of 7.62mm rounds slammed into his back, lifting small brown puffs of dust off his ragged white shirt.

The pilot allowed his gunners the pleasure of spraying the shack with several hundred more bullets. Then a secondary explosion from inside burst the walls of the building outwards, tossing four occupants through the roof like discarded Raggedy Ann dolls. Grinning, he swung the helicopter back around toward Da Nang.

They were now safely inside the city, flying low over the rows of hootches clustered along the western edge of Da Nang. The curly, redheaded door gunner relaxed his grip on the handle of the machine gun and swiveled the barrel downwards. He settled back into his canvas seat and sighed.

McShane leaned closer to the doorway and smiled. They were approaching the Special Forces FOB (Forward Operational Base). The gunner reached into the left pocket of his baggy jungle fatigue pants and pulled out a crumpled pack of non-filtered Camels. He offered one to the lanky, blond sergeant sitting to his right.

Pulling one from the pack, McShane studied the cigarette. He started to light the end of the twisted, crescent-shaped Camel but hesitated. Somewhat reluctantly, he flicked the cigarette out the door, remembering that he had quit his fifteen-year habit in the hospital. Thanking the puzzled gunner, McShane abruptly turned his attention to the FOB compound below. It looked even better than before, he thought.

Nearly three months ago, a commando team of VC sappers had slipped under cover of the black moonless sky into the still, warm waters of the South China Sea from their rickety fishing boat. Over a half mile from shore, the sappers had clung to their black market-purchased styrofoam rafts and had quietly paddled toward the tiny twinkling lights of the FOB.

An hour later, the VC abandoned the rafts on the beach and crept stealthily over the low sand dunes lining the beach between the bay and the concertina wire that wrapped the Special Forces camp in security. Each carried a pair of small canvas bags crammed with plastic explosives and bits of scrap metal.

Since the bay had always been considered an unlikely avenue of attack, there had never been any reason to post guards on that side of the camp. For the sappers, it was simply a matter of clipping the concertina with wire cutters, slipping undetected into the shadows of the barracks that dotted the compound, and hurtling the charges through open doorways and windows.

It was hard for McShane to believe, peering out over the FOB, that just a few months ago the camp had been the scene of such shattering destruction and death.

Two men standing on the outer edge of the concrete heli-pad shielded their eyes against floating particles of sand whipped up by the backwash from the Huey's rotors. McShane smiled. It had been a long time since he had seen his two close friends. As the chopper landed on the heli-pad, rocking gently, he grabbed the small, battered Samsonite suitcase he had carried on his three tours to Viet Nam, and an olive green duffel bag. He stepped out onto the concrete.

"Steve!" shouted the first man to approach, adjusting his beret. "Damn, it's good to see you! The way you looked last August I thought you'd probably retire in that damn hospital. You were a mess. But you're lookin' good now!"

"Damn right I look good," replied McShane, peeling a flake of skin from his sunburned nose. "Gonna take more than a slope sapper to put me under."

As McShane spoke, he studied his friend's puffy red-rimmed eyes. "You look terrible, Chris. I can see you haven't changed much."

Chris Dean was one of the FOB medics. He was a few

11

years younger than McShane, and heavier. He wore his black hair clipped short. Raised on a Navajo reservation in Arizona, he had joined the Army after flunking out of the local community college and then volunteered for Special Forces.

"So how the hell are you, Chris?" McShane demanded.

The chubby Indian grinned, "Still the same. Haven't gotten laid in weeks. Guess that's my fault. The last bitch gave me the clap so bad, I spent two weeks givin' myself penicillin shots."

"That must have been something to see," McShane chuckled. "You humped over in front of a mirror, jabbing yourself in that fat brown ass."

He took a few steps forward to help his other friend unload a box of medical supplies from the chopper. "Hi, Ron. How have you been?"

Ron Engals, a tall medic with sun-bleached blond hair, took McShane's hand and shook it vigorously. "Same as my Indian buddy. Except a lot more careful who I sleep with."

They all laughed and then turned from the sudden blast of hot air from the Huey's rotors as the craft lifted off. The door gunner waved to McShane.

"Let's go to the club for a beer," Dean suggested as he held on to his beret. "It's too damn hot out here."

Nodding agreement, McShane and Engals followed Dean down the wooden walk that zig-zagged over the sand. They laughingly hashed over old times as they strolled leisurely to the club at the eastern end of the compound. The small, one room club was used exclusively by FOB recon team members and their guests.

Dean opened the door, allowing Engals and then McShane to step into the air-conditioned lounge. It felt good to them. A half dozen tables with five chairs spaced evenly around each were scattered around the room. At the bar stood seven tall stools. The men were the first customers.

"Where the hell is everybody?" Dean asked. "Usually they're trippin' all over each other trying to get a table. The war's not over, is it?"

McShane said quickly, "Hope not. Got to settle a few things with Charlie first."

Sliding his suitcase and duffel bag under the empty table, McShane fell into a chair. Dean and Engals walked up to the bar and ordered three beers from the skinny Vietnamese bartender. The man bent over, pulling three cans from the cooler filled with cracked ice. He opened each with a can opener dangling from a string attached to the cooler.

Grabbing the beers, the two friends walked back to the table. Dean handed McShane one of the icy drinks, then sank into a chair across from him. Engals plopped down next to McShane. They raised their beers in a silent toast and then drank eagerly.

The day had been hot and cloudless as were most days during Vietnam's dry season, McShane thought, or the wet season, or anytime in Vietnam.

Dean interrupted the silence. "How was that hospital in Japan? When we didn't hear from you we thought you'd run off with a Geisha girl." Dean leaned closer to McShane. "By the way, Steve, did you get any of that slant-eyed stuff?"

"Once, but I was so damn sore and stiff from all the operations that I couldn't really get into it."

Rocking back on the legs of their chairs, Dean and Engals laughed at their friend's play on words.

"They dug so much scrap iron out of my legs and arms, you'd have thought I was gonna retire from the Army and start my own salvage business."

Dean, pounding his fist on the table, roared with laughter.

13

"Did they give you a convalescent leave?" Engals asked.

"Yeah, three weeks. So I took a military hop out of Atzugi Air Base to Travis, and then from there another hop to Fort Bragg. Thought I'd check up on the ol' lady. Only got a letter from her once while I was in the hospital."

"Did you get to see her?" Dean wanted to know.

"Well," McShane continued, "she'd moved from our apartment on Branson Street to a rundown old house on Sanbourn Road."

"Why the hell should she move?" interrupted Engals.

"Seems that my ol' lady was shacked up with some damn leg cook. Caught 'em both half undressed; they'd left the front door wide open. I probably would have killed the guy, except he looked so damn pathetic, standing there in blue polka-dot skivvies and yellow and blue argyle socks with his food-stained white cook's shirt on. That cracked me up. She started yellin' at me sayin' I had no right comin' by without phoning first. She was my damn wife. What the hell did she mean, call first? Then she told me she was goin' to divorce me and that's when I turned around and walked right out the front door without ever saying a word to her."

McShane took a swallow from his beer and then continued. "After that I was so damn pissed that I went to the 3rd Group Transportation Officer and asked him to put me on the next flight to Nam. He took a look at my orders and said, 'Hey, Sarge, you've got three weeks of convalescent leave.' I told him I changed my mind, that I had some important business to take care of in Nam. Next morning I was on my way back to Travis. The following evening I was sittin' next to a Pan Am stewardess in the first-class section of a 707 headed for Cam Ranh Bay."

"If it'd been me," Engals said, "I think I would've slugged your ol' lady."

"Not me. I would've kicked that greasy cook square in the nuts," Dean declared.

They all laughed and then finished their beers.

"Hey, Mai!" Engals shouted, waving his empty can of Schlitz. "Bring us three more of the same."

McShane turned to Dean and asked, "What's goin' on with the FOB now? Still runnin' missions across the DMZ?"

"The situation has gotten tough up there. Seems like every time an RT (Recon Team) or ST (Spike Team) is inserted into an area, they bump into a company of NVA (North Vietnamese Army) regulars. I think we're gonna be in a world of shit come Tet."

"Have we lost anyone from the FOB?"

"Yeah, a black guy. Can't remember his name, but the RT he was with was on the way to set up an ambush. Well, they walked right into one that the NVA had set up for some Marines. The poor bastard caught an AK round through his Adam's apple. The two other Americans were hit, too. One of the Cambodian mercenaries got zapped and a couple of others were wounded.

"The wounded radio operator called for an extraction. Then the team leader and the radio operator somehow managed to carry the black guy back to the LZ (Landing Zone). NVA probably would have wasted the whole team, if it wasn't for the fact that they weren't fully into the position for the ambush they were settin' up for the Marines. Hell, thirty more minutes and they'd have shot up the grunts instead of the team. Far as I'm concerned, you can give the whole DMZ to the jarheads."

Mai was standing off to the side of the table, holding a trayload of beers. As soon as Dean stopped talking,

15

she stepped up to the table and placed a can in front of each of the men. A slim, attractive Vietnamese, she wore a light blue Ao Dai, the traditional Vietnamese dress. Reaching over, Dean took her hand and kissed it.

"Be nice," she said, pulling her arm free. "You numba ten G. I." Turning abruptly, she sauntered back to the bar. Dean slapped McShane on the back and winked.

The men sat in the cool comfort of the air-conditioned club for better than an hour, swapping war stories and drinking. Eventually, the talk got around to that night in August. Dean filled in the missing pieces for McShane, telling him the story of the sappers.

Once they had cut through the concertina wire, the sappers struck the east end of the compound. With everybody there asleep, they had no difficulty entering through the main door of the individual ten-man barracks. Charlie Simmons and John Parker, just back from a five-day mission above the DMZ, were the first hit. A two-man sapper team entered their barracks and crept cautiously up the hall that ran its length. Simmons's and Parker's door was the first one on the right. They had left it open, allowing the ocean breezes to cool their stuffy room.

The lead sapper crouched low on his birdlike legs and waddled quietly to the open door. He stood up slowly along the left side of the jamb. The second VC took up position to the right of the door, waiting for the command from his comrade. Silently, the lead VC shifted the satchel from his left to his right hand. Understanding the move as his signal, the second sapper lowered his hand to the bag he was carrying in his left. Together they triggered the ten-second-delay detonator attached to each of the bags of plastic explosives, then slowball pitched them into the silent room.

The first charge landed underneath Parker's bunk. The other fell in the center of the room, between the two bunks. Quietly, the two assassins hurried back down the hall and out the front door into the night, to join their comrades.

The explosives under Parker's bed detonated first. The blast lifted it off the concrete floor with such force that it rammed the steel-framed bunk up into the ceiling, eight feet above. The impact shoved Parker's face into one of the wooden rafters, crushing his head in two.

The twisted O. D. frame fell in a heap near a corner of the room. Bits of blackened mattress lay scattered about. Parker fell to rest on his right side, facing the wall. Plum size holes had been torn through his back and legs from the scraps of metal crammed into the satchels by the sappers' wives. A ragged strip of aluminum from a beer can protruded from the back of his neck.

Before the explosion, Simmons had been asleep on his left side, facing the barracks wall, with his back to Parker. He was holding his pillow over his head with his knees drawn up tight to his stomach.

The blast from underneath Parker's bunk slammed the front of Simmons's body into the wall. He was lucky. The pillow protected his face. He bounced off the wall and onto his back. Confused by the deafening roar of the explosion, he tumbled onto the floor and began crawling aimlessly around the room. He could hear other explosions and small arms fire somewhere outside.

His hands found something on the floor. He started to brush the object aside. Suddenly, there was a second blast from inside the room; he never moved again. It took personnel from the Vietnamese clean-up crew assigned to the U. S. Army Grave Registration detail most of the next day to clean up Simmons's and Parker's room and to gather up all the pieces.

II

House-22 had been built in the late 1940's for a wealthy, French rubber plantation owner and his family in an attractive residential section of Da Nang. The family later sold the plantation and the house and moved back to Paris after the fall of Dien Bien Phu in '54. The house stood vacant for ten years until it was bought in the middle '60s by MACV (Military Assistance Command, Vietnam). It was immediately converted into a safehouse for 5th Special Forces Group personnel assigned to the newly created special projects that operated out of four FOBs in the I Corp, and II Corp areas of South Vietnam. Men enroute to a FOB spent two or three days at the private retreat while they awaited an Air America flight to their particular destination.

The building underwent extensive remodeling when the new owners took over. Upstairs rooms were partitioned off to provide sleeping areas. Three double bunk beds lined the walls of each of the bedrooms. The bathroom was enlarged and a long, low urinal installed for the relief of the beer-drinking green berets. The one small shower and tub was replaced with a much larger, tiled shower stall able to accomodate several men.

The floor plan downstairs remained unchanged. The living room was converted into a game room with a pool table in the center, cue stick racks along the west wall, a chess board in the north corner, and a soft drink and candy machine were located opposite the cue sticks.

A 25 inch RCA color console occupied most of the far corner of the den. Heavily worn, overstuffed sofas and chairs, abandoned by the former owners, were lined up a dozen feet from the TV. A small bar was constructed in the foyer and operated by a civilian clothed ex-recon team sergeant who also filled in as manager and bouncer.

Dean drove the dusty, one-quarter ton jeep past the large, two story off-white plaster, French colonial style home to the rear entrance of the house. He entered the grounds through a rusted, wrought iron gate opened by a Vietnamese guard. An eight foot high stucco wall with bits of broken glass cemented to the top surrounded the property, a precautionary measure instigated by the French landlord to protect his property and family against roving bands of Viet Minh terrorists in the early '50s.

Coming to House-22 had been Dean's idea. After a supper of leathery-tough liver buried under a mound of greasy, limp onions, and served with dry instant mashed potatoes, he had suggested they sign out a jeep from the motor pool and drive to the safehouse for an evening of drinking. "To wash away the bad taste in my mouth," was his reasoning. Of course, neither McShane nor Engals balked at his logic. It was as good a reason as any.

He parked the jeep next to the garage now used as a storeroom. Stepping hurriedly out of the vehicle, the three men hastened up the concrete steps that led to the back porch. They could hear "Purple Haze" playing on the jukebox as they strode through the door into the smoke-laden room. A group of men huddled around the pool table were observing two players. A tall, slender, sandy-haired Sergeant standing among the spectators looked up from the table and stared at the three as they walked across the room.

"Dean!" shouted the Sergeant.

Dean spun around and peered at the group. He picked out the Sergeant waving his arm. "Harper!" he yelled back, grinning. "What the hell you doin' in this den of iniquity?"

Dean, closely followed by his two companions, walked over to Harper. "I'm on my way to the FOB in Kontum. Hey, let me buy you guys a beer and I'll tell you all about it."

They left the crowd at the pool table and walked over to the bar and ordered their drinks and sat down at a table next to the jukebox. "Purple Haze" was playing again.

"Is this thing stuck?" Dean shouted to the bartender. "Got any Hoyt Axton on that damn jukebox?" The bartender shrugged and finished pouring two Seagram-7's for a couple of crusty looking Sergeant-Majors from Phu Bai.

"Oh, yeah," Dean said, suddenly remembering his companions. "John, this is Ron Engals, a medic who works with me at the dispensary. And Steve McShane. He just arrived back in-country today from Zama hospital. Steve got screwed up pretty bad the night the sappers hit the FOB."

Everyone smiled, shook hands and then took a few sips from their beers.

"So what's cookin' in Kontum, John?" Dean asked.

"I've been the one-zero of a Recon Team in Ban Me Thuot the last four or five months. Mostly runnin' missions into Cambodia. My tour was up last month, so I extended for another six months. Just got back from a thirty-day leave in the States.

"Well, while I was in Nha Trang last week, I stopped by 5th Group S-3 (Operations) to bullshit with an ol' intelligence sergeant I once knew with Delta Project, in '66. We had a few beers at the NCO club. He told me that the FOB in Kontum needed experienced recon men. Couple of their teams had walked into a real shit storm in Laos — an A. O. (Area of Operations) they code named Hotel-9. Evidently, this is a real hot area." He stopped for a moment and took a drink.

"The first RT, it seems, stumbled into the defensive perimeter of a Company of NVA Regulars. The team tried to pull back gingerly, but a couple of NVA saw 'em and sounded the alarm. The radio operator was able to call in their position before the shootin' started. When the bastards started firin', it was bad. The two Americans, the one-zero and one-one, were hit right off. The teamleader died on the spot and the radio operator died later at the 5th Evac in Pleiku. The Cambodian mercenaries lost a couple, too. The remaining Cambodes carried the Americans and their own dead back to the LZ, where they set up a hasty defensive perimeter and waited for the choppers. They were extracted about a half hour later."

Harper paused long enough from his war story to drain his beer. He ordered four more from the bartender and then continued. "They bombed the hell out of the place that afternoon and most of the night. 4th Infantry Division Artillery even used the place for target practice. Two days later they sent in another RT to do a body count and assess the damage."

The bartender interrupted, "Here's your beers, Sarge."

Harper pushed back his chair, stood up and walked over to the small bar. He tore a $1.00 chit from his MACV chit book, handed it to the bartender and said, "Thanks." Grasping the beers in both hands, Harper carried them back to the table and set them down.

"Anybody thirsty?" he asked.

Without answering, the three reached for an open beer. They sat quietly, content with just guzzling the icy brew.

Putting his beer down first, Harper clasped his hands behind his head and rocked back on the legs of his chair.

"Well, the second RT didn't find a single body. The slopes had completely cleaned the area of bodies and equipment. They found bunkers and trenches, but no sign of life. It must've been spooky as hell. There were some blood trails, however.

"Anyway, the one-one found some documents the commies had overlooked, stuffed into a corner of one of the bunkers. Interpreter read 'em. Said they had somethin' to do with troop movements from the North. The team radioed the FOB and told 'em what they'd found. Kontum suggested they follow the blood trails. They broke for lunch and rested awhile. The trails led off into the jungle in a westerly direction so that's the way the RT went.

"The mission went well for the first couple of days. They traveled slowly and damn carefully, maybe walking a klick a day, with stops several times an hour to listen for signs of any NVA. Also radioed in their position regularly. Occasionally a team member would find a torn piece of uniform hangin' on a branch or a button lying in the dirt. One dumb son-of-a-bitch had even dropped his canteen.

"Well, shortly after lunch, on the third day, they heard what sounded like heavy equipment several hundred meters to the north. The team changed their direction, and moved quietly towards the sounds. The closer they got, the louder the noise got, naturally. The one-zero brought the team to a halt and sent one of the mercenaries ahead to investigate. He came back about twenty minutes later, waving his arms around and excited as hell."

Harper stopped abruptly and got out of his chair, "I gotta piss like a race horse. Be back in a sec."

"You idiot, John!" Dean shouted. "Right during the excitin' part, you gotta piss." Harper stalked off towards the latrine, chuckling.

"I might as well piss, too," said McShane.

"Me, too," added Engals.

Dean demanded, "Well, hell! I'll order us another round."

A few moments later, the bartender motioned Dean over to the bar to pick up his beers. He pushed himself out of his chair and sauntered to the bar. He handed the manager four twenty-five-cent chits and then clasped the cans with his large brown hands and carried them back to the table. He sat down and drank heartily. He felt loose. Pleased to be a part of Special Forces. Pleased to be listening to war stories with his friends. Pleased to be in Vietnam, far from the hassles of the world back home. God, he dreaded the thought the war would one day be over. Then what?

Down the hall, he could hear McShane, Harper and Engals singing a drunk, disjointed melody. They had their arms around one another's shoulders. Dean choked on his beer, blowing a fine mist of suds over the table. "Get your ass over here, Harper, and finish that bullshit story of yours."

They plopped into their chairs and drank quietly. After several gulps, Harper set down his can. "Okay. Well, the interpreter asked the Cambode what he saw. The mercenary explained that there was a road about seventy meters ahead. The interpreter questioned him about the noises they had been following. The Cambode became very excited again. Finally, the interpreter calmed him down and the Cambode said he saw tanks! Dozens of them.

"The one-zero grabbed the radio handset from the one-one and called the FOB. Told him their present location and what they'd found. FOB wanted 'em to set up a road watch, get some pictures with their half-frame Olympus. So, the one-zero moved his team slowly up to the road, stopping about five meters from the edge. The team eased to the ground and watched. The one-zero pulled the camera from his pack and waited. The road was just wide enough to accomodate a truck or a tank. Pretty soon, out of nowhere it seemed, a tank came haulin' ass through the jungle."

Harper stopped talking and glared towards the den. The big color TV was showing a re-run of "Gunsmoke"—all television programs were reruns from the States, and broadcast twice a day, once in the afternoon and again at night. The volume was turned to an excruciating level. Several men sat leaning forward on the couch with elbows dug into their knees and chins resting on the palms of their hands. They were screaming at the picture. Marshall Dillon had just punched a bank robber in the mouth.

"How the hell can a guy talk with that crap turned up so loud?" Harper yelled. "Hey, bartender, can you get those bums to turn that son-of-a-bitch down?"

He looked up from his Playboy on top of the bar and glanced passively towards the den. He walked around from behind the bar and strode over to the doorway.

"Hey! Can you guys turn that thing down some? Can't concentrate on my reading!" A short Sergeant with receding red hair reluctantly took his hands from his chin, leaned forward and turned the volume to a more tolerable level.

"How's that?" asked the short Sergeant.

"Much better, Sarge." The bartender turned from the doorway, walked back to the bar and continued his reading.

"Thanks," said Harper. "At least a guy can hear himself think, now. You guys ready for another round?"

"Might as well," Dean agreed. "You could be all night with this tank story of yours."

"Let me get this round," said McShane. "Four more over here, Sarge."

Once again the pudgy Sergeant in civilian clothes lifted four beers out from underneath the heavy cooler lid and stood them up on the formica bar top. He expertly punched each can twice with the Coors can opener he had brought from back home in Durango, the last time he was on leave. He loved this job and would probably extend his tour another six months when it ended next month.

Harper leaned from his chair and grabbed two of the beers from the counter and passed one to Engals and the other to McShane. He snatched the remaining two cans, keeping one for himself and passing the other to Dean. They lifted the frosty cans to their lips and drank contentedly. Shortly, Harper clanged his beer on the table and resumed his story.

"They were Russian PT-76 amphibious tanks. Well, the team lay there about as quiet as a bug in a rug, although the engine noise must've been deafening. The tanks rolled along about fifty meters apart. They counted about two dozen tanks during their twenty or thirty minute watch. The one-zero called the FOB and told 'em about the tanks. FOB told 'em to head back to the closest LZ, and they'd have the choppers on their way for an extraction before dark. The one-zero found an LZ about a klick southeast of their position. He radioed the FOB with the coded map coordinates, and led his team toward the LZ.

"About halfway to their destination, they spotted an NVA squad movin' up a wash. The same wash the team's walkin' down. There's no time for the RT to take cover, because the gooks are maybe only ten or fifteen meters away, but completely at ease and unaware with their AK-47's restin' on their shoulders. Our boys do about all they can. They flip their CAR-15 selector switches to full auto and open fire. Kill every one of 'em. Now they know they're in a world of shit.

"They change their route and cut through the jungle, making a ton of noise. But they know all they have to do is reach the LZ. It also turns out that the squad they wasted was the point element for a NVA company. It wasn't long before the Company was in hot pursuit of two humpin' green berets and their ragtag lot of multinational mercenaries. Would have made a great scene in a movie. The one-one was screamin' into the radio that they'd made contact and needed an extraction ASAP. All the while, the slopes are right behind 'em. Must've been one heart pumpin' son-of-a-bitch.

"Well, they made it to the LZ, such as it was, and set up a quick defensive perimeter. Seven guys aren't much of a defense against a Company of mad rice heads. A few minutes passed and then the first couple of gooks came bustin' through the jungle. The team opened fire and nailed the suckers in place. It was quiet after that. But the RT could sense movement all around. The NVA were gonna surround 'em, just like the Indians in an old John Wayne western.

"About then, they thought they could hear the choppers off in the distance. The one-zero yelled into the handset to the pilot to step on the gas, the team was surrounded. Probably about this time the RT wished they could disappear up their own assholes. The chopper pilot called back and said they'd be there in five minutes and asked the one-zero if the LZ was big enough to set down in. 'Hell, yeah it is!' the team leader screamed.

"Now, they could hear and see the choppers flying in formation, coming from the east. One slick and four gunships. But, at the same time they were checking out the choppers, the jungle opened fire. The RT tried to return fire, but the NVA's automatic weapons fire was so intense that the team had to lay low. One of the Indig was hit in the ass and legs when he tried to crawl to a downed tree. A buddy ran to help him, but was knocked to the ground by an AK round through the chest.

"The team's shit was lookin' weak, like maybe the cavalry wasn't gonna make it in time to save the pioneers. Then the one-one took a round in the shoulder when he raised up to fire. The gooks must've seen the choppers bearin' down on 'em, because they stopped shootin'. Our boys took the opportunity to open up on the slopes.

"The gunships began their descent. They came swoopin' down on the NVA behind the tree line, lettin' everything go at once: rockets, miniguns and M-60's. The noise must've been deafening. It went on for three or four minutes and then the slick came in. Well, those sleazy slopes hadn't given up, despite the gunships. When the team, carrying the wounded, made a dash for the slick, the gooks opened fire on 'em. The one-zero went down with the top of his head splattered all over the ground. Another Cambode was hit. The door gunners on the slick had their fingers glued to the triggers of their M-60's, firing over the heads of the RT. The gunships came in for another pass. The medic flying chase jumped from the slick to help drag the wounded one-one.

"Finally the NVA eased up. Don't see how they could've kept up the fight for as long as they did, with those damn rockets burstin' all around 'em! And those minigunners are enough to put the fear of God into anyone. I mean four thousand rounds a minute — shit!

"Well, they finally got the wounded aboard. The one-zero couldn't have been much deader. He lay on the chopper floor, the whole way back to Kontum, with only half a head. That must've given the team the creeps. Anyway, they got out.

"I flew over to Pleiku the next day to visit the one-one in the hospital. His name was Sam Livingston. Any of you guys know 'em?"

Dean, Engals and McShane shrugged.

"He was a pretty good commo man. Had a nice safe job back at the FOB. But, he wanted to see some action, so he'd have somethin' to tell his girl and the boys back home. He had lots to tell 'em now. Poor bastard was in a world of hurt the next day. The AK round through his shoulder broke his collar bone. Another bullet busted some ribs when he was hit in the side while runnin' to the chopper. All he could talk about was gettin' out of the FOB, out of Special Forces, out of the Army and back to the States. He wanted no more of this sneakin' around spook crap. He got his wish. They medivac'd him to Japan and then to an Army hospital near his home town."

Harper paused, letting out a slow sigh, "My throat's dry and so is my beer. I'm ready for another."

There was nothing but silence from his audience. They were staring at Harper, who was now looking around for the bartender. He glanced back at the three Sergeants.

"So, that leaves four immediate openings," he concluded. "I'm hoppin' a C-47 day after tomorrow for Kontum City to fill one of those openings."

Harper finally saw the bartender coming out of the latrine. He held up four fingers and yelled, "Four more, Sarge." The manager nodded his head.

"Do you know how may of those four slots they've filled, John?" asked McShane.

"Last I heard, and that was yesterday from the Da Nang FOB Sergeant-Major, there was one. Me. You thinkin' about goin' down there, Steve?"

McShane scratched the top of his head and frowned, "Well, I haven't really signed in yet. Just got here this afternoon. Stoppin' by the orderly room in the morning to check on my assignment. Kontum would be as good a place as any. Besides, I always did like the Central Highlands and the Montagnards. Maybe I could catch the flight you're takin' on Friday."

Harper smiled, "That might work out okay. It leaves at 0830 hours on Friday. You'd want to be here around 0700 hours. That's the time the transportation leaves for the airfield."

"I'll see what happens tomorrow," McShane answered.

"Hey!" Dean shouted suddenly. "It's almost twelve. We'll never make curfew."

"Let's spend the night upstairs," Engals suggested. "Leave early in the morning. The Sergeant at the motor pool won't know the difference."

"My ass, he won't know the difference. He's probably standin' out front of his office checkin' his watch. I know the guy all too well. His name is Jim Simpson."

"What do you suggest then, Dean?" McShane questioned.

"Maybe I'll call him. Give him some bullshit story about a dirty carburetor or somethin'. Think that's what I'll do. Only instead of calling Jim, I'll leave a message with the C. Q. That'll be easier. Be back in a minute."

Dean pushed back his chair, grabbed a beer from the bartender, then stood and staggered over to the phone.

McShane lifted his beer into the air, "How 'bout a toast?" He thought for a moment, staring at the table, then said, "Here's to 5th Group, the war, and all those lovely toothless whores."

Harper and Engals clanged their beers into McShane's. They downed the liquid in unison, drinking until the cans

29

were empty and then slammed them down on the table, crinkling in the sides. They ordered more and waited for Dean to return. He had just hung up.

Dean fell into his chair and sighed, "Jim was the C. Q. and he was pissed, but there wasn't much he could do. So, looks like we're bunkin' upstairs till the mornin'."

"Hope we can find empty bunks," Engals said.

"If we can't, then we'll just have to empty some," Dean added jokingly.

* * *

They continued talking and drinking well past midnight. The manager had closed up the bar earlier and left a sizeable stack of beer on their table. They were down to their last four cans when Dean suggested they take the jeep for a drive downtown. Fortunately, McShane was still sober enough to explain to him that Da Nang had shut down hours ago and that its occupants were long since asleep.

Engals suggested that they could watch TV, but then everyone remembered that the AFVN (Armed Forces Vietnam) network stopped broadcasting at 2200 hours. Finally, they came to the realization that the only alternative was sleep. And once they stood up, quite a task in itself, they knew it would be the best alternative.

It was rough going as they tackled the chore of climbing the staircase. Dean passed out on the sixth step. No one noticed. the others managed to make it to the top and then stumbled into the dark bedrooms. They collapsed into the first bunks they found unoccupied.

Sometime during the night, Dean awoke, with his head hanging over the edge of the stair tread. He slowly pulled himself up to the railing and then staggered up the stairs, twice falling to his knees. Not as fortunate as his friends, Dean picked an occupied bed to crawl into resulting in the occupant's elbow shoved into Dean's stomach. He checked the next bunk more carefully before claiming it as his own.

Engals awoke to the sounds of trucks passing along the street below. He rolled over, wrapping his sheet around his head, trying to escape the unwanted noise. He peeked at the luminous hands on his watch from underneath the sheets. It was 0630. Time to face reality, the reality that another lousy day had begun and that he and his friends must get back to the FOB. Time to rise and shine, he thought, with a distasteful grin. "Shit," he said aloud.

He pulled back the sheet, knowing that getting out of bed was going to be as big a chore as climbing the stairs had been just a handful of hours earlier. How much did we drink last night Engals wondered. He thought about the question for a moment, then swung his boots — of course, no one had bothered to undress — over the side of his bunk and down onto the wood floor.

Slowly he pushed his upper body up with his forearms until, after what seemed an eternity, he sat on the edge of the bunk. Blinking a couple of times, he tried to focus on McShane, sleeping quietly on the bunk against the wall. Engals rubbed his eyes. Finally, he stood and walked uneasily over to McShane and shook him lightly.

"Steve! Steve! We've got to get back to the FOB. Dean and I have to be at the dispensary by 0800."

McShane, who was asleep in a fetal position, rolled his head on his pillow and looked up through slits at the blurred figure standing above him. "What's the racket outside?" McShane moaned.

"It's a troop convoy, goin' north I think. Hey, look,

31

I'm gonna find Chris so we can get out of here."

"Yeah, okay."

McShane lay on his back staring at a ragged crack in the plaster on the ceiling while Engals looked for Dean. As he followed the crack on its twisting route, he thought about the unpleasantness of signing in at the orderly room. No doubt, there would be forms to fill out. He would be assigned a new code name. His last one had been given to someone else when it was learned that he wouldn't be returning from the hospital. But he had.

He wanted to make damn certain to talk to the FOB Sergeant-Major about an assignment in Kontum. He had always liked the Central Highlands and knew the FOB there was smaller and less regimented than Da Nang. Actually, he didn't care where he went, just so he got back to work soon and into a bunk of his own with clean sheets.

Engals grimaced as he bumped into the door jamb on his way back into the bedroom. McShane sat rigidly on the corner of his bunk with his eyes only half open.

Engals plopped down on his bed and said, "Found Chris draped over a bunk in the room down the hall. Had a hell of a time waking him. He's up now. Trying to find the keys to the jeep. Harper's already up. He's downstairs makin' coffee. I'm goin' down myself to get some. Want me to bring you up a cup?"

McShane yawned. "Yeah, that sounds good. Think I'll be in the shower."

"Okay, but we're leavin' in fifteen minutes."

"No sweat, I'll be ready."

McShane stood up and walked into the bathroom. He quickly undressed, stepped into the shower and turned on the water. The warm water ran down along his neck and back and finally out onto the bathroom's blue and white tile floor. It felt good.

Minutes later, Engals found him standing under the

shower head. "Hey, Steve. Got your coffee," he hollered from outside the shower.

Reaching behind his back, McShane pulled the hot mug into the shower. He managed one sip before the cup overflowed with warm sulphur tasting water. He turned the shower knobs to "off" and leaned against the tiled wall, slurping diluted coffee. After he could no longer stomach it, he stepped from the shower, grabbed a towel hanging from a nail in the wall above the john, and dried off.

He walked over to the heap of clothes he had thrown into the corner. They reaked of stale beer and good old Nam sweat. He sat down on the long bench bolted against the wall and pulled on his wrinkled fatigue pants. Grabbing his shirt from the pile, he stuck his arms, first the left and then the right, through the sleeves and buttoned up the front.

Engals called from the bedroom, "You ready to go yet? I've got to get back in time to change my fatigues before I show up at the dispensary."

"Yeah, I'm ready." He stood up, rubbed his eyes, and walked into the next room. "Chris find the keys yet?"

"Found 'em on the stairs."

"Good, let's go."

III

The early morning drive to the FOB was pleasant. The sun's fury was as yet unleashed. The men knew it would be twenty degrees warmer in another three or four hours, with steaming humidity. Commuters on buzzing Honda 90's weaved in and out of traffic on their way to work. Dean nearly pressed two Vietnamese "Cowboys" on one such Honda between a douce-and-a-half carrying Marines and his jeep, when the motorbike cut sharply in front of him.

The young truck driver had to slam on his brakes to avoid smashing into a couple of children who had run out into the street. The Vietnamese delinquents skidded into the back of the truck. Dean swerved his jeep to the right and bumped to a halt on the sidewalk. The Marines cheered.

Except for a few minor bruises and scratches, the "Cowboys" were okay. The motorbike suffered little damage, and started right up when the driver pumped hard on the kick starter. They flipped the jeering Marines the bird, climbed aboard their Honda, and drove off at a much reduced speed.

Dean backed the jeep off the sidewalk and said, "What the hell was I thinkin' about? Nearly screwed up the jeep; maybe us too, trying to avoid those punks on that bike. I should have smeared their scrawny asses all over the street. Damn, I'm pissed!"

He slammed the shift lever into gear, revved the engine and then popped the clutch. "Those chicken shit son-of-a-bitches ought to be out fightin' their northern brothers instead of clownin' around causin' accidents."

They drove the rest of the way in silence. McShane enjoyed the city of Da Nang and spent the remainder of the drive watching the people scurry about. Street vendors were setting up their black market wares. Children were walking to school with their lunches clutched tightly in their skinny hands. Europeans were strolling to God-only-knew where, while Vietnamese women dressed in Ao Dais stood talking in groups on the street corners. American troops were everywhere. McShane loved it all and wished that it would never end.

They rolled through the FOB gates at 0730. Dean waved to the guards as they passed. He could see Jim Simpson standing by his office door talking to a First-Lieutenant. As they pulled to a stop in the jeep's designated slot, Simpson strode over to them. Dean frowned.

"You guys have a good time?" Simpson asked, sarcastically. "Find lots of girls? Maybe all of ya will catch a dose of the incurable syph the jarheads have been comin' down with."

Dean tried to laugh. "Naw, all we did was have a few beers."

"A few dozen, the way my head feels," Engals added.

"That's a real shame," Simpson drawled, "Well, I want one of you clowns to wash the jeep."

"Engals and I have to get over to the dispensary right away. Steve used to work at a car wash in high school.

35

He'll shine her up for ya real nice. What do ya think, Steve? Shouldn't take ya much more than twenty or thirty minutes. Besides, you ain't got that much to do today, anyway.''

"Sure, I'll wash the jeep. No sweat. Well, maybe a little. It's startin' to get hot. Where's the sponge and bucket, Sarge?''

"You'll find everything you need in the shed over by the threequarters,'' said the grinning motor pool Sergeant.

"Hey, Jim. Thanks for the use of the jeep. Buy you a beer tonight at the club. Oh, yeah, guess who we saw at House-22 last?'' Dean asked.

Not waiting for an answer, he continued, "John Harper, from the FOB in Ban Me Thuot. He's on his way to Kontum. What a story he told us about a couple of RT's in Hotel-9! Do you know Harper?''

"Nope,'' Simpson replied, not really caring.

"Well, I guess me and Ron better get our asses over to the dispensary. Got a bunch of Montagnard recruits comin' in for physicals. It's gonna be a busy day.''

"I'll stop by after I finish in-processing,'' said McShane. They nodded, then turned and hurried towards the dispensary.

McShane walked over to the shed and rummaged through its contents until he located a sponge and a bucket. He found some detergent on a shelf. He looped a hose, coiled on top of the hood of a jeep, around his arm and carried it over to the water spigot jutting from the side of the motor pool. He screwed the end of the hose onto the threads of the spigot and uncoiled the hose, dragging it over to the jeep.

It was only a few minutes before eight and already it was hot. He hastily washed the jeep's dusty exterior, stopping twice to drink from the hose. He couldn't decide which was worse: the taste of the sulfur water or the beer scum coating his tongue. He swept most of the dirt from the interior with a small, frayed whisk broom. Returning the bucket, hose and broom to the shed, he hurried directly to the safety of the air conditioned mess hall to escape the sun's wrath on an already damaged body.

Vietnamese K.P.'s were busily washing the stainless steel counter, scrubbing pots and pans and dragging cans of foul garbage through the back door. McShane found the Mess Sergeant sitting alone at the rear of the mess hall drinking coffee and reading the latest "Stars and Stripes."

"Looks like I'm a little late for breakfast, huh, Sarge?"

The heavy set Sergeant looked up from his newspaper long enough to catch a glimpse of McShane's infectious smile. "'pears so." He returned to his paper.

Not giving up, McShane asked, "Think there might be a chance I could fry up a couple of eggs for one damn hungover and hungry son-of-a-bitch?"

He thought he saw the Mess Sergeant begin to smile. Without looking up from his paper the Sergeant replied, "Might find an egg or two in the fridge. But get Hai over there to cook 'em. I don't want you screwin' up my kitchen."

"Right, Sarge. Thanks a lot." Feeling victorious, McShane sauntered over to a squat Vietnamese woman with Betel-nut stained teeth.

"Chou ba. (Hello, ma'am). Umm. Trung si say you numba 1 cook. Maybe you cook me two eggs, okay?"

Without a word, she shuffled to the refrigerator, opened the door and pulled out two eggs. She continued her shuffling to the stove, slopped grease with a wooden brush over a large griddle and then expertly cracked the eggs. McShane sat at an empty table close to the stove and waited with a cup of coffee.

Breakfast had filled his stomach, but McShane couldn't help but wonder what kind of chickens had laid such dreadful eggs. Or maybe, he thought, they had been shipped frozen from a chicken farm in California last year and stored in freezers in Da Nang until this year. Anyway, he needed something to wash away the taste of old eggs and burnt coffee. But what he really needed he couldn't get until the club opened.

Before checking in at the orderly room, he stopped by his temporary quarters and changed into his last clean pair of fatigues. He shoved the dirty pair he had removed into his duffel bag. Rummaging in his toilet kit, he found a rolled up tube of Colgate and a toothbrush with frayed bristles.

The latrine was located in a centralized area of the FOB, about fifty meters from his quarters. He found it deserted this time in the morning. He plopped the toothbrush and toothpaste on a small wooden shelf above a sink and ran a comb through his closely cropped hair. In-country was too hot a place to think about long hair and, besides, the Army frowned on it.

After brushing his teeth, twice, he sat down in one of the stalls and took a long shit. He felt much better.

The walk to the orderly room took McShane past his old quarters. The missing chunks of concrete block from the explosives and small arms fire during the sapper attack had since been filled with mortar. But it couldn't cover up the memories of that night, the memories that suddenly flooded his thoughts as he stood there staring at the blocks.

He had passed out at around 2300 on his bunk, after spending several hours in the club drinking with Dean and Engals. He had been awakened by an explosion sometime after 0100 that nearly rocked him off his bunk. His roommate was on R & R and McShane was alone and scared.

What the hell was going on, he had asked himself. How could they be shelling us? Have the NVA captured Da Nang? Questions raced through his mind as he rolled off the bed onto his stomach and crawled to his CAR-15, leaning against his rucksack in the far corner of the room.

Another blast, outside the window, shook the building as he reached for the CAR. He grabbed his web gear hanging from a hook on the wall, buckled it around his waist, and then slapped a 20 round magazine into the shortened M-16. He pulled back the slide bolt and released it, locking a round into the chamber. He moved the selector switch to full auto.

He crawled low and moved cautiously across the floor. Poking his head slowly around the door jamb, he whispered as loudly as he dared to the open door across the hall. "Johnson, you in there? What the hell's goin' on?"

Johnson, a tall black from Monterey, whispered back, "I think Charlie's blowin' up the FOB."

"Well, I don't want to get wasted in this chicken coop. Let's get outside in the fresh air. Got your CAR?"

"You bet, man."

McShane was about to push himself up when he saw movement down the hall by the front door.

"Looks like they're comin' in for us, Johnson. Anybody else in their rooms?"

"I don't know."

"Okay. Get ready."

Two small, crouched figures slowly crept through the door and then up the hall. They carried little bags in their right hands. One of the sappers quietly opened the door to the first room. They both began to pitch the bags in.

"Now, Johnson!"

They swung their CAR-15's around through the doors and opened fire. The figures jerked violently and slammed into the wall. The bags fell from their hands.

McShane and Johnson ducked back in their rooms.

Two deafening explosions blew out the front screen door, smearing bones and bits of flesh on the walls and ceilings.

A moment later...

"Johnson, how you doin'?" McShane shouted.

"Oh, doin' great boss," he answered shakily.

"Let's get out of here before their buddies come lookin' for 'em."

The two men poked their heads back around the door jambs, shoved fresh magazines into their weapons, and quickly glanced up and down the hall. McShane led the way down the hall to the front door.

"Man, it's slippery in here! Shit! Think I stepped on one of those bastards' hands," Johnson screeched. "I want out of this damn place, man." He brushed past McShane and hurried through the front door.

Outside was total confusion. Automatic weapon fire was coming from every direction. Johnson and McShane found cover behind a low dune. They fell to the cool sand and pointed their CAR-15's towards the beach. Flares burst overhead, casting long, spooky shadows. From their position they could see a pair of silhouettes running across the sand, fifty meters away.

"Looks like a couple more of those bastards," whispered McShane.

They fired three short bursts. One of the silhouettes performed a loose marionette's dance and then collapsed in a heap. The other form, seeing his buddy go down, fell to the sand and lay motionless. Johnson and McShane waited in darkness for another flare so they could finish off the loathsome sapper hugging the sand. Finally, three 81mm flares burst overhead. They took aim at empty space; the sapper was gone.

Johnson turned to McShane, "Where'd that little fart go?"

"Maybe back to the beach. Or, maybe over to that hootch. Let's check it out before he screws somebody up."

They crouched low and sprinted to the suspected barracks, keeping a ten-meter interval. McShane reached the building first and glanced around quickly for the terrorist. Johnson soon joined him. They caught their breath and then moved quietly around the back side of the hootch. Waiting at the corner of the barracks, the two men surveyed the darkness.

McShane heard something, turned his head and peered over his shoulder. There was movement to the rear, where they had just been. He tapped Johnson on the shoulder. Just as he began to turn, an arm quickly appeared from around the corner and tossed something in their direction.

McShane's mind raced. The goddamn sapper was behind us, he said silently. Must've been hiding around the corner or underneath the building. We've had it now.

"Run, Johnson! Satchel!" he screamed.

The charge landed a few feet from their position. Pivoting on the balls of his feet, Johnson moved to round the corner as McShane broke to his left. The explosion caught them in midstride.

A large chunk of pot metal smashed through Johnson's arm, tearing the limb from his shoulder. Another smaller piece forced a hunk of flesh from the back of his head, exposing grey goo. He stumbled to his knees, then pitched forward and died.

McShane was picked up by the blast and hurled through

41

the night air, landing on his back in the cool sand. He gazed up at a flare and watched it fall slowly. Gradually, he lifted his head to see if he was intact. Nothing showed but blood. He didn't hurt, he was just numb. Maybe I'm going to bleed to death, he thought. Wouldn't be such a bad way to go. As long as there wasn't any pain. Why not? He passed out.

He awakened sometime later to men's voices. The firing had stopped and he couldn't hear any more explosions. For a second, he thought the voices were VC, coming to finish him off. But as they neared, he recognized one of them.

"Here's a couple more over here," the voice said. "It's Johnson! Oh, man, he's all screwed up. How 'bout the other guy?"

McShane felt someone touch his shoulder. He blinked his eyes open.

"This guy's alive. Bring that stretcher over here."

It's Chris Dean, thought McShane.

"Steve, Steve," Dean said softly. "Is that you? There's sand all over your face."

He lied. It was mostly blood. He didn't want to scare him to death, literally. "Hey, man, you're okay," he continued. "Just shook a little. We'll wash that sand off your face, get some clean fatigues on ya and you'll be good as new."

The medic and two others rolled the wounded man onto a stretcher. McShane looked up at Dean's comforting smile as he walked alongside the stretcher holding his hand. Thank God all that damn noise had stopped, he thought. He closed his eyes.

McShane had awakened the following morning in the German hospital, half a mile up the road from the FOB. Dean was sitting by his bed when he opened his eyes.

"Good morning, Steve," Dean said quietly. "Glad to

see you back with us. Had us a little concerned last night when we brought you in."

"I've been unconscious all this time?" McShane demanded, a little groggily.

"Off and on. Doc says you're gonna be in good shape, though."

"Am I still in one piece? I mean, do I have my family jewels and everything?"

Dean laughed. "Yeah, you've got your family jewels and everything. You mostly received frag wounds on your legs and back, a few on your neck and a couple on your forehead. I almost shit when I first saw you. You were a mess. Blood from head to toe. Lost about three pints. Doc says you'll get to have a nice rest in Japan."

"What about Johnson? He was with me when it happened. Did he get that gook we were trackin'? I remember, we nailed his buddy good. But the flare burned out and then we couldn't find him."

"Uh, no, he didn't find the other gook. Actually, it was the gook who found you two. He's the one who threw the satchel charge."

McShane interrupted, "Well, what about Johnson?"

He knew from Dean's expression what the answer would be.

"He caught the biggest chunks of scrap. He was pretty screwed up when we found you two. I'd guess he was killed instantly. You were luckier. Just a whole bunch of little pieces. The girls are gonna love those scars." He grinned wickedly.

"What about the rest of the FOB? Many casualties?"

"The sappers went through the compound quickly and efficiently. Lots of guys were asleep. If it hadn't been for a few late nighters comin' back from the club, some guys playin' poker down at recon company and Murphy, the commo man on duty that night who grabbed an M-60 machine gun, it might have been a lot worse. Yeah, Murphy must've looked like John Wayne, firing the M-60 from the hip. Shot up three or four sappers as they were about to blow up the C. O.'s hootch. Needless to say, the Ol' Man put him in for a Silver Star.

"Still, I guess we lost about fifteen men, KIA, and a dozen or more wounded. The dispensary looked like Bellevue Emergency in New York City on Saturday night."

A knock on the door interrupted Dean. "Yes, come in."

The tallest, slimmest and prettiest nurse Dean had seen during his three tours in Vietnam, opened the door. She was pushing a cart carrying a stainless steel pitcher, some paper cups, a vase of freshly cut flowers and a plate of doughnuts.

"Good morning," she said with a pert smile. She replaced the wilting flowers on the night stand next to his bed with the fresh ones from her cart. She offered Dean some juice and doughnuts.

"I'm sorry, Sergeant McShane, but the doctor wants you on a liquid diet for awhile. Would you like some juice?" Her English was flawless. She must have gone to nursing school in the States, thought McShane.

He couldn't help but to stare into the clear, blue eyes of the Germanic beauty. "Umm, yes, please," he replied somewhat self consciously.

She poured the juice into a Dixie cup and put it in his outstretched hand. Just as he was about to take a drink she took the cup from his hand and placed it next to the flowers on the night stand. She then took a thermometer from the top pocket of her starched white uniform, shook it several times, and placed it underneath his tongue.

"I'm sorry. I should have taken your temperature first."

"That's okay," he mumbled.

44

IV

That was the last time he had seen the pretty German nurse. He was medivac'd to Japan the next afternoon aboard an Air Force C-141 jet. And now, nearly three months later, he was standing before his old room. He shuddered.

He turned and continued his walk on the wooden slat sidewalk to the orderly room. It was after 0900 and the heat and humidity were nearly unbearable, making breathing difficult.

The orderly room was just inside the main gate to the FOB. Above the front door was a sign that read simply, "Orderly Room." McShane opened the door and walked in. It was refreshingly cool inside. Besides the club, mess hall, dispensary, and C. O.'s quarters, the orderly room was the only other air- conditioned building in the compound. A young black Sergeant looked up from his typewriter when the spring-hinged door slammed. McShane stood in front of the clerk's desk.

"Can I help you, Sarge?" asked the young Sergeant.

"Yeah, I'm Sergeant Steve McShane. I got in yesterday from the hospital at Camp Zama. Well, actually,

Travis. I had a three week convalescent leave."

"Do you have your 201 file?"

"It's right here." He handed his personal record file to the clerk. He hadn't remembered seeing the Sergeant before. Probably new, he thought. There were lots of new faces walking around the FOB.

Thumbing through the file, the clerk asked, "You haven't been to 5th Group Headquarters in Nha Trang yet?"

"No, I haven't. Didn't want to. Group is too much like Bragg: spit shined jungle boots, brassoed belt buckles, pressed jungle fatigues and starched berets. Makes me nervous seeing all those puppets struttin' around."

"I'm afraid you're gonna have to go anyway, Sarge. You have to in-process through Group Personnel and Finance. Want to get paid, don't you?"

"That could take a week or more by the time I hang around that damn Da Nang airfield for a flight to Nha Trang. And then trudging from station 1 to station 2 to station 3 until you fill up a typed form with checks and x's and initials to prove you've really been there. Bullshit!"

"You don't have to try and do it all in one day. Relax, go to the NCO Club or to the beach. They've got three nice beaches in Nha Trang."

"I've been relaxing. For three months. I've been to clubs. I've been to the beach. I've got to move on before my joints stiffen up on me."

James Stanley, the tall, greying FOB Sergeant-Major, had overheard McShane's conversation with the clerk from his desk at the rear of the orderly room. He sighed, stood up, and walked over to the clerk.

"What's the problem, Sergeant Kinney?"

"Well, Sergeant-Major, umm, Sergeant McShane hasn't processed through 5th Group yet. I can't process him through FOB until he does."

"Yes, I know," frowned the Sergeant-Major. "Hate to see you have to go to the Group. I avoid the place as much as I can myself."

He took McShane's record file from the desk and flipped through the pages. He thought for a moment. "The only thing Sergeant McShane probably really cares about is his pay. Now, I'm going to Nha Trang next week. I could drop his pay records off at Finance; I know the Sergeant-Major there. I'm sure we can figure something out. Wouldn't mind if I forged your signature to a few forms, would you, McShane?"

McShane grinned. "Not at all, Sergeant-Major. What about the rest of my records?"

"There's nothing really important here that you have to do. You can in-process the next time you're in Nha Trang. We'll hold your records, in the meantime, for safekeeping. Think that'd be okay, Sergeant Kinney?"

"Sounds good, Sergeant-Major."

"Very well." He handed the records back to Kinney. "Just remind me Monday to take his finance records to Nha Trang."

"Yes, Sergeant-Major."

"Now, is that all we can do for you, McShane?"

"Well, Sergeant-Major, I was talkin' to a Sergeant Harper at House-22 last night, and he was tellin' me they were short a few men in Kontum. Thought maybe I'd check with you. Think I could be assigned to their FOB?"

"Hmmm." He pondered the question for a second, then answered. "Don't see why not, McShane. Sergeant Kinney will type up some travel orders for you. I'll call Sergeant-Major Fields in Kontum and tell him to be expecting you."

"Thank you, Sergeant-Major."

The Sergeant-Major nodded and returned to his desk.

McShane sat down in a chair next to the clerk's desk and waited patiently while Kinney typed his travel orders.

"When would you like to leave, Sergeant?"

"There's an Air America flight leavin' Da Nang Air Base tomorrow morning. I'd like to be on it, if it's possible."

Kinney shuffled through papers stacked neatly on the upper left-hand corner of his desk. Finally he slipped a flight manifest from the bottom of the stack. He stared at it for a few seconds, then looked up.

"Yeah, there's an Air America Flight that leaves approximately 0830. Want to be there at least an hour early. Those pilots don't keep accurate schedules. They could take off early or late."

"That must be the flight."

"Okay, then." Kinney went back to his typing. He was quick and efficient. Might be a corporate executive or something, someday, McShane reflected.

He yanked the papers, in triplicate, from the carriage of the typewriter, handing one copy to McShane and placing the other two on top of the stack.

"You might want to stay at House-22 tonight. They provide transportation to the air base. Get you there in plenty of time." Kinney stood up from his chair and stuck out his hand. "Good luck, Sergeant."

McShane pushed off the arms of his chair and rose to face him. He took the friendly Sergeant's hand and gave it a vigorous shake. "Thank you, Sergeant Kinney. You've made this very painless. Think I'll go over to House-22 this afternoon."

"Anytime, Sergeant McShane."

He released the clerk's hand and turned to walk out the door. "Good luck in Kontum, Sarge," shouted the Sergeant-Major from the rear of the room.

"Thanks, Sergeant-Major."

McShane walked out into the brilliant sunlight. He stopped momentarily on the "Welcome" pad to put on his sunglasses. It felt even hotter outside after being in the comfort of the air-conditioned orderly room. Well, he would get used to the heat again, he mused.

He strode briskly down the walk toward the dispensary, pleased with the morning's outcome. A six-man RT was boarding a Huey slick, on their way to Phu Bai to link up with the gunships that would escort them to their destination, somewhere across the DMZ. The missions into North Vietnam were classified and only the one-zero and one-one on the team had been briefed by S-2 and S-3 (Intelligence and Operations) as to their exact destination. The mercenaries didn't care. They were along for a fight.

In front of the dispensary was a long line of Montagnards waiting quietly in new tiger fatigues for their physicals. McShane walked to the front of the line and pulled open the door to the dispensary. Inside was the FOB doctor, Captain Spring, and several FOB medics poking and probing a half dozen or so nude Montagnards. McShane spotted Dean shoving a hypodermic needle into an unsuspecting Yard's ass.

"Hey, Chris," McShane hollered. Dean pulled the needle from the Yard's rear. "Got my travel orders. Leavin' for Kontum in the morning."

Dean looked up and smiled broadly. "That's good news. Me and Engals are gonna miss you."

"Oh, bullshit! You've got your butts and half the whores in Da Nang to take care of. You'll be too busy to miss me."

"You're right," said the medic with a chuckle. "What time's your flight leave in the mornin'?"

"0830, hopefully."

"Goin' to stay at House-22 tonight?"

McShane nodded. "Probably go over there after lunch. Maybe you and Engals could stop by for a few beers."

"Yeah, maybe. Have to figure a way to get there, though. After last night Simpson won't let us use the jeep. How you gettin' there?"

"Probably hitchhike. It's pretty easy to catch a ride into town. Maybe hitch a ride with some Marines from down the road."

"Ron and I could hitch a ride, too. Have supper at the outdoor cafe up the street from House-22. Could ask some of them German Frauleins to join us."

"Dream on, Chris. Couple of toothless whores would be more like it."

Dean laughed, "Speak for yourself. I'm going to line me up one of them blonde nurses."

"Good luck. Hey, I'll see ya at lunch before I leave."

"Right. I've got to get back to these Yards. There's still a shit pot full of 'em outside. See ya later."

"Okay." McShane turned and walked toward the front door, pausing long enough to allow another half dozen Montagnards to pass through. While he waited, he put his sunglasses back on. After the last recruit had moved passed him, he strolled through the door and once again into the bright light.

He spent the remainder of the morning reading a paperback, THE NEW LEGIONS, by Donald Duncan, and rearranging his duffel bag. He gave his dirty fatigues and underwear to one of the mama-sans to wash and dry before he left. One thing for sure about Vietnam, it didn't take long for clothes to dry.

A few minutes before noon, McShane closed his book and stuck it between a pair of faded Levis and a red plaid shirt folded neatly in his Samsonite suitcase. He sat up on the edge of his bunk and shoved his feet into the O.D. canvas and black leather jungle boots he had taken off to air. Slowly, he laced the boots, hoping the mama-san would have his clothes ready in time. He guessed she would.

Outside, the sun was high overhead. The humidity made the simplest of tasks a chore. Sweating profusely, McShane moved steadily up the walk to the welcome relief of the air-conditioned mess hall. A team was sitting on lawn chairs in front of their one-zero's hootch cleaning their CAR-15's and picking through a case of lurp rations. Dean and Engals were on their way out of the dispensary and saw McShane coming their way.

"Hey, Steve," Dean yelled. "Goin' to chow?"

"Yeah. Guess so."

"Shit, am I ever tired of lookin' into dirty Yard ears, snotty Yard noses and stinkin' Yard asses. I bet I've looked at a hundred of them since we opened this mornin'!"

"You know you love it, Chris. Could always go back to the reservation and treat your own people. I'm sure they could use a good medic. You'd be chief medicine man."

"I already tried that. At the end of my first enlistment, two years ago, I thought I'd go back to the reservation and be a civilian. The cops gave me fifteen citations for speeding, reckless and drunken driving. Landed in jail five or six times. After six months of that bull, I re-up'ed. Been back a couple of times for Christmas and that's it. Guess I'm what you'd call in this man's Army a 'lifer'."

"Even look like a 'lifer' with that white side wall haircut," Engals chuckled.

When they arrived in front of the mess hall, there was a short line of men waiting outside the front door. Dean stopped momentarily to talk with a short black Sergeant at the head of the line. McShane and Engals went on to the rear of the line and waited for Dean. The sun beat savagely on their backs. McShane glanced at his black-faced Seiko. It was a couple minutes until noon. He faced Engals.

"Damn, that Mess Sergeant would just as soon let us fry out here like a couple of his raunchy eggs than let us in a few minutes early."

"He must've heard you, Steve. See, he's opening the door."

"And there's even a minute to go. Must've seen us startin' to pass out."

The line moved rapidly through the open doorway into the cool mess hall. Dan was already seated at a table near the milk machine. He motioned for McShane and Engals to join him. As they pulled their chairs to the table, Dean introduced the black Sergeant also seated there.

"Hey, guys, this is Sam Adams. Sam, that's Steve McShane and Ron Engals." Adams stood up and McShane and Engals shook his hand. After the formalities they plopped into their chairs.

"Patched Sam up a few weeks ago. I was flyin' chase when Tom's team made contact with some NVA Regulars. He was hit in the shoulder. Just back from Cam Ranh Bay."

"Where you goin' now, Sam?" asked McShane.

"To Bangkok. Do a little catchin' up. I've got a two week convalescent leave."

"Maybe we'll go along," McShane said, winking at Dean.

"Hell, no! This is just for us niggers. Some other brothers from Phu Bai are goin' with me. It's their R & R. Savin' my R & R for Hawaii. Goin' to see the ol' lady and three kids."

"Well, you watch your step over there, Sam," Dean said. "I don't want to see you in my dispensary with a social disease. Might just be out of penicillin. Hate to see

52

you visit your wife in a tender condition. Be a little hard to explain, don't you think, Sam?''

Adams let out a deep, hoarse laugh, "You wouldn't do that to a poor dumb nigger, would ya?''

"Never can tell, Sam.''

"I don't think you have to worry, Chris. I'm takin' a gross of Trojans. Probably have to get another box before the week's over.''

"What are you goin' to do, have the girls line up outside your hotel room for fourteen days?'' asked Engals.

"I'm going to do my best. I want to go out with as many as I can before I have to go back out on those damn missions again.''

"You can always quit, you know,'' McShane pointed out.

Adams turned and stared at McShane. "Yeah, and so could you. I heard how bad you got screwed up, and Dean tells me you're goin' to Kontum to do it over. How come you ain't quittin'? Because you can't. You hate it and you love it. Just like me. Ain't that right, Steve?''

"Maybe so,'' McShane agreed quietly.

"Look, Sam,'' Dean interrupted. "Why don't you come on over to House-22 with us tonight? Steve's leavin' tomorrow morning for Kontum and you're takin' off for Bangkok with your Trojans. We could have a little farewell party. I think the club still has a few bottles of champagne left over from a party we had last month. We could really do it up right! What do you think, Sam?''

Adams scratched his chin, "Well, sounds like a pretty good time. How we gettin' there?''

"That's a good question. Steve's leavin' this afternoon. Goin' to hitchhike. I reckon we could do the same after work. We could stay the night again.''

"Okay, Chris,'' Adams grinned. "I'll meet you at the gate around 1700 hours.''

"Fine," replied Dean.

"We aren't goin' anywhere if we don't get something to eat," McShane growled. He spun around in his chair and scanned the room. He spotted one of the serving girls standing by the counter and yelled, "Hey co, lai day." The young Vietnamese server shuffled meekly over to the table.

"What you want?" she asked.

"Right off hand," said Dean, "I think we want something to eat. You know, some of those mashed potatoes with gravy and a couple slabs of meat loaf. Now, di di mau len." The girl frowned and then scurried off to the serving counter.

"Damn these servers. 'What you want?' ", mimicked Dean in a high, squeaky voice. The men laughed at his imitation and then McShane turned to the black Sergeant.

"How were you hit in the shoulder, Sam?"

"That's a long story. But I'll try and make it short. I was the one-zero of a six man RT. S-3 wanted us to investigate a hunk of territory just across the Cambodian border that had been heavily pounded by B-52's and artillery for several days. The Operations Officer told me that a battalion of NVA Regulars was supposed to have been bivouacked there and he wanted my team to go in, assess the damage and get a body count. Well, I've been on those wild goose chase body count missions before, and they're pretty much the same. You find a few blood trails, maybe a finger or two, but usually you don't find a damn thing."

"Yeah," Dean interrupted. "Kinda like the team John Harper was tellin' us about last night at House-22. But that team found tanks instead of bodies."

"Well, we didn't find tanks, but plenty else. They dropped us in at the eastern edge of the AO early in the morning. We tromped around most of the morning without findin' a shred of evidence that anyone had ever been there. But there was plenty to show that our fire power had been there. Bomb craters as wide as this mess hall and huge fallen trees that made it damn near impossible to walk.

"At noon we took a short break for lunch. I called in our position to the FOB relay station and told 'em what we'd seen, or rather what we hadn't seen. After lunch, we continued weavin' around the craters, sometimes walkin' right on down through the holes when there wasn't any other way around 'em. I tell ya, I was sure glad it wasn't me at the receivin' end of those B-52's.

"About an hour later, we got a whiff of somethin' we've all smelled before. Rottin' gooks. We followed the stench, which got stronger and stronger, for a half hour or so. Suddenly, one of my Indig, a Cambode, stopped and pointed to something up in one of the trees. There, thirty feet up, was a leg hangin' on a limb. We looked around on the ground, but couldn't find the body that went with it. The NVA had done a job cleanin' up. But the stink was gettin' worse. We had to find it."

Adams was interrupted by the young server, carrying four steaming trays. She placed one in front of each man and promptly left. The men all took a couple of bites of the meatloaf, washing it down with gulps of grape Kool-Aid.

"It didn't take us long before we found out about the stink," Adams finally went on. "We came upon some bunkers that had somehow escaped the bombing. The slopes had cleaned them out pretty well, but on the west end of the bivouac area we found something I hope never to lay my eyes on again. Stacked up in neat little piles, four high, four deep and ten long, were the bodies of roughly a hundred and sixty gooks. My one-one was carrying an Olympus half-frame S-3 had given him, so I had him take pictures of the stacks and some of the bunkers. I was beginnin' to get a little nervous standing around the open. I knew somebody had to still be in the area watchin' over all them bodies and I didn't want him to find me standin' around takin' pictures of his buddies.

"After about a dozen pictures I moved the team out towards the LZ. I had the one-one call for an extraction. I didn't want to have to be waitin' around at the LZ for choppers. 'Bout two hundred meters outside their camp, we started takin' rounds from a sniper up in the trees. That's when I was hit in the shoulder. My M-79 man fired a Willy Peter round into the tree and well, need I say more? I crammed a field dressing into my shirt and we double-timed it back to the LZ. The choppers arrived 'bout the same time we did.

"Kept thinkin' the whole way back to the LZ that I'd look over my shoulder and there'd be a hundred sixty rottin' bodies, missin' arms and legs, chasing us. I was never so happy to be on a chopper headed home."

Everyone laughed at Adams, who was washing down another mouthful of meatloaf with Kool-Aid. "Yeah, well, you should've been there. You wouldn't have thought it was so funny." But then Adams began chuckling, "I guess maybe it is a little funny."

"Damn right it's funny," said Dean.

McShane, who had been busily eating during the account, pushed his tray to the side of the table and began picking his teeth clean with a toothpick from a dispenser in the middle of the table. When he had finished, he broke the toothpick in half and tossed it onto his empty tray. He scooted his chair back from the table and stood up. The three men gave him puzzled looks.

"I've got to get my ass in gear. Still need to do some packin' before I hitchhike into Da Nang. So what time you guys think you'll be comin' over?"

56

"Engals and I won't be able to leave until after work. What about you, Sam?"

"I reckon I'll wait for you two."

"Okay, then. I'll see you guys tonight."

V

It wasn't long before a deuce-and-a-half, bellowing black smoke, carrying a squad of Marines to the PX on the other side of town, stopped in front of McShane. He was sitting on his duffel bag, once again reading THE NEW LEGIONS. The driver poked his head out the window of the truck and grinned. One of his front teeth was missing.

"Where you goin', Sarge?" asked the driver in a thick Southern drawl.

"Into town," McShane replied, hoping the young driver would let him ride up front. He wasn't overly excited about the prospect of riding in back with twelve cantankerous grunts.

"We're goin' right through town, buddy. Hop aboard. You can ride up front with me. Too dusty in back."

"Okay, thanks." That's a break, he thought. He stuffed the book into the deep pocket on the left side of his jungle fatigue pants.

"Need a hand with your gear, Sarge?"

"That's all right," he said, throwing the duffel bag over his shoulder. "It's not much." He grabbed his weathered suitcase and walked around to the passenger side of the truck. The driver flung the door open and leaned over the seat, taking hold of the duffel bag as McShane stepped up onto the side of the cab. The driver pulled the bag into the cab and propped it up on the seat next to him. McShane slid onto the seat, holding his suitcase on his lap and slammed the door.

"All set, Sarge?"

"Yeah."

"Well, then, let's get this baby rollin'. Da Nang, here we come." He let out a short rebel yell, then floored the accelerator. McShane didn't think he used the clutch once, as he ground through the gears.

"Where you from, Sarge?"

"California."

"Where 'bouts in California?"

"Crescent City."

"Never heard of it." He sounded like he didn't really care, anyway. "I'm from LaPines, Alabama. Know where that is?"

"South of Montgomery, isn't it?"

The driver flashed McShane his toothless smile. "Hey, that's pretty good. You're the first in a long time to know where LaPines is. How come you know where it's at?"

"My wife's from Montgomery. Think she had a cousin livin' there."

"You married, huh?"

"Sort of." McShane was thankful the drive into town was a short one. He was tiring of the conversation with the Marine. He was also tired from the long night, and he looked forward to a nap before Dean showed up.

"Thinkin' about gettin' married myself. Got me a real nice girl in town. She don't even charge me nothin' either. She likes me to bring her C-rations. Hell, that's easy enough. I work in supply. I take her four or five cases a week. She has a real big family, ya know."

"She's probably sellin' 'em out on the black market, too."

"Not my Suzy."

"Suzy?"

"Yeah, I renamed her Suzy, because I couldn't say her real name. Suzy has a real nice sound to it."

Half the whores in Vietnam were renamed Suzy, thought McShane. He was beginning to feel sorry for this poor southern Alabamian. He doubted the Marine's family would be very receptive to their son's bringing a Vietnamese girl home with him. And what about their offspring? Mama's not going to take kindly to a bunch of 50-50's running around her house in LaPines, McShane mused.

The kid's only chance was to have his C.O. refuse to okay the paperwork. Or maybe something else would come along. Like a transfer.

"Have you asked your C.O. about marrying...umm, Suzy?"

"Not yet. But I'm goin' to. Probably this week."

"Well, good luck." McShane pointed ahead. "You can drop me off at the corner. I'll walk the rest of the way. It's only a couple of blocks."

"I can take you if you want."

"No, that's all right. Need the exercise."

The driver steered the large truck over to the curb and stopped. He turned and faced McShane. "Here you are, Sarge."

"Thanks for the lift."

"Sure thing, Sarge."

McShane kicked open the door and stepped down to the street with his suitcase. The Marine pushed his duffel bag across the seat into the waiting hands of his passenger, who then tossed the bag onto his shoulder.

The driver pulled the door shut and waved. McShane nodded. The truck eased slowly away from the curb, spewing ugly smoke from its exhaust.

Balancing the bag on his shoulder and carrying his suitcase in his right hand, McShane crossed the street, stopping a time or two to allow a bicyclist or motorcyclist to pass. It felt good to be out walking in the city he enjoyed so much. But it wasn't long before the enjoyment turned to displeasure as his muscles ached from the brisk walk and the strain of carrying the duffel bag on his shoulder.

The long days of confinement in the hospitals had softened him. And then, once he had been able to move about, there were the nights at the NCO club drinking and swapping war stories with the other patients. He had actually gained weight in the hospital during the past months, and he knew that soon enough it would be time to start trimming. After tonight.

Fifteen minutes later, McShane was walking up the steps to House-22. The club manager was sitting on an aluminum folding chair on the front porch. McShane dropped his bag in front of the door.

"How far did you have to walk, Sarge?"

"Few blocks."

The manager extended his hand. "I'm Sergeant Winston. Where you headed?"

McShane took his hand and gave it a vigorous shake. "Steve McShane. To Kontum. Want to catch the flight leavin' in the morning."

"No problem. Here, let me give you a hand with your gear and I'll get you signed in."

Winston stood up, taking hold of his guest's duffel bag, and together they walked through the doorway into the entry hall and up the short flight of stairs that only a dozen hours earlier had seemed so long and treacherous.

Winston, panting heavily, stopped at the top of the steps and pointed to the room on the right.

"Think there's an empty bunk over in the corner. You can put your gear in one of the lockers. I'll get you a lock and key if you need one." The pudgy Sergeant released the handle of the bag, letting it fall to the floor in front of the room.

"Yeah, I could use a lock."

Winston turned and walked slowly back down the stairs, stopping once to catch his breath. The many years as a Mess Sergeant and Club Manager had taken its toll. McShane thought he was at least fifty pounds overweight.

While waiting for Winston to return, McShane opened a locked door, propped his Samsonite against the inside of the metal wall locker and slammed the door shut. He slid his duffel bag underneath the bunk in the corner, wrapping the bag's canvas strap around the leg of the bed and then refastening it to the metal clip on the side of the bag.

His bunk was one of the new models with an innerspring mattress. It certainly felt more comfortable than the old non-spring style. He laid back on the mattress, resting his head on the palms of his hands and closed his eyes. He slept for better than three hours.

* * *

Sergeant Winston was stocking shelves behind his small bar with bottles of Cutty Sark from an open box set up on the counter of the bar. Tonight was Friday and he knew men from the FOB and Da Nang B-Team would more than likely stop by for a drink or two, renewing old acquaintances and swapping yarns. House-22 could be a lively night spot if the right people happened by.

He remembered two men from Project Sigma who had spent the night a few months back. They brought four female dancers they had met on a flight from Saigon with them. Somehow, they convinced the four girls to drive them in their borrowed '66 VW Microbus to House-22.

When the girls arrived in front of the old French home, their two passengers invited them inside for a drink. Winston was rearranging furniture in the den that particular Friday afternoon and was surprised to hear females giggling in his club so early in the day. He stopped what he was doing and went into the hall to investigate, expecting to find a couple of mama-sans squatting on the front porch chewing betel nut. Needless to say, he was just a little surprised to find four, young and attractive Caucasian girls standing by the front door, laughing at two Green Berets, dancing arm in arm on the sidewalk.

He leaned against the wall and observed the girls watching the sidewalk antics for awhile until one of the girls noticed him staring at them. She smiled. The Sergeant, embarrassed, introduced himself.

"Hi, I'm Sergeant Winston, the manager. Can I fix you girls a drink?"

"Hell. We're the guests of Sergeant Abbot and Sergeant Henry. My name's Stormy and that's Jennifer."

A tall, luscious, red-head stuck out her hand. Winston shook it daintily. She introduced the others as Bonnie and Lucy. He shook their soft hands as if he was handling his mother's crystal wine glasses. "And, yes, we'd love a drink."

He mixed the girls gin and tonics in tall glasses he had frosted in the freezer. The Sergeants from Sigma drank beer.

"What brings you girls to Da Nang?" Winston asked.

"We're part of a USO show that's touring military

63

bases in Vietnam," Stormy explained. "We were in Saigon last night and tomorrow night we'll be performing at the Air Force Base in Da Nang. Maybe you'd like to come?"

"Well," Winston blushed, "maybe. If I can find someone to look after the club for a few hours. What exactly do you girls do in the show?"

"We go-go dance," Jennifer said promptly.

Winston tried to act nonchalant. "Oh, yeah. That's nice. Hey, maybe you girls would like to stick around for awhile. Put on a little show for the guys. After months in the field," he lied, "they'd really appreciate it."

Stormy looked over at the others who were sipping their drinks. "What do you think?" The girls thought for a moment then nodded their approval.

"Sure, I guess so. But we can't stay late. We've got to be bright-eyed and bushy-tailed for rehearsal in the morning."

Winston just bet they were bushy-tailed. "That's great. We can push the jukebox into the pool room and maybe use the pool table as a dance floor as long as you don't wear shoes."

An hour later, the place began filling up. Everyone wanted to buy the girls a drink. Abbot and Henry had a hell of a time fending off the drunks' crude passes. But the girls loved it. They had seen THE GREEN BERETS with John Wayne, on the flight to Saigon from San Francisco, and were very familiar with Barry Sadler's "Ballad of a Green Beret." To be among so many horny males suited them.

While the jukebox was being pushed into the pool room, the girls went upstairs to change into skimpy, tasseled dresses. Somebody plunked a quarter into the machine and played "Born to Be Wild" by Steppenwolf. Down the stairs they came, bumping and pumping, twirling the colored tassels that covered their breasts. The men let out whoops that could probably have been heard all over Da Nang.

The girls gyrated through the hall into the pool room. There was no shortage of volunteers to help the girls up onto the makeshift dance floor. The pool table wasn't really large enough for both girls, but nobody seemed to care; in fact, it made the show more amusing. Stormy tripped and bumped Jennifer off the table. She landed safely in the outstretched arms of a grinning admirer. Another fan took Jennifer's position next to Stormy and began stripping, throwing his clothes out into the drunken audience.

For close to an hour the girls entertained the men. Winston had been surprised at their conduct; only one fight had erupted and that was broken up almost immediately. The girls ended up staying longer than they had anticipated. They hadn't really minded, not with all the drinks they were fed. Abbot and Henry finally had to carry them to their VW and drive them back to the air base. It was probably about the best time Winston could remember having at House-22.

He doubted tonight would be one of those nights. Just the usual, he thought. Half a dozen guys watching TV. Few more playing pool. And some just sitting around at a table bullshittin' and drinkin' beer.

As he put the last of the bottles on the shelf, he heard a jeep door slam outside. Glancing over his shoulder, he saw three Sergeants walking up the steps. They looked familiar to Winston, but then after two years as House-22's manager, everybody in Special Forces looked familiar.

"Is Steve McShane stayin' in your fine establishment?" Dean asked.

"He's asleep upstairs," Winston said. "Been sleepin'

for about three hours."

"How 'bout John Harper? He was here last night."

"Harper's been out all day. Don't know where, though."

Dean looked upstairs. "Well, then, let's wake up Steve. He's got a party to go to."

Adams sat down at the table and drank a cold beer while Dean and Engals sprinted up the stairs to look for McShane. Damn, Adams thought, as he set the frosty can down, this guy Winston must have the coldest beers in Da Nang or maybe in Vietnam.

They didn't find McShane asleep on his bunk, but standing nude in front of the mirror in the bathroom drying his hair with a dog-eared towel he had found wadded up on the floor. A small puddle had formed at his feet from water dripping off his body.

"So there's Sleepin' Beauty. Checkin' himself out in the mirror. Have a nice nap?" Dean asked.

McShane turned and smiled. "Yeah, and a nice shower, too. I was just goin' to close my eyes for a couple of minutes. Next thing I knew it was three hours later. Thought I'd read my watch wrong when I first checked the time. Had to look at it again just to make sure. Feel a helluva lot better now. It's a good thing I took a nap. We could be up a long time. Have you told John about our little farewell party? He's leavin' tomorrow, too."

"He's been out today. But you can be sure he'll be invited when he gets back."

"Too bad we can't get a few women to join us," Engals added. "Might liven things up."

"Winston probably knows where we can find a couple," said Dean. "Hey, Steve, hurry up and dress. We've got to get started."

"What's the hurry?"

"I'm just thirsty."

They left McShane standing in front of the mirror brushing his teeth. Adams was finishing his second beer when they walked up and sat down at a table. Winston brought over a bottle of champagne and three plastic glasses.

"Sergeant Winston, you are really on the ball," said Dean. "Would you like to join us?"

Winston grabbed another glass from behind the bar, pulled a chair out and sat down.

"Thank you. Think I will."

Dean peeled the silver foil from around the top of the bottle and tossed it into the trash can next to the bar. He untwisted the wire holding the cork and aimed the bottle at the front door, easing the cork out with his fingers. There was a loud POP and the cork shot out of the bottle and through the doorway, landing on the street, a few feet from a startled vendor who quickly rolled his cart of hot noodles to safer territory. The party goers nearly laughed themselves out of their chairs.

"Hey, you missed," Engals laughed. "Next time, I want to try and hit one of them dinks."

"If I can't hit one, nobody can," Dean challenged.

"Five bucks says I can."

"And I'll throw in a five that says you can't," Adams added.

"I'm stayin' out of this," said Winston. "I'm here to drink."

"First, we have to finish this bottle," Dean declared. "Then we'll see what kinda shot Ron is."

It didn't take long for the three experienced drinkers to polish off the bottle. They were all anxious to test Engals' skill, which he certainly wanted to prove was superior to Dean's.

"Winston, if you'll get us another bottle, I'll demonstrate to these gentlemen the way it's done."

67

It only took him a few seconds to pull another bottle from the refrigerator and bring it over to the table.

"Okay, hotshot," Dean encouraged, "let's see what you can do."

Engals took the bottle from Winston and began unwrapping the gold colored foil. "The first thing I need is a target."

The men surveyed the street and sidewalk. The noodle vendor had moved out of range. A few people were riding bicycles and motorbikes along the street. Engals finally found a victim standing beneath a tree, talking to an attractive Vietnamese girl.

"Let me get this straight," Engals said as he adjusted his aim. "You guys are each bettin' me five bucks that I can't hit someone with the cork from this bottle of champagne, right?"

"Remember, I'm stayin' out of this," Winston reminded him.

"That's right, Ron," Dean said. "Now show us how great you are. I'm thirsty."

"See that G.I. across the street with his back turned to us, talkin' to the Vietnamese chick?"

Dean scanned the street until his eyes fell on the G.I. with the girl. "That's Harper!" he exclaimed.

"Right. I'm goin' to nail him in the back."

Suddenly, Winston shouted, "Here's another five that says you can't!" He reached into his front pocket, pulled out a crumpled bill and threw it onto the table with the other fives.

Engals smiled. Slowly, he unwound the wire from the top of the bottle. Harper leaned motionless against the tree as the girl gestured wildly, flailing her arms about. Engals handed the wire to Adams. He angled the bottle in the direction of his prey and began working the cork loose with his thumbs.

All eyes were riveted to Harper's back, twenty-five meters away. Engals readjusted the bottle slightly to the left and then once again eased the cork forward. There was another loud POP. The men leaned forward in their chairs as they watched the cork arc its way over the street, hitting its target with uncanny accuracy in the small of the back.

Harper spun around, looking for the culprit who dared throw a rock at him. At his feet, however, lay a champagne cork. Puzzled, he looked across the street and saw three grown men laughing and jumping about in the open doorway like the little spider monkeys in their cages at the Da Nang zoo.

He picked up the cork and shook it madly in the air. The girl laughed hysterically.

The men moved to the front porch. "John, come on over and join the party. Bring your friend with you."

The girl, apparently understanding English, shook her head and whispered something to Harper. Climbing on her bicycle, she rode off leaving him standing there with the champagne cork still clutched tightly in his hand. He stepped from the sidewalk onto the street and ambled over to his friends.

Engals met Harper on the top of the steps. "Sorry about that, John. We had a little bet goin' that I couldn't hit someone with the champagne cork. When I was lookin' for a target, I saw you across the street talkin' to that girl. Just couldn't resist that broad back of yours."

"Well, it was a helluva good shot. How much did you take these bums for?"

"Thanks. I used to open champagne for my parents. They used to throw these big parties couple times a month during the summer. When no one was lookin' I'd pick out a large apple in our apple tree in the back yard and try and hit it. Got pretty good at hittin' 'em at almost any reasonable distance. Anyway, I took these clowns for fifteen bucks."

"I'm ready for a drink; let's go inside," Harper suggested.

They found McShane standing at the bar pouring beer into a glass. He had changed into fresh fatigues. Looking up from the glass, he said, "What was all the racket about?"

"We were havin' a contest to see if I could hit Harper with a champagne cork," Engals explained. "Why don't you dump out that beer and have some of the good stuff? After all, it's your farewell party."

He left his beer on the bar and sat down with the others at their table. Engals refilled everyone's glass, emptying the bottle.

"At this rate, we'll finish off a case before dark," Dean said. "That is, if it doesn't finish us off first."

"Yeah. Well, me and John don't want to miss that flight to Kontum in the morning," McShane added.

"Don't worry about that. Sergeant Winston here will make sure you're on it."

"Let's have a toast," Adams proposed. They raised their glasses into the air. "Here's to my trip to Bangkok and to Steve and John's new assignment in Kontum. And I sure hope it's a safe one."

* * *

Dean's prediction came true. They finished a case before dark. But that hadn't stopped their drinking. They simply switched over to beer until midnight when everyone staggered to bed. Actually, everyone except Dean, who crawled.

70

Winston had to awaken Harper and McShane at sunrise. He informed them that their transportation to the air base would be leaving at 0700. That's when Harper tried to convince the manager to let him sleep and he would catch the next flight. But there wasn't a flight for another week, explained Winston. It was finally McShane who talked him into getting out of the rack and into a cold shower.

Actually, McShane didn't relish the thought of a roller-coaster ride in a rickety old C-47 nor did he fancy the idea of hanging around House-22 for another week, drinking into the wee hours of the morning. The past two nights had been enough.

A few minutes before 0700, Winston pulled up out front in a new Dodge three-quarter. McShane and Harper sat on the front porch sipping scalding black coffee. Winston honked the horn a couple of times and they stood up uneasily. They dragged their duffel bags down the steps to the curb and then flung them into the back of the idling truck. McShane placed his suitcase more carefully next to his bag. As they were the only two passengers that morning, Winston allowed them both to sit up front in the cab. Besides, he was aware of their delicate condition, and sitting in the back could be disastrous.

The ride to the air base took less than fifteen minutes. Winston dropped them off in front of the main terminal and suggested they check their reservations and the departure time. He wished them luck and drove off.

The Da Nang air terminal was small by comparison to Tan Son Nhut in Saigon or Cam Ranh Bay. But it was still one of the largest in Vietnam and certainly the largest in I Corp.

A company of Marines stood in formation on the lawn with their packs and M-16's, waiting to be flown to Hue. McShane felt sorry for the young grunts as he and Harper strode past. They were always given the shittiest jobs. Not that RTs weren't given some dirty assignments, but at least they had all the air support they could ever use and had the luxury of flying in and out of operations by chopper. Marines had to hump into a flight and then hump out, unless maybe they were lucky enough to be wounded and then they had the luxury of flying out in a medivac. If it arrived.

Lieutenant Stevenson was carefully unfolding Miss November as McShane and Harper approached the terminal information counter. Trying not to look embarrassed, the Lieutenant casually closed the magazine and eased it under the counter. McShane had read the same issue just before he left Bragg.

"Good morning, Lieutenant," McShane said cheerfully. "Do you mind if we take a look at Miss November?"

"Umm...well, I suppose it's all right." The officer nervously glanced around and then pulled the magazine from underneath the counter. "I really think Miss October was better lookin'," replied the Lieutenant, as he fumbled through the pages searching for Miss November. He found her sandwiched between an article by Timothy Leary and "Sex in the Cinema." Stevenson spread her open on the counter.

"She's certainly a tasty treat," observed Harper.

"I think she'll do in a pinch, anytime," McShane agreed.

"Uh, Sergeant, can I help you?" the young Air Force Officer abruptly closed the magazine and stuck it once again under the counter.

"Yes, you can. We're scheduled to leave on the Air America flight to Kontum, departing at 0830. We wanted to make sure we're on the manifest."

"Let's see now," he said, running his forefinger down along the row of names on the manifest. McShane winked at Harper.

Flustered, the Lieutenant looked up from the list and asked the two Sergeants matter-of-factly, "Could I have your names, please?"

"Lieutenant, I thought you'd never ask. I'm Steve McShane and this is John Harper."

The names on the manifest were typed in alphabetical order, enabling Lieutenant Stevenson to find their names quickly. "Yes, you're both on the manifest. And it's still scheduled for 0830. Just listen for the announcement over the PA."

"Well, thank you, Lieutenant," McShane said. "We won't take any more of your time. We'll let you return to your reading."

Still visibly rattled, the Lieutenant replied, "Oh, you're not taking up my time. It's my job to help you."

"Right, I guess we'll be on our way. See you next time we're back through Da Nang."

They left the red-faced Lieutenant and walked across the waiting room to an empty bench and sat down. Rows and rows of long benches crisscrossed the floor, filled with G.I.'s in various positions of rest. Some tried to sleep, some to read and some to talk, while others simply sat motionless and bored, staring at the large round terminal clock, waiting for their particular flight to be announced. McShane and Harper spent their time observing the information officer, who had now reached back under the counter for his magazine and reopened it once again to Miss November.

"Looks like he's at it again, Steve," Harper observed.

"Not for long. This should be real interesting. He's too busy slobbering on November's thighs to notice those two nurses walking up to his counter."

In fact, he didn't notice the nurses until one, a tall brunette, cleared her throat, nearly causing the startled Lieutenant to snap Miss November closed in the nurse's face. Fortunately, she jerked her head back out of the way just in time, catching a brief glimpse of an overly endowed platinum blonde.

A loud, echoing roar of laughter could be heard throughout the terminal from two men sitting on one of the benches. Everyone looked around the room to see what was so funny, not knowing that what had happened was over.

That was all Stevenson could take. He apologized to the young brunette and her friend and then excused himself to the men's room. On his way, he dropped the magazine on a sleeping marine's lap.

After several minutes, another Lieutenant returned and explained that Lieutenant Stevenson had gone to breakfast and wouldn't return for an hour. "Could I be of assistance?" he asked the nurses.

Harper and McShane were still chuckling over the incident with Miss November when their flight was announced over the PA. They grabbed their gear and headed for the departure gate. The wait had been far more enjoyable than either had ever expected.

VI

The blue and white twin engined C-47 dropped through a hole in the thick cloud cover that had enveloped Kontum Province the last couple of days, and settled into its final approach.

Sergeant-Major Fields sat in his jeep, tapping the steering wheel with the knuckle of his forefinger as he watched the Air America plane slowly and carefully make its approach.

He had received a call from the Da Nang FOB Sergeant-Major just yesterday, informing him that two experienced one-zero's had requested assignments in Kontum. Could he use them, the Sergeant-Major asked.

"Goddam right I can use them," he yelled into the phone.

"Well, you've got them," the Da Nang Sergeant-Major had shouted back. "They'll be on tomorrow morning's flight from Da Nang. Have someone meet 'em at the air field."

Well, he wanted that someone to be himself. The FOB had lost four good men, and experienced one-zero's just weren't that plentiful. He wanted to make a good first impression on the two men by showing up personally instead of sending the usual shuttle driver, Sergeant Hedges, the mail clerk. Besides, he needed to butter them up for some of the nasty missions MACV had been throwing their way. Missions that had been causing a lot of casualties.

The C-47 touched down beautifully on the new concrete runway, built by the Seabee's only the year before. It had been recently rocketed by local VC entrenched in the surrounding hillsides and the pilot had to dodge craters created by the 122mm Russian-made rockets.

Sergeant-Major Fields waited for the plane to complete its taxi to the east side of the runway before starting his jeep. He had been given a pretty good description of McShane and Harper. Anyway, they would be the only two who looked like a couple of lost puppies.

Vietnamese ground personnel rolled an aging set of stairs up to the C-47 as the co-pilot unlatched the heavy passenger's exit door. Several Vietnamese women departed the plane with their children and walked carefully down the rickety stairs. McShane and Harper stood in the doorway of the plane, surveying the lush green hillsides of the Central Highlands, and waited for the stairs to clear.

Fields knew right off that the two men standing on the stairs were his boys. He started his jeep and drove up to the plane stopping within a dozen meters of the stairs.

McShane spotted the Sergeant-Major waving his arm. He elbowed Harper, whose attention had wandered to a group of college age Vietnamese girls. "Hey, John, snap out of it. I think our ride's here. See that skinny Sergeant-Major in the jeep?"

Harper nodded.

"Let's go then."

They walked briskly over to the waiting jeep. Fields

climbed over the side of the door and extended his hand. "I'm Sergeant-Major Fields. I hope you're the two I've been hearing so much about from Sergeant-Major Stanley." he said, shaking each of their hands.

"If you've been waiting for Steve McShane and John Harper, then we're your boys," grinned McShane.

"Great. You guys have any gear?"

"Yeah," Harper said. "Think they're unloading it now." The same two Vietnamese who had rolled the stairs to the plane were now passing out luggage to the Vietnamese passengers.

"Hop in the jeep and we'll drive over and pick it up. It's too damn hot to be carryin' anything."

They drove the short distance to the C-47's cargo door. Their duffel bags and suitcases lay off to the side on the concrete. McShane and Harper pulled their bags into the jeep and then grabbed their suitcases.

"That all you have?" asked Fields.

"That's all," Harper replied.

"Let's go on back to the FOB. I'll give you a little guided tour through town; such as it is."

"Sounds good," McShane smiled. He was looking forward to his new assignment at the FOB. And already he found this tall, wiry Sergeant-Major to be quite likeable. But then maybe he was a good PR man. Sergeant-Majors had a knack for spreading bullshit just the right way. He doubted if Fields was much different from most of the others he had come across during his ten years in Special Forces. He supposed that time would tell.

Such as it was, the guided tour through Kontum City was interesting enough. The main street was composed primarily of little shops run by East Indian merchants and Vietnamese jewelers. McShane had never seen so many jewelry stores on such a short street. He also noted a bar in the middle of the street with a rather small sign swinging over the front door with Suzy's Place written across it. Thinking back to the young marine, he knew he wouldn't have any difficulty remembering the name in the future if he was looking for a little diversion. Besides, it was the only bar in town.

Next to Suzy's Place, on a large dusty lot, was an open-air market. Individual stalls covered with scrounged plywood and discarded lumber from an abandoned 4th Infantry Division Battalion headquarters at the north end of town, formed the market place. Vietnamese women sold black market American goods from behind their makeshift counters, while women from the local Montagnard villages sold beautiful multicolored bolts of hand-woven cloth, straw baskets and crossbows made by their husbands. The whole scene reminded McShane of pictures he had seen as a kid of the huge bazaars in Turkey.

Once through town, they drove north on Route 14, a main dirt road that linked Kontum to Dak To, sixty kilometers to the north, and Pleiku, thirty-five kilometers to the south. It was roughly three klicks from town to the FOB on Route 14 and the drive was miserably hot and dusty. The only scenery along the road was vast stretches of rice paddies on either side that seemed to extend forever.

Fields drove the jeep at breakneck speed, showing little regard for local travelers walking into town and often missing them by mere inches as tires spewed dust and gravel on the cursing villagers.

Fortunately, the ride was short and McShane finally saw the FOB compound ahead. They passed through a row of small hootches running perpendicular and on either side of the road. He later learned that many of the civilians working at the compound lived in the houses.

Route 14 split the FOB into two sections. The main area, on the west side of the road, contained the barracks for the RT's as well as the motor pool, headquarters building, chopper pad, indigenous barracks, and the C.O.'s quarters. The club, mess hall, dispensary, and barber shop were clustered together on the east side of the road.

Fields turned through the gate leading into the main compound and drew the jeep to a stop alongside some green sandbags stacked waist-high in front of a narrow one-story building with a blackboard nailed to a post supporting the roof. McShane glanced up at the blackboard. Neatly written in white chalk was the inscription, 30 NOV '67 - HAPPY BIRTHDAY WHITE - PX RUN 1300 HRS - THOUGHT FOR THE DAY: DEVOTION TO DUTY.

"This is the FOB Headquarters Building," Fields said as he opened the door of the jeep. "We'll get you signed in and then find a room for you."

He led the men past the sandbag entryway and through the front door of the building into a blast of freezing air. The shock of the cold almost made McShane forget about the dull throbbing in the front of his head. It had been with him ever since he woke up. He knew better than to drink so much champagne, and he cursed the rotten hangover.

They walked down a long corridor, passing a door on the left with "Major Alex Fernwood — Commanding Officer" written in yellow block letters on a blue sign hanging over the door. Continuing down the hall, they came to another door with a similar sign that read "S-3." Fields pushed it open and allowed McShane and Harper to enter first. A Sergeant well over six feet and weighing an easy two hundred pounds, stood by a desk in the middle of the room reading a report in a manila folder marked "CLASSIFIED -- TOP SECRET." He quickly closed the folder when he saw the two unfamiliar looking men come in.

"Relax, Owens," chuckled the Sergeant-Major. "These are our two new one-zero's from Da Nang: John Harper and Steve McShane. This is Dick Owens, our Operations Sergeant."

Owens smiled and shook their hands.

"Dick will assign you code names and brief you on our mission here. It's not too much different from Da Nang's, just a different AO. Be back in about fifteen minutes, Dick, and then I'll take 'em across the street to S-1.

"Okay, Sergeant-Major," replied the S-3 Sergeant. Fields turned and walked out into the hall, gently closing the door behind him.

Owens rolled two grey swivel chairs from behind the desk in the corner and pushed them towards the standing men. They each fell into one of the chairs, exhausted from the long day and night. He then produced a typed list of names from a stack of papers piled in a safe against the wall.

"Here's a list of available names you can choose from. Most of 'em were guys who've rotated back to the States or to other FOB's.

He handed the list to McShane, who read the names thoughtfully. They sounded like characters from a cheap spy thriller: Ambitious, Dynamic, Killer, Mad Dog, Kamikaze, Lunatic, Clown, Dynamite, Prince, Invader, Headache...Headache would be perfect for now, he thought.

"I think I'll take 'Dynamic'," McShane said looking up from the list. "It's a pretty good description of me."

"Bullshit," Harper grinned. "Gimme that damn list."

He snatched the paper out of McShane's hand and scanned it slowly until he came across a name that suited him. "How's this — Generous? The girls in Saigon used to call me 'Numba one generous G.I.' If they were good in the sack, I'd pay 'em more. They liked that. Gave 'em a little incentive. Found a couple who could really work you over."

Owens laughed. "Generous and Dynamic it is." He took the list from Harper and penciled through the names they had chosen. He placed a 3 by 5 card into his typewriter and began banging at the keys with his index fingers. "What's your middle initial, Steve?"

"A."

Owens hammered at the keys a few more moments then jerked the card from the carriage and stuck it into a metal file box on the left edge of his desk. He repeated the process on a card for Harper.

With the task completed, the S-3 sergeant leaned back in his chair and sighed. "Okay," he began. "Please bear with me for a couple of minutes. It's SOP (standard operating procedure) that I give all incoming personnel a briefing on just exactly what we do here at the FOB. I know you both have probably heard everything I'm about to say at one of the other FOB's, so I'll make my little speech as brief as possible.

"Naturally, due to our sensitive crossborder operations, our missions are classified Top Secret. We obviously want to avoid any nasty political repercussions with the doves sitting back in their fancy offices in Washington." McShane and Harper exchanged sly grins.

"We utilize two types of teams for the missions. Recon teams or RT's and spike teams or ST's. The primary difference between the two, as I'm sure you're well aware of, is their size. An RT is comprised of two Americans: a one-zero who acts as the team leader and a one-one, the radio operator. In addition to the Americans there are four indigenous team members. Here at the FOB we use Cambodians, Laotians, Montagnards and Vietnamese.

"An RT's mission is to recon an AO that MACV thinks

is a likely area for NVA infiltration and troop build up. By monitoring trails and roads a team can gather valuable intel on enemy movement and troop strength. MACV likes to keep tabs on the North Vietnamese so they can inform local infantry units as to the most probable points of NVA infiltration in to the South. The Air Force also uses the intel to direct their B-52 strikes on suspected enemy sanctuaries. RT's are also inserted on BDA's (Bomb Damage Assessment) following an Arc-Light strike. In some cases, they'll be utilized for a prisoner snatch and even assassinations.

"Now," he said, clearing his throat, "An ST is larger. They have three Americans and six or more Indig. Their missions are much the same as an RT's but because they are bigger they're better able to hold off the enemy in tight situations. They'll be called upon to make a prisoner snatch, recover a body or perhaps help out a team that's stepped in the shit.

"All our missions take place, across the fence, so to speak, in Laos which is code named, Prairie Fire." Owens paused, and studied the two men slumped in the chairs. "Are there any questions at this point?"

"Who decides whether we're on an ST or RT?" Harper asked.

"Actually, S-3 decides. Right now I need two RT one-zero's. Lost two a few weeks ago."

"Yeah, we heard the stories in Da Nang," McShane remarked.

Owens nodded. "Steve, I'm going to assign you to RT Illinois. John, you'll be taking over RT Rhode Island. Couple of commo men downstairs want to get out in the fresh air and see a little action. They'll be your one-ones." He opened a notebook and began flipping through the pages. "Let's see. I'm going to assign Dave Wormington as your radio operator, Steve. He's been with us for about four months. Real conscientious kid. I think you'll like him. Charlie Hamilton will be your one-one, John. He's a good buddy of Wormington's.

"Well, that's it. As soon as you check in with Personnel and get settled, I'll have Wormington and Hamilton move their gear out of the Headquarter's barracks and into your team rooms. Any questions?" he asked, replacing the notebook on the desk.

"Not really," Harper replied.

"When do we meet the Indig?" inquired McShane.

"In the next day or so. It'll give you a chance to get settled and learn your way around. Okay?"

"Fine," said McShane.

VII

Harper and McShane stood in front of a screen door. Drawn above the door on a large plaque was a skull and crossbones with RT Illinois printed in red over the skull. Smiling, Harper looked down from the plaque and turned towards McShane, "This looks like your new home. Let's put your bag inside and then we can look for my family crest."

The door squeaked on old rusty hinges as McShane pulled it open. They stood in the middle of the room and inspected its sparse furnishings. In one corner was a bunk with mosquito netting draped over the top. In the other stood a white, four drawer dresser and a tall, single doored metal locker. McShane walked over to the bunk in the left corner, slid his duffel bag and suitcase underneath and sat down on the mattress. He bounced up and down, testing it.

"This one feels pretty good." He turned and looked out the small screened window. "Got a great view of the bunkers and mortar pit. I'll be right on top of things if Charlie decides to pay us a visit."

They found Harper's room at the other end of the

building. RT Rhode Island was printed on a small sign nailed over the door. "Looks like we're neighbors, Steve."

Harper's room was identical to his buddy's. He stuffed his bag into the locker to the right of the door and flung his suitcase onto the bed. "Actually," he said, "this is kind of spooky, taking over the rooms of two teams that aren't around anymore. Particularly since we know what happened to 'em."

McShane frowned. "It's best not to think about that shit. Bad luck. We don't want it interfering with our own missions." Glancing down at his Seiko, he said, "Hey, it's 1700. We haven't eaten all day. Let's go across the street, get a drink, and wait for the mess hall to open."

"Sounds good," Harper grinned.

The club, mess hall, and barber shop were located in a U-shaped building at the east end of the compound. Situated in the middle of the U was a large, covered, screened-in patio with a pool table standing in the rear. The patio was used as an open air theater for the nightly feature length movies that were passed from camp to camp in the II Corp area. Occasionally, "smokers" purchased on R & R in Hong Kong or Bangkok were shown following the main feature. On Saturday nights, barbecues made from split 55-gallon drums were set up to cook steaks.

As they opened the screen door to the patio, McShane noticed four large rectangular holes along the exterior of the wall of the club. He nudged Harper in the side and pointed. "Wonder what those are for?"

"Let's go inside and ask the bartender," Harper suggested. They strolled across the concrete patio, past the pool table and through the open double doors of the club.

The lounge was about twenty-five feet square with a small, raised platform in the right corner. On the left, along the wall, was the bar. Several round tables with Captain's chairs were randomly scattered about the room. A pretty young Vietnamese girl was leaning over the counter, flirting with the bartender. A few early arrivals sat talking at one of the tables.

Harper and McShane pulled a couple of barstools up to the counter and sat down. One of the men seated at the table shouted for the girl to bring another round of beer. The bartender placed four Millers on her tray and she left.

"What would you boys like today?" asked the bartender with a million dollar smile.

"How 'bout two Schlitzes?" Harper grinned in return.

"Okay. Two ice-cold Schlitz comin' right up." He reached underneath the counter into a cooler filled with crushed ice and pulled out two cans of beer, placing each into a hand operated beer opener.

"Twenty cents please."

"I'll get this one," McShane said as he tore two ten cent chits from his Da Nang FOB chit book.

The bartender glanced at the chits. "You boys from Da Nang?"

"I am. My partner's from Ban Me Thuot," McShane explained. "We just got in today."

"Well, great. My name's Harv. Actually, it's Jim Harvey. But people been callin' me Harv ever since I was in high school. I'm a bartender here when I'm not chasin' slopes. I'm one-zero for RT Hawaii."

"I'm Steve McShane." He shook Harv's hand. "And this is John Harper. He's takin' over Rhode Island and I've got Illinois."

"Yeah? I knew the guys on those teams pretty well," he said, a little sadly. "In fact, the one-zero and one-one from Illinois used to play poker with me and my one-one in our team room. Theirs was right next door. The guys in Rhode Island were also good friends of mine back at Bragg. Got a postcard from the one-one, Sam Livingston, last week. He's still recovering from his wounds, but happier than hell to be home with real round eyes. He did mention, however, that he missed the FOB and my Mai Tais. Bet you guys anything, after a few more weeks in that hospital, he'll be changin' his mind 'bout gettin' out of the Army and S.F. Probably be back at the FOB inside six months. Wait and see."

McShane and Harper had finished their beers and were waiting for Harv to finish talking before they ordered another. The good-looking bartender in his red and blue Hawaiian shirt had a way of making them feel relaxed when he spoke. He put the two newcomers at ease in the unfamiliar surroundings. But then maybe it had something to do with the beer on a totally empty stomach.

"It's such a damn shame," Harper said, heavily. "Me and Steve have lost our share of buddies over the years and we're goin' to lose some more before the show's over. C'est la vie, as the French say. How 'bout a couple more of those cold beers and you can fill us in on the FOB."

Harv dipped his tanned hands into the melting ice and fished around until he found two Schlitzes towards the bottom of the cooler. He pulled them up through the slush. "You're goin' to like this FOB," he said, opening the cans. He set them in front of his customers.

"We've got a movie every night. Last night we saw BONNIE AND CLYDE. Boy, I'd give a month's pay to get into the gal's pants who played Bonnie." Harv made a quick pelvic thrust. "On Saturdays we have a steak barbecue with french fries and a nice Da Lat green salad, washed down, of course, with plenty of my specially-chilled beer. The chow's good the rest of the week, too. Then we've got the club to drown your sorrows away. That's where I come in, when I'm not out trackin' gooks."

"How often do you pull a mission?" asked Harper.

"Well, that depends. Maybe once every two or three weeks, depending on the weather. Go out for up to five days. That is, if you don't make contact. Rest of the time is pretty much your own. You can go into town and horse around, stop by the MACV PX or their club. It's nice, but they don't think much of us and frankly, we don't think much of them in their starched fatigues and spit shined jungle boots. Our boys have a tendency to look a little scruffy at times and that pisses them off."

"I noticed a bar in town called Suzy's Place," McShane remarked. "What's it like?"

"You want to steer clear of Suzy's," Harv said quickly.

"Why's that?"

"First of all, the girls who work there have the clap so bad that it'd take a deuce-and-a-half load of penicillin to cure them or you. Second, their mixed drinks are watered down and cost a buck, four times what we charge. Thirdly, the ARVN (Army of the Republic of Vietnam) use the place as a watering hole. Those guys cannot drink. One beer or one of those diluted drinks and they are blitzed. Last month, two guys from the FOB stopped by Suzy's for a beer. An ARVN Lieutenant and one of his Sergeants were sitting at a table, chugging beer. They could barely keep their scrawny asses in the chair, they were so loaded.

"The two sergeants from the FOB, Williams and Dixon, could clearly see the ARVN's were smashed, so they sat at the bar to avoid any hassles and started talking to a couple of the bar girls. Well, this pissed off the slope Lieutenant. Apparently, he'd been trying to put the make on one of the girls all along, but they wouldn't have anything to do with him. The girls knew the ARVN were ill paid, even a Lieutenant. And all they were interested in was a free shot of crack.

"Williams and Dixon bought the girls a drink and then put their arms around the girls' shoulders. That did it. Somehow, the Lieutenant stood up and staggered over to the bar. He pulled Dixon's arm off the girl's shoulder. Dixon casually turned his head towards the slope and looked him up and down. Kinda like, "Who's this little fart think he is, Napoleon?"

Harper and McShane chuckled at Harv's remark.

"Dixon was really cool. He took the glass of beer he was holding and slowly raised it over the Lieutenant's head and then tilted it and poured. The Lieutenant was wearing a brand new pair of starched tiger fatigues. The beer ran down along his shoulders, the front of his shirt and crotch of his pants.

"The girls nearly fell off their barstools, they were laughing so hard. Even the ARVN Sergeant was laughing. Well, Dixon turned his head on the soggy Lieutenant, ordered another beer, put his arm back around the girl and began kissing her neck.

"The Lieutenant stood there for a few seconds, staring down at his beer-soaked fatigues. Oh, the guy was pissed! He knew this big American had humiliated him in front of his own Sergeant and his own people. And he had to show 'em. This is when things ceased to be funny. The ARVN pulled his .45 caliber automatic out of its holster and tapped Dixon on the shoulder. When he turned around, the Lieutenant leveled the automatic on Dixon's mouth. Dixon just smiled. He motioned his head towards the front door and pointed towards the .44 magnum he wore in a shoulder holster.

"The shit got real serious. The girls tried talkin' to the Lieutenant; said he could have a free lay. Both of 'em, if he wanted. But he wasn't listening. He wanted to settle the score with the guy who'd wrecked his shiny new fatigues."

Harper interrupted, "What about Dixon's buddy, Williams?"

"What about him?" Harv countered.

"Well, didn't he try and stop Dixon?"

"Hell, no! Why should he? He knew his buddy could handle himself. Probably thought Dixon was goin' to knock the .45 out of the lieutenant's hand."

"Is that what happened?" McShane asked.

"Not quite. The little Lieutenant led the way to the door with Dixon grinning confidently, following a few steps behind. When the Lieutenant opened the door, he smiled at Dixon, allowing him to pass through first. Before anyone had a chance to shout a warning, the little shit raised the .45 and fired two quick shots into the back of Dixon's head. At that close range with a .45 automatic you can imagine what happened.

"The girls, the bartender and ARVN Sergeant just stared in disbelief. But not Williams. He pulled his .44 from its holster, slid off the stool, and pointed the magnum at the Lieutenant's back. His Sergeant yelled something in Vietnamese. The Lieutenant whipped around and Williams fired all six rounds. Brains, guts, and flesh blew all over that damn bar room."

Harv paused, poured himself a shot of tequila, and tossed the liquid down his throat.

"What happened next?" Harper asked. His eyes were wide with anticipation.

"Well, Williams put his .44 back in its holster, grabbed a towel from behind the bar, walked over to his dead buddy and placed the towel over what was left of his head. Then he picked him up, carried his body to their jeep parked across the street, laid him in the back seat, and drove back to the FOB."

"Damn!" McShane gasped as he crumpled the empty beer can with his hand.

"Yep, it was definitely a bitch. The C.O. put Suzy's Place off-limits and confined all personnel to the FOB compound for a week, unless you had official business in town. He didn't want our boys goin' into Kontum and shootin' up their allies."

"I can see his point," McShane frowned.

"Probably the hardest thing for the C.O. was the letter he had to write to Dixon's wife. I mean, how do you tell Mrs. Dixon that her husband was shot in the back of the head by a South Vietnamese Lieutenant? Aren't they supposed to be on our side?"

"What did he write?" Harper asked.

"Never saw the letter, but a friend of mine who works in the message center saw the teletyped copy that was sent to Da Nang. The C.O. wrote his regrets and explained that her husband had been killed by a sniper while on patrol. Hell, what else could he tell her?"

"Yeah," McShane said softly.

"What happened to Williams?" Harper asked.

"They shipped his ass back to the States before anyone could get their hands on him. He's with 10th Group in Bad Tolz."

McShane sighed, "Think I'll stay away from Suzy's. You hungry yet, John?"

"Not as hungry as I was. Harv's story left a bad taste in my mouth that only beer can wash away."

"Let's get a quick bite and then we'll come back."

They told Harv to hold their seats and stack the cooler with more Schlitz. As they walked toward the club door, Harper turned and asked, "Hey, Harv, what are the holes in the wall for?"

Harv chuckled and replied, "Air conditioners. We ordered 'em 'bout six months ago. Think they must've been sent to some General in Saigon. That's why I keep my beer so cold."

"Yeah, right," Harper chuckled.

* * *

Two weeks went by, and McShane and Harper had still not been assigned an indigenous team. Dave Wormington and Charlie Hamilton had moved in with their one-zeros the day after their arrival. The four had become close friends during the days that followed, and, it seemed, were inseparable. They ate together, drank together, watched movies together and whored together. Few of the other teams were as close as RT Illinois and RT Rhode Island.

It was during their third week at the FOB when McShane was approached by Owens. He and Wormington were sitting at a table outside their room, cleaning their CAR-15's they had been firing at the range earlier that morning at the "Yard" camp. This was the first time McShane had seen Owens outside the mess hall, club or movies, and he hoped that he was bringing good news.

Owens sat down at the table next to Wormington. "You guys ready for a little action?"

This is what McShane had hoped to hear. He sighted down the barrel of his CAR, inspecting for minute particles of carbon he may have missed. Pleased with the job, he laid the barrel carefully on the table and smiled at Owens, "I thought you never were goin' to ask."

"Yeah, well, we wanted to give you time to get settled; find your way around, meet some of the other teams. You know, relax a little bit."

"Hell, I was settled after the first two days. And if I relax any more, I'll forget how to walk. Damn right we're ready for a little action! How 'bout John's team?"

"They'll be your backup if you need 'em."

"What about the Indig team members? Dave and I can't go in by ourselves."

Owens laughed. "Don't worry, we've got a good team

92

for you. Few of 'em were on leave so that's why we couldn't get you guys together earlier. The team has been together for a long time and they know the NVA and how they operate. Trang will be your zero-one and interpreter. He fought with the French as a teenager against the Viet Minh in the early '50s. He's a topnotch soldier and interpreter.''

"So when do we go in?''

"Couple of days. I want you to get together with Trang today and meet the rest of the team. Then tomorrow I'll give you a briefing and if all goes well, we'll get you in the next day, Friday.''

"That sure doesn't give us much time to train with the Indig," McShane noted.

"Like I said before, Trang's team's a good one. They know what to do. They've been out dozens of times.''

Standing up from the table the big Sergeant said, "I'll see you boys at the briefing Thursday morning, 0900.'' He turned abruptly and walked away.

McShane watched Owens for a moment as he strode towards the headquarters building. Wormington returned to the task of disassembling the CAR's receiver group. McShane faced his one-one and asked, "What do you think, Dave? Ready for a little hike in the woods?''

"You bet," he replied enthusiastically. "That's why Charlie and I volunteered: to get out of that windowless commo shack and out into the boonies.''

"We've both been granted our wish," McShane said a little solemnly. "Come on, let's get the CAR's back together and meet our new team.''

They reassembled their weapons quietly and efficiently. McShane had waited over three months for a chance to run a team and now, in less than three weeks, he would be leading his new team on its first mission. They would depend on him for five days and five sleepless nights. He felt both exhilarated and scared. Scared shitless.

After returning the weapons to their room, McShane and Wormington walked briskly over the dusty parade field to the indigenous barracks at the west end of the compound. It was over a hundred feet long and fifty feet wide, much larger than any of the American barracks, and was used to house all the teams' mercenaries. The one large room was broken up into smaller cubicles with portable wooden partitions segregating the men into their respective teams.

Coming from the bright sunlight, it took them a moment to adjust to the dimly lit room. Finally, McShane was able to make out the team names on little signs nailed to the partitions. They walked slowly down the long row of cubicles, reading each of the signs. All the teams had been named after States of the Union, out of patriotic duty, McShane had guessed. They found RT Illinois at the end of the building.

Peering around the corner of the partition, he saw four men huddled around a makeshift stove constructed from an old C-ration can with a chunk of C-4 plastic explosive as fuel. A young, boyish looking Laotian was emptying the contents of a squid and rice lurp ration from its olive drab plastic package into a pot sitting on the stove.

McShane cleared his throat. The Laotian looked up from the stove and gave McShane a big grin. His two front teeth had been capped in gold.

"I'm looking for Trang," McShane said.

An older man, seated with his back to the Americans, stood up and turned around. "My name Trang. You new one-zero?"

"Yes, I am." He spoke slowly and deliberately. "My name is Steve McShane and this is Dave Wormington, the one-one."

Trang stretched out his skinny arm and shook their

hands. The other team members were standing now and McShane figured that their average age must have been twenty. No doubt all had volunteered to fight with Special Forces rather than be drafted into the South Vietnamese Army at a quarter of the pay.

He began introducing the rest of the team to his new bosses. The Laotian was Loc, a tall Cambodian was Billy, probably so nicknamed because his real name had been unpronounceable to a former one-zero, and a Vietnamese with longish black hair named Ngo completed the team. Only Trang and Ngo could speak English.

"Trang, tell the team we go on mission, maybe Friday. Also, tell them I want to inspect their M-16's and packs tomorrow morning."

"Okay. No sweat, Trung Si Mac. I check myself first. Make sure numba one."

"Thanks, Trang. See you tomorrow."

"Okay."

The young mercenaries squatted around the stove and tended to their freeze-dried squid, while Trang stood watching McShane and Wormington walk quickly to the barracks door, anxious for a breath of fresh air.

Outside, McShane breathed in heavily. "Damn, that shit stunk. I need a beer."

* * *

Thursday morning, McShane awoke to a knock on his screen door. Peering through the green mosquito netting, he saw his petite, young Montagnard maid, Aness, standing with an armload of clean folded underwear and fatigues. Aness came by every morning at 0800 to return and pick up any dirty laundry. Occasionally she swept out the room. It was still worth the ten dollars it cost each man in the building per month for the service. He glanced down at his watch, realizing instantly that he had overslept.

He yanked the netting back and jumped to his feet, unconcerned about modesty as he stood naked next to his bunk, fumbling through the top drawer of his chest of drawers looking for clean underwear.

"Come in, Aness," he shouted into the drawer.

She opened the door and tiptoed across the worn plywood floor to his bed, stacking the clean clothes on the unoccupied top bunk. McShane stepped into a pair of G.I. boxer shorts and slipped on an O.D. undershirt.

Aness began to pick up the empty beer cans stacked in a huge pyramid in the middle of the floor that he, Harper, and their one-ones had constructed the night before. She placed them one by one into a tem gallon plastic garbage can in the far corner of the room. She was probably the prettiest Montagnard — a Jeh from Dak Pek — he had ever seen.

McShane grabbed one of the empty cans and tossed it at Wormington, still asleep, hitting him on the stomach. He bolted upright, smacking his head into the springs of the top bunk. Aness giggled.

"Good morning, Dave. We'd better get to the mess hall before they close. Got that briefing at 0900."

Wormington rubbed his eyes with the palms of this hands. "All I want's a cup of coffee."

"Well, that's up to you. But we've got a big morning ahead of us. You might want to eat somethin'."

Without answering, he got out of bed, bent over and picked out a clean set of fatigues from the pile Aness had set on the bunk and dressed.

When they left for breakfast, Aness was still cleaning up the remnants of the party. It had been Harper's idea for an early farewell party, for tonight they wanted to try and get a good night's sleep. Only McShane knew better. He seldom slept soundly the night before a mission. At least, they would wake up without the benefits of a hangover.

After a breakfast of powdered eggs, spam, toast, grapefruit juice and a gallon of coffee, they met Owens at Operations for their S-2 and S-3 briefing. Lieutenant Jim Anderson, the intelligence officer, stood next to a large wall map of Southeast Asia. Owens introduced McShane and Wormington to the tall, slender, blond officer and then motioned for them to sit down in a pair of chairs set up especially for the occasion.

The mood seemed a little somber to the new one-zero. The Operations Sergeant took a seat behind his desk and slipped a blue folder from out of the top drawer of the desk and handed it to the Lieutenant who opened the folder and read silently for a moment.

"Okay, gentlemen," he began, looking up from the folder. "Let's get on with it."

No shit, thought McShane. Sounds like a damn court-martial proceeding.

"Now, we all know that the NVA's AK-47 Assault Rifles are supplied to their men by the Chinese and Russians. We know this both by the differences in construction and serial numbers."

He paused momentarily, as he flipped to the next page. "MACV has received an intelligence report from 4th Infantry Division G-3 indicating that one of their lurp teams captured an AK-47 northwest of Dak Seang with a serial number unlike that of the Chinese or Russians. MACV wants us to get our hands on one of those weapons to confirm the G-3 report. They think that the assault rifle was manufactured by one of the Warsaw Pact countries. They feel, that if in fact, an Eastern European country is supplying weapons to the North Vietnamese, then the U.S. can somehow bring up the subject before the U.N. and get them to make a formal protest to the country in question."

Is that all, thought McShane. MACV wants to risk the lives of six men to confirm a hunch? And so what if Bulgaria or East Germany or Poland was supplying the enemy with arms? The NVA's money was good.

"When do we leave, Sir?" McShane inquired.

"Tomorrow morning at first light," Anderson replied, pointing to the map with a freshly sharpened pencil. "You'll fly by chopper from the FOB to Dak To, where you'll link up with two Huey Blackbird gunships. From there you'll travel west until you reach the AO, code named Romeo-3."

The pencil came to a stop on a five kilometer square area, circled in red, along the Ho Chi Minh Trail. "You and your team, Sergeant, will set up an all-day watch along one of the trail tributaries. Until, by whatever means, you capture a weapon with the serial number in question."

"Sir," interrupted McShane. "It could be a cold day in hell before some poor slob stumbles across our path with one of those AK's. Hell, maybe the NVA planted the weapon the lurps found just to confuse our intelligence."

"That's possible, but not likely, Sergeant McShane. But that's what we want to find out. If after five days you don't come across the weapon, we'll pull you out and inform MACV that we were unable to locate their AK."

McShane stared at the little red circle surrounding Romeo-3. Sitting along a trail for five days, waiting for a squad of NVA to come marching by with special AK's was not exactly his idea of a good time. A squad, his team could handle, but ambushing them would no doubt compromise the mission and surely would bring a world of shit down upon his team. There had to be a simpler way. At least, a better way.

"Sir," he said. "We aren't goin' to get that many chances at a hit, and once we make one or, maybe I should say if we make one, we'll have to move quickly."

"We understand that," Owens said. "S-1 will supply you with two silenced .22 caliber Hi-Standard pistols. When a squad happens by, you can quietly hit the last man, pull him back into the brush and check his AK."

"What if his AK is just an ordinary assault rifle? Then what? Won't be long before his friends miss their comrade and start backtrackin'. We're goin' to have to be long gone by then and we for damn sure can't be humpin' a dead slope through the jungle."

"You'll have to conceal the body the best you can," Anderson said tersely. "Then move your team to another trail. This mission is important to MACV."

"Yes, Sir," McShane sighed, feeling helpless. "We'll be ready to go at dawn."

Thumbing through the folder, the Intelligence Officer said, "Okay. The serial numbers we're interested in begin with SA, followed by four digits." He closed the folder and looked at McShane. "Any questions?"

"No, Sir, don't believe there are."

The two men rose from their chair as Lieutenant Anderson offered them his hand. "Good luck, Sergeant McShane and Sergeant Wormington."

"Thank you, Sir," they replied together.

Owens walked them to the door and wished them luck, too.

"Damn," McShane muttered to his one-one as they strolled to the Indig barracks. "I've waited all this time for a mission, and now that I get one, it ends up being a crazy weapons snatch. If it was a prisoner snatch, we could at least interrogate the son-of-a-bitch. Maybe find out where they've been gettin' any new weapons. Shit!" He kicked at the dusty parade field.

Trang's men were standing outside their barracks with their entire issue of equipment spread out neatly on a canvas tarp. Each man stood behind his own gear with his M-16 at inspection arms. McShane couldn't believe it. He felt like a drill instructor inspecting new troops at basic training.

Trang marched up to his team leader and gave him a snappy salute. McShane returned the greeting.

"Trung Si Mac. Men are ready for inspection," he said in his best authoritative voice.

"Very good, Trang. Let's take a look."

They followed Trang over to the men standing rigidly at attention. If nothing else, McShane mused, I've got the best disciplined team in the FOB. I hope they can fight as well.

Trang stopped in front of Ngo first. He grabbed the M-16 out of his hands, poked his right eye over the muzzle of the barrel, and put his little finger into the chamber so the fingernail could reflect light up the barrel. Satisfied with his inspection, he handed the weapon to McShane who quickly peered down the muzzle. It looked as though it had been cleaned with a Brillo pad. He gave the rifle back to Trang, who returned it to Ngo's waiting hands. McShane smiled at Ngo and said, "Very good." Ngo grinned back, pleased with himself.

Crouching down next to the tarp, McShane randomly picked through Ngo's gear: a clean set of fatigues, three pairs of extra socks and enough freeze-dried lurp rations for seven days. His web gear held twenty-five 20-round magazines for his M-16, four canteens, and a small first aid pouch. Six HE (high explosive) hand grenades hung from the webbed shoulder harness. In addition, each Indig carried one red, green, and yellow smoke grenade in their rucksack. Everything was in order, thought McShane.

McShane and Trang repeated the brief inspection with each man. The Cambodian, Billy, carried a 40mm M-79 grenade launcher. In place of the M-16 magazines, he carried thirty of the inch-and-a-half diameter HE rounds, five white phosphorus and five grape shot cannister rounds. Trang told McShane that Billy was the best M-79 man in the compound.

The two Americans saluted Trang and congratulated him on his men's preparedness. McShane told him to have the team at the chopper pad at 0600 the next day. He would keep the details of the mission from the team until after their departure from the FOB. This prevented any intelligence leaks, accidental or intentional.

They spent the remainder of the day signing out additional equipment essential to the operation: the silenced .22's, a 50 round box of .22 long rifle hollow points, a PRC-25 radio with four extra batteries, and maps of the AO. They packed their individual rucksacks with twelve lurp rations, two anti-personnel claymore mines, ten pounds of C-4 with various time delayed fuses and loaded as many magazines as they could carry. The one-one also had the burden of the additional weight of the radio on top of his rucksack.

It was after dark when they finished their packing. McShane sat back on his bed and leaned his head against the cool concrete block wall. He gazed out the window into the darkness. He worried about tomorrow and the following week and Wormington. It was his first mission. He turned and studied the young radio operator as he fitted the radio into his ruck. He recalled his first mission and the nervousness he felt before going out. Wormington seemed cool, perhaps a bit too cool, thought

McShane. The realization that they would be miles from any friendly troops and over a half hour's flight from help in Dak To, had probably not sunk in. He was too young for this crap anyway, thought McShane. He should be in college somewhere, chasing those tasty co-eds.

He closed his eyes and fell asleep, dreaming about his honeymoon so long ago, it seemed, in Hawaii.

VIII

Black hills slowly turned orange as the sun's first rays bathed the Highlands with a soft glow. The Americans of RT Illinois sat quietly on the edge of their bunks and watched the spectacle, waiting for the time to pass.

McShane checked his black faced Seiko. It was 0555. Five more minutes. He glanced over at Wormington. He was staring at his freshly oiled jungle boots. " 'Bout ready, Dave? It's almost time!"

Wormington nodded. He stood up and unhooked his web gear from the nail above his bunk, slipped it over his shoulders and buckled the belt snuggly around his waist. McShane grabbed his radio operator's rucksack lying on the floor and held it up for him. He backed into the ruck, shoving his arm through the padded straps. Next, he helped his team leader with his ruck.

They gave each other a quick spot check of their equipment and then grasped their CAR-15's propped in the corner of the room. McShane kicked open the screen door, and the two men stepped into the cool, Central Highlands morning air. Deros, the camp dog, jumped up on Wormington's leg and licked his hand. He gave the mongrel pup a pat on his black head, then pushed him aside.

Trang and his men were waiting at the edge of the chopper pad as the Americans walked toward the helicopter a little unsteadily under the heavily loaded rucks. The Indig appeared quite comfortable with their loads, as though they had been carrying heavy packs all their lives, which wasn't entirely untrue.

The pilots of the Huey UH-1B were making a final check of their instruments and flight controls, as the two door gunners busily loaded cans of belted 7.62mm ammunition for their M-60 machine guns, affixed to bipods on either side of the Huey slick. Ground personnel fueled the chopper from a thousand-gallon tanker truck.

McShane took Trang aside and briefly explained their mission. His face was expressionless. It didn't seem to bother the wiry veteran that their mission was fruitless and likely to end in casualties. But rather as a challenge. An adventure. Something to replace the tedium of camp life. His men enjoyed a fight no matter what the mission entailed. On the contrary, McShane wanted to avoid contact.

As they were boarding the chopper, Harper ran up to the team. He slapped McShane on the arm as he was helping the young door gunner feed a belt of ammo in his M-60. Spinning around, he broke into a broad smile, pleased to see his buddy, grinning that Harper grin.

"Thought you'd try and rush off without tellin' ol' John goodbye, huh?"

"Well, I tried. Didn't think you'd be up this early."

"Yeah." Then with a more serious tone, "Hey, look, I want you to take care of that ass of yours. I don't want you back without it."

"Don't worry, John. I ain't comin' back without it. Wish me luck, you sentimental bastard."

The grin reappeared. "You bet, Steve. Good luck, and you, too, Dave. There's nothin' like your first mission."

Wormington had been sitting on the floor of the slick, dangling his feet over the side, "Thanks a lot, John. You're a big help."

"Hey, ease off the kid. This little hike is screwed up enough as it is."

"How do you mean?" asked Harper.

"Don't have time. Tell you about it when we get back, Christmas Eve."

The huge rotor blades began to turn as the pilot kicked over the turbine engine. "Have an egg nog waitin' for me," he yelled above the noise of the rotors.

"Sure."

McShane shook his hand and then joined his team on the floor of the Huey. He gave the pilot a thumbs-up and waved to Harper as he stepped back from the increasing rotor blast. The chopper vibrated noisily as the rotors picked up speed. McShane leaned back and closed his eyes. The mission had begun.

* * *

The flight to Dak To to link up with the UH-1F gunship escorts from the 20th TASS (Tactical Air Support Squadron) had been breathtaking that morning. Nothing was quite as magnificent as a sunrise over the mountains of the Central Highlands from three thousand feet up in a chopper. McShane had seen it many times and each was still unique and just as beautiful.

Now, deep into NVA territory, the gunships formed a ring of protection around them as they neared the landing zone McShane has chosen from the map as the most suitable. They had already made two blind insertions at other possible LZ's in an attempt to throw the enemy off. Everyone aboard hoped this LZ was cold.

The gunships banked sharply, corkscrewing towards the LZ to draw any enemy fire. The Huey slick circled above and waited. Finally, the gunships returned to the side of the slick. The gunship pilot radioed, "Tomahawk one-six, looks like a cold one."

"Roger, one-five."

The slick turned and made a steep descent. The team hastily shoved magazines into their weapons, and moved to the edge of the open doorway. The Indig grinned like kids with a new toy at Christmas time.

The pilot eased back on the control stick as the chopper neared the LZ. It was half the size of a basketball court and pocked with bomb craters. The slick hovered four or five feet off the ground. McShane and Trang, standing on the right skid, jumped first, landing between two craters. Wormington and the remainder of the Indig followed closely behind. The team sprinted to the tree line, fifteen meters away and set up a quick defensive perimeter.

The slick joined the gunships and flew off towards the eastern horizon. They would stay in the immediate area, but out of sight, for another twenty or thirty minutes in the event the team made early contact.

Wormington pressed the handset of the PRC-25 to his dry lips and depressed the push-to-talk button. "Tomahawk one-six, this is Hidden Valley."

"Go ahead Hidden Valley," replied the gunship pilot.

"Still cold at our end."

"Roger, Hidden Valley. That's what we like to hear. See you at the club. Out."

Wormington hung his handset on the strap of his rucksack and leaned back against the tree. McShane pulled the map, wrapped in plastic, from the bottom right pocket of his fatigue pants and traced the route he had planned the day before with his forefinger. It would take the team roughly three kilometers northeast of the LZ to a point where he hoped they would find one of the many subsidiary trails that branched off from the famed Ho Chi Minh Trail.

The team waited while Trang and Ngo fanned a hundred meters out into the jungle to recon their course. The first thirty minutes or so were critical. If the NVA were aware of the insertion, they would be coming to investigate. No one-zero wanted to rush his team into a confrontation with a company of NVA regulars.

Ten minutes later, Trang and Ngo returned. McShane was relieved to find his zero-one smiling. So far, the mission was running smoothly.

Sitting close to his one-zero, Trang whispered, "Okay. No NVA." McShane signaled for the team to move out.

Trang led the way over the same ground he had traveled minutes previously. McShane followed with Ngo behind him, then came Wormington, Billy, and Loc. They kept a good ten-meter interval between them while they walked cautiously through the triple canopy jungle that blocked out all but a few rays of the intense sun climbing overhead.

Every two hundred meters or so, Trang signaled for the team to come to a halt. The team, standing motionless, listened for any unusual sounds that might indicate enemy movement. This careful maneuvering allowed the six men to travel undetected through the dense jungle.

At approximately 1200 hours, McShane stopped the team and motioned for the men to move off the wash they had been traveling along for the past hour and into the jungle for lunch.

McShane and Wormington sat down beside a large rubber tree and eased the rucks from their sweaty backs. The Indig formed a defense perimeter a few meters out from the tree and settled into a crouch with their backs to the Americans, eyeing the surrounding jungle for signs of impending danger.

One at a time, so as to keep any noise to a minimum, the team members opened the flaps on their rucksacks and pulled lurp rations from the top. As it was neither practical nor safe to heat water, the men simply poured a few ounces of tepid water from their canteens into the olive drab foil package and let the contents sit until the freeze-dried chunks softened enough to eat.

McShane sat leaning against the tree, munching on hard beef hash and potatoes. He added more water and stirred the ingredients with a plastic spoon. By evening, the mess would have softened enough to be at least tolerable. The rations were actually quite good when cooked with a little tabasco sauce.

After a half-dozen bites, he folded the package and slipped it back underneath the flap. Pulling the map from his pocket, he laid it on the ground between his outstretched legs. They had traveled a little over a kilometer the past three hours, following the narrow washes created by the heavy rains of the monsoon season. The terrain was primarily densely vegetated slopes.

McShane found their general position on the map and pointed out the coordinates to Wormington. He would call in their position to the relay station, located high on a peak in eastern Laos, using the coded Kak-pad he had been given by the S-3 for the month of December. Presently, they were atop a long ridgeline that would take them down to a narrow valley, where McShane hoped to find the trail.

The Indig didn't mind their lurps and ate better than half their packets before returning the contents to their rucksacks. They stood up, stretched, and put the heavy loads back onto their shoulders. They were anxious to get started.

Their one-zero sighed and slowly rose. He grasped the straps of his pack and jerked it up, thrusting his left arm through the webbed band and then his right arm. He shrugged his shoulders until the load settled into a comfortable position. Wormington went through a similar ritual, made more difficult by the awkwardness of the thirty-pound radio sitting high in the rucksack.

Trang led the team back to the wash and the RT continued silently along the ridge that he hoped would eventually lead them to their destination.

* * *

It took the team the remainder of the afternoon to reach the valley. Ngo had been sent ahead to recon a likely spot to set up camp for the night. He had discovered some three hundred meters from the base of the valley a cluster of bomb craters with several fallen trees laying across the holes. Upon their arrival at the site, Trang found the craters entirely suitable for the night as they afforded excellent cover and were nearly undetectable. McShane agreed with Trang; it was an ideal camp and base of operations for their sorties.

He slid through an opening in the branches and down the bank to one of the craters. The downed trees alone provided excellent camouflage for any NVA who happened by, and this, McShane felt, was unlikely as there was little need for the enemy to stray from the beaten path. After all, this was their territory and American troops were miles away.

McShane whispered for Wormington and Trang to join him in the hole.

"Okay," he said to the two men as quietly as possible while still being heard. "We'll stay here, at least for now. Dave, maybe we can monitor some of their radio transmissions. It's possible sometimes, if they're using captured radios. Be great if we can pick up a little intel while we're here."

Wormington nodded in agreement.

"Trang, have Billy and Loc find a suitable location for a listening post forty or fifty meters from the craters. Have them put out claymores. I want Ngo to stay with Dave while you and I make a quick trip down to the valley. There's still a couple of hours of daylight left."

Trang nodded his approval and scurried up the dirt bank to relay the orders to his men. He reappeared minutes later with Ngo. "We won't be gone long, Dave. Try the radio for those NVA transmissions. Ngo can interpret."

"Right, Steve. Take it easy and don't get lost."

McShane smiled and then the two men crawled together out of the crater. Ngo squatted beside Wormington who sat cross-legged in the dirt, fingering the frequency knobs of his PRC-25.

Trang and McShane stood on a narrow bluff a short distance from the camp. The valley stretched below like a tiny green pit viper as it wound its way north and south between the steep slopes of the mountains. The small valley was no more than a quarter mile across and maybe a mile long. Most of the valley was covered with lush green foliage. According to his map, a little creek was located somewhere amidst the greenery. A perfect place, thought McShane, for the NVA to pass through and rest.

The two men wove their way cautiously down the slope to the valley. Working their way through the brush, they finally came to the creek on the map. Stepping across the narrow stream, they turned north and continued their search for a trail. Only an hour of daylight remained and McShane knew they would have to return in the next fifteen or twenty minutes if they didn't come upon something.

Suddenly, Trang, a few meters to McShane's front, raised his hand and came to an abrupt halt. The one-zero froze. The mercenary motioned for the team leader to come forward. Moving as carefully as a cat stalking a sparrow, he joined Trang, who was now lying on his belly and crawling through a hedgerow. With McShane at his side, they slithered a couple of body lengths and then stopped.

The Vietnamese faced the American and smiled. Before them, entirely camouflaged from the air by the dense undergrowth, lay a wide sidewalk-sized trail. Looking south, the trail ran straight for twenty-five meters, then twisted easterly. Looking north, the trail continued for another fifteen meters until bending sharply to the west.

Glancing up and down the trail once again, they pushed themselves up and stood along the edge of the trail. With McShane covering the rear, they hastily walked up the trail to the bend. Making an almost ninety-degree turn, the trail narrowed to a path no more than a foot-and-a-half wide and then continued up a slope several meters before turning north again. It was ideal, thought McShane. They would start tomorrow.

* * *

Ngo sat with his knees scrunched under his elbows as he rested his chin in his dirty hands and stared at the man with the radio. For better than an hour, Wormington had been listening to static through his handset as he changed frequencies, hoping to pick up something of interest. He wanted to run through the bands one more time before hanging it up, then maybe try again after dark.

He rubbed his eyes and then, startled by movement outside the crater, looked up to see McShane and Trang standing above him. They slid down the bank. Trang whispered in Vietnamese for Ngo to return to the listening post.

"Any luck with the radio?" the one-zero asked softly.

"Nope. Maybe I'll try tonight."

"It's a long shot. But still worth a try," McShane speculated.

"How was your walk? Find anything?"

"You bet. Got really lucky. We stumbled onto a trail about a half a klick east of here. It's perfect, Dave. The trail narrows around a sharp bend and then continues a ways up a slope, then turns again. I figure we can hide the team in the heavy brush that lines the path and wait for a patrol to come along. As they round the bend and out of sight, we wait for the last man in line and then hit him before he turns the corner with his buddies."

"Maybe," said the one-one, "we can split the team up and make two hits, the last and next-to-last man. Grab 'em and meet back here. That way, we'd double our chances at finding the AK. We could bury the bodies in one of the craters."

Rubbing his cheek, McShane said, "Could work. We'll have to play it by ear. We'll set up in the morning. Right now, I'm goin' to dine on some left over beef hash."

He turned to Trang, squatting next to him. "Tell the men to break for chow. Leave one man at the listening post and one up top."

Trang nodded and climbed out of the hole.

Wormington took a fist size chunk of C-4 from his pack

112

and broke it into two pieces. He placed one piece under a metal cup that McShane had filled with water and now held by its handle. He lit the explosive with a match, then sat back and gazed at the orange glow.

Trang returned with Ngo just as the water began to boil. They crouched in between the two Americans with their half empty lurp rations, left over from lunch. McShane poured a few ounces of the boiling water into each man's package, saving a little for himself. It was a real treat to have hot water to mix with lurps.

"Ahh," McShane said, stirring the water around in the packet. "There's nothing like reheated, freeze-dried beef hash in a B-52 bomb crater after a nice hike through the woods."

They all chuckled and then ate their meal in silence.

* * *

As usual, McShane only grabbed snatches of sleep. He had always found it difficult to sleep in the jungle, away from the relative security of a guarded camp. But it was just as well. The insomnia provided him with time to think out an operation. It also doubled the guard against a possible enemy probe, as each man pulled an hour's watch.

At first light, he reached over and shook the arm of his one-one who lay comfortably curled in a fetal position in his makeshift poncho and poncho liner sleeping bag. He awoke instantly and sat up.

"Rise and shine, Dave. Time for breakfast. You have choice of squid and rice, chicken and rice, tuna and rice or the house special, beef hash."

"Shit! What difference does it make?" He yawned,

kicking the liner off his legs. "They all taste the same. What time is it?"

"Six o'clock. We want to be set up on the trail and ready before the gooks start moving."

."What if today is their day off?"

"Fat chance. Those guys don't know what a day off is." He looked at his watch again, "I'm goin' to check on Trang and the boys. I want to leave in half an hour. Heat up some water for breakfast."

The Indig were up and eating as McShane ambled up to the listening post. Loc stood guard, leaning against a tree several meters from the team with his M-16 cradled in his arms. Trang smiled at his one-zero as he crouched beside him. "Good morning, Trang." He smiled, "Tell the men we leave in twenty-five minutes."

He gave a quick nod.

"Hear anything last night?"

"Billy think maybe he hear trucks somewhere. But not know for sure. Maybe airplane flying over mountain."

"Maybe." He decided now would be a good time to explain his plan to his interpreter. "We'll set up along the trail we found yesterday. We'll wait for the NVA to come. Then Wormington and I will shoot the last two men. You and the men run out and pick up the bodies and carry them back here. Okay?"

"Why not capture NVA? Get beaucoup information."

"We're only interested in their weapons."

Trang simply shrugged. It was all very confusing. What good were two enemy weapons? Besides, he liked the M-16 better, anyway.

Wormington thought the chicken and rice he was eating for breakfast tasted suspiciously like the beef hash he had eaten for lunch and the chili con carne for dinner the day before. He imagined the manufacturer probably spiced all the meals the same. Hell, who cared, as long as they weren't cold!

He looked over at McShane, who had just returned from talking to Trang. He was eating a squid ration; the least appetizing to the Americans but the favorite of the Indig who would gladly trade any of the other rations for a squid. It made him shudder to see McShane scoop the rice and bits of chopped tentacles into his mouth.

"What are you lookin' at, Dave? Haven't you ever seen anyone eatin' squid and rice for breakfast?" He shoveled another spoonful into his mouth. "Nothing like it."

"Bullshit!" chuckled the radio operator.

Smiling, he checked his Seiko. "Ready to move out?"

"Yeah."

Before leaving the security of their bomb crater, Wormington pulled the Kak-pad from the sleeve on the flap of his rucksack. Turning to the coded page for the day, he called in a brief message, informing the relay station that they were moving to a new map coordinate to set up an ambush.

The mercenaries were on their feet, itching to move out, as the Americans approached the listening post. All signs of any human presence had been picked up or covered. He was pleased with his team's thoroughness at keeping the mission covert. A simple slip-up like a discarded lurp packet or wooden match could be disastrous.

Trang and McShane took the point and led the team over the same general route they had followed the evening before, frequently varying their course to foil an enemy ambush attempt, however unlikely. The morning was cool and pleasant as the men of RT Illinois cautiously picked their way through the jungle.

Upon reaching the tiny creek, they quickly filled their empty canteens with the icy mountain water and dropped a halozone purification tablet into each. Then, they split into two three-man teams. Trang was to take Billy and Loc and position themselves at the narrow bend in the trail, while McShane, Wormington, with the silenced .22s, and Ngo would set up at the curve in the trail where it widened.

Trang's men would be able to signal McShane at the first signs of an oncoming patrol. As the patrol passed Trang's position, he would again signal them either a thumb's-up, indicating the end of the patrol or a quick thumb's-down, meaning more men on their way. With a thumb's-up, McShane and Wormington would pick off the last two men in the file before they reached the sharp twist in the trail and out of sight of the other patrol members who would have rounded the bend.

McShane's half of the team found excellent cover behind a large, rotting rubber tree that lay hidden underneath a heavy strand of vines from a tree above. From this position, they could clearly see Trang's hand signals through an opening in the brush, twenty meters west. Wormington lay beside his team leader while Ngo, crouched in a bamboo thicket a few meters east, studied the long, wide stretch of trail. From his vantage point he would be able temporarily to hold off the NVA if they suddenly turned to investigate the disappearance of their missing buddies. All that was left was the long, agonizing wait.

* * *

"How the hell we supposed to get in the Christmas spirit when outside it's ninety degrees in the shade with ninety percent humidity?" joked Harper as he sat with Charlie Hamilton, drinking a gin and tonic in a tall glass and staring at the silver colored, plastic Christmas tree someone had bought two years ago while on R & R in Hong Kong.

"Damn, wouldn't it be somethin' for those *Stars and Stripes* reporters to write about if it snowed in downtown Saigon this year on Christmas Day?"

"Never happen," said Hamilton, taking a sip of his San Miguel.

"Yeah, well you never can tell what might happen in Saigon on Christmas. Hey, Sergeant-Major, hear anything on McShane this afternoon?" he asked Fields, who had just sat down with Owens at the next table.

"Just got a report from the relay station. They're about to pull up stakes for the day and return to their base camp. Waited all day for an enemy patrol. Nothin'. Goin' to give it another shot tomorrow. They feel certain somethin' will come along. The trail they're covering has been well traveled."

"I hope they can pull it off, Sergeant-Major. I promised Steve I'd buy him an eggnog when he got back. Don't want him steppin' in a pile of NVA shit and then have my team sent in to bail his ass out on Christmas."

"McShane's an experienced one-zero," reassured Fields. "He'll make it back in plenty of time for an eggnog."

Harper held up his glass. "Well, here's to Steve McShane and RT Illinois. Wherever you are, Merry Christmas."

* * *

McShane took a drink from his canteen, then wiped the drips of tepid water from his chapped lips with the back of his hand. He glanced at his watch. It was 1730. They had spent the entire day lying in the dirt waiting for a Vietnamese patrol. The mosquitoes were their only distraction from the sweltering heat and tedium of the trail watch. Forming miniature mountains were dozens of mosquito carcasses piled next to Wormington's and McShane's exposed left forearms. The score appeared even as McShane carefully squished one last victim between his thumb and index finger. He would have to save the game for another day. It was time to get the team back to the craters and settled in before dark.

The team leader reached over the log, grabbed the end of a vine and pulled his aching body up. He stood on the rail, then walked stiffly over to Trang, who sat crouched on the side of the trail. McShane pointed to his black faced Seiko watch and waved his arm in the direction of the craters. Trang slowly rose and moved up the path to inform Billy and Loc, who, hidden in a thicket, obediently watched the trail. They exchanged glances and smiled when Trang motioned for them to move out.

At the creek, the team paused long enough to sink their faces into the cool spring water, washing away the day's sweat and grime. Ngo and Billy waited their turns as they kept a watchful eye for intruders.

McShane reflected on the mission as he mechanically placed one weary foot before the other up the long, steep slope to the craters. He had already tired of the operation. It seemed pointless and far too risky. The sooner he made the hit, the sooner he would be back in Kontum, drinking at the club with Harper. Maybe their luck would change tomorrow.

The RT arrived at the craters an hour before sunset. They ate a quick meal before turning in for the night. Wormington made a final radio report. McShane took advantage of the last brief moments of daylight and began hastily but methodically field stripping the silenced Hi-Standard single shot .22 pistols, first used in World War II by members of the OSS. The pistols had to perform flawlessly if they were to pull off the mission successfully.

He finished cleaning the .22's under the last bit of dwindling light and placed them under his poncho. He pulled a poncho liner out of his rucksack and wrapped it around his shoulders, then leaned back against the ruck and instantly became lost in thought as he began mulling over the details of tomorrow's operation.

IX

McShane was washing down a mouthful of mushy, freeze-dried meat balls with stale, blood warm water when a squadron of B-52 sized mosquitoes landed on his bare left forearm and began sucking. Quickly, he rubbed his arm against the inside of his left thigh. He picked them off and dropped them onto the pile. The addition of the new bodies to the stack left from yesterday clearly put him in the lead. He stared blankly at the half dozen or so red welts rising on his arm then turned his attention to the trail. He gazed up its empty length.

Wormington was about to turn the radio on for the noon transmission, when McShane, out of the corner of his eye, saw Trang frantically waving his arms. At last, he thought, someone was finally coming down the trail. The RT pressed close to the dry earth. McShane waited for Trang's signal as the first members of an NVA patrol straggled past their position.

Only it wasn't just a patrol. For the better part of an hour, armed men dressed in the standard uniform of the North Vietnamese Army — khaki fatigues and white pith-like helmets — carrying heavy packs and AK-47's, sauntered down the trail. McShane was able to observe the troops undetected through narrow openings in the brush. He counted close to a hundred soldiers during the next twenty-minutes.

He began to worry about the increasingly painful cramp in his upper left thigh. He tried readjusting his position. But it was in vain. The only satisfactory position was an upright one. He looked over at Trang, hoping to see the all clear signal that would allow him to stand and stretch. Trang only stared impassively at the trail and the moving men. McShane chewed on a twig and tried to think about something else. Even Wormington was becoming restless. He began to fidget, rubbing his neck and lower back. McShane prayed it would be over soon.

Then suddenly, glancing at Trang once again, he noticed the little Vietnamese become more alert. Trang leaned in the direction of Billy, hidden from McShane's view. Billy pointed towards the trail, then made a slashing motion with his right hand across the throat. Trang turned back and gave his team leader a thumbs-up.

McShane elbowed Wormington, who was following an overweight beetle with a sharpened stick. It was crawling slowly in front of his left hand. The radio operator glanced up. McShane was reaching for the silenced .22, dangling from a two foot lanyard looped around his neck. Wormington twisted his makeshift spear through the crunchy black body and grabbed his Hi-Standard.

Trang held up five fingers for the American and began subtracting a finger at a time. Five men left, four, three...there was a three man lag between them and Trang. McShane waited for the soldier Trang had started with and then picked up the count. With a seven-to-eight meter interval between each NVA, McShane hoped that the third to last soldier would be well aroung the bend in the trail when they made the hit. Even then, it was going to be risky.

The Americans moved cautiously to a kneeling position. The third soldier was about to walk in front of them. They pulled back the hammers on the .22's. The third man passed and began to round the corner. Wormington sighted on the next to last NVA while McShane aimed at the last. Suddenly McShane saw movement to his right. He cocked his head. Through the brush, he saw Trang wildly waving his arms. When he knew he had his team leader's attention, he gave him a thumb's-down. What the hell, McShane wondered.

But then McShane heard it. A loud, gruff voice shouting in Vietnamese. And now, glancing once again at Trang, he saw that the interpreter was giving him a thumb's-up. Now he was really puzzled. The voice came yelling around the curve near Trang's position and down the long stretch of path leading past the concealed Americans. McShane poked his head over the log and peered through an opening in the hedgerow.

What he saw made him chuckle softly to himself. The voice belonged to a craggy, old North Vietnamese Army Sergeant. He was scolding two young soldiers, probably for lagging behind, surmised McShane. Every couple of steps the Sergeant would stop and lecture them. The Privates would bow their heads in apparent shame. Then, satisfied his words had taken effect, he would continue stalking down the trail, only to stop again a few meters later to give them hell.

McShane found the situation ideal. The rest of the enemy troops were by now several hundred meters ahead of the three strays. This fact allowed the team more time for the ambush and increased their chances of success. They would shoot the two Privates and snatch the old man. He could be a valuable source of intelligence.

Cupping his hands around Wormington's ear, McShane quickly whispered, "We'll hit the two Privates. Then grab the old man. Don't let him scream."

He nodded. McShane firmly gripped the pistol and sighted on the first of the two privates. Wormington followed the second soldier. The three NVA stopped directly in front of their position. The Sergeant again reprimanded the young soldiers. They were so close now, McShane could have stuck his hand through the brush and untied the old man's boot laces.

The Sergeant turned from his men and began to walk away. McShane and Wormington stood erect. They leveled the silenced Hi-Standards over the chest high hedgerow and fired two, unheard shots. The hollow point round from McShane's pistol entered through the first private's left ear canal, mushrooming as it traveled through his brain and exited, with his right eye in a brilliant red mist of bone fragments. He crumpled to the ground. Wormington's slug struck the back of the second soldier's head, just below the knowledge bump, blowing shattered teeth and half a shredded betel nut-blackened tongue onto the shoulders of the Sergeant.

Before either man had come fully to rest on the trail, Wormington had lunged from hiding and encircled his left arm around the Sergeant's neck and squeezed the mouth shut with his right hand. Leaping from his position, Ngo took the man's feet and helped Wormington carry him into the jungle. The Sergeant seemed too surprised and shocked to put up a fight.

Trang and Loc ran down the trail. They each grabbed one of the bodies and, half carrying, half dragging them, followed Wormington and Ngo into the brush. Billy remained behind as a lookout.

McShane scraped the teeth and tongue off the trail with the edge of his boot. He kicked dirt over the blood and brains. Then he ran up the path to get Billy. The young mercenary grabbed him by the arm, yanking the startled

American into the brush. The M-79 man held his index finger up to his lips. McShane heard the clanking of canteens.

The two men crouched low and waited. McShane hoped the rest of the team made their way back to the creek and continued on up the slope to the craters as planned. But he knew Trang or Loc would probably return to investigate their team leader's tardiness. He frowned as a file of NVA strode down the trail.

Fortunately, it appeared to be only a small security squad. They moved past them. Billy and McShane started to stand, but then the North Vietnamese stopped just before the bend. One of the soldiers stooped down. He unsheathed his bayonet and began scraping at the dirt. From what McShane could see it appeared that the shuffling feet of the squad had unearthed the pool of blood he had hastily covered moments earlier.

Puzzled, the soldier followed the stream of strange-looking mud with the tip of the bayonet. He started poking around at the base of the bush where McShane had kicked the teeth and tongue. Billy and his team leader paled when the NVA laid down his bayonet and fished under the foliage with his hands.

McShane repositioned the selector switch on his CAR-15 to full-auto while Billy raised the M-79 to his shoulder. They prayed the squad would move on before they found the grizzly remains of their comrade.

But the NVA soldier was persistent. He had two other members of the seven men squad on their hands and knees, rummaging in the underbrush. Oh, Christ, thought McShane, it's only a matter of time.

The first soldier brought his hands out, clutching a couple of broken teeth still clinging to strands of red gums. He let out a gagging scream, flinging the clump of gore into the air. One of the other men found a few more teeth and the tongue. The squad looked around nervously. The first soldier shouted something in Vietnamese, and Billy squeezed the trigger of the grenade launcher. At 20 meters, it was a cinch.

The 40mm HE round struck the ground just in front of the feet of the three investigators. A sharp, deafening explosion roared through their ears as they felt themselves helplessly lifted off the trail and catapulted into the hedgerow.

The other squad members lay screaming and writhing in mortal pain from the dozens of tiny spring steel fragments that had twisted through their flesh. Two of the men managed to get up. Three five-round bursts from McShane's CAR slammed the soldiers back onto the trail, killing them and putting the others out of their tortured misery.

Wormington and Trang had just crossed the creek with Ngo and Loc carrying the dead NVA when they heard the explosion and the automatic weapons fire. Wormington ordered the two Indig to drop the bodies and return to the trail. He unhooked the radio handset from his pack strap. Trang held the handcuffed and blindfolded prisoner tightly by the arm. Wormington had planned to wait for the whole team to rendezvous at the craters before calling for an extraction, but the surprise skirmish forced a change in those plans.

"Contact! Contact!" He shouted excitedly into the handset, disregarding the coded Kak-pad procedures which were senseless now, anyway; their mission had been compromised. "This is Hidden Valley. Have made enemy contact. Have one prisoner. Need extraction ASAP at primary Lina Zulu, over." There was the usual radio clutter, then a faint voice gabbled in the earpiece.

"Roger, Hidden Valley," replied the relay station. "We'll have the choppers in the air ASAP."

He replaced the handset and waited with Trang for the return of his one-zero and the Indig.

Just as they crossed the creek, Loc and Ngo met their team leader and Billy storming through the jungle. They were carrying seven AK-47's. Weighing more than ten pounds apiece, the weapons were a heavy and cumbersome load. McShane looked drawn and was instantly pleased to see the two mercenaries. Grinning, he gave each of them two weapons and then led them across the creek.

They found Wormington and Trang standing uneasily with their prisoner in a thick grove of trees fifty meters north of the creek. They smiled nervously as the four men approached.

"The choppers are on the way, Steve," Wormington said quickly. "Probably take them about forty-five minutes. We're going to have to hustle. All these extra AK's ain't helpin', either."

"The prisoner's not carryin' anything," McShane noted. "Let's load him up with three of the weapons. That'll leave one apiece for the Indig."

Trang passed the word on to the team. Ngo and Billy hurriedly tied the slings of the AK's to the old Sergeant, arranging them so he could still travel freely.

"Okay," McShane said. "That's good enough. Let's get the hell out of here. Not going to be long before this place is crawling with dinks."

* * *

Owens found Harper with Hamilton and their team filling sandbags on the east perimeter of the FOB compound. His shirt was off and he was bent over at the waist, holding an olive drab sandbag open. Hamilton, perspiring heavily and woozy from a long night at the club, shoveled dirt from a pile left over from the Seabees after they had dug a large pit for a new underground communications center.

"Hey, Harper," shouted the S-3 Sergeant. Harper let go of the bag and straightened up, arching his upper torso as he rubbed the small of his back.

"What's up, Owens?" he asked, wiping sweat from around his mouth.

"You'd better get that eggnog mixed for McShane," he replied.

"He called for an extraction?"

"About five minutes ago," Owens confirmed. "Choppers are in the air. You best get your men into their gear just as a precaution. Stand-by pilots have been alerted in case there's trouble. Meet 'em at the chopper pad in fifteen minutes."

Harper and Hamilton, along with the Indig, double-timed to their barracks. It took the Americans only moments to grab their packs and snatch their CAR's.

"Charlie," Harper said, out of breath. "Take my CAR. I'll meet you at the choppers."

"Where are you goin'?" he asked, puzzled.

"Never mind. Just get the team to the choppers," he replied, running out the screen door.

* * *

RT Illinois made no attempt at a stealthy return to the LZ. It was an all assholes and elbows retreat. On several occasions the team heard an NVA patrol in hot pursuit as they crashed through the scrub brush. McShane knew they would probably have to confront the patrol before the afternoon was over.

Whereas it had taken them nearly a full day to cover the three kilometers from the LZ craters, it now took them only forty minutes to return. They hoped the choppers would be on time; it seemed as though a division of NVA were now following them along the ridge to the LZ.

About a hundred meters from their destination, McShane signaled the team off the wash they were traveling along and led them into a thicket that surrounded the LZ. He stopped the team and motioned for them to crouch down behind a stand of tall elephant grass. They tried to control their labored breathing. There was no sign of the choppers.

McShane took the radio handset from Wormington's back strap and depressed the talk button, "Tomahawk one-six, this is Dynamic." Releasing the button, he waited a couple of moments, then tried again. "One-six, one-six, this is Dynamic. Do you copy? Goddamn, where are those guys? We've got half the North Vietnamese Army on our asses!"

Finally, "Roger, Dynamic," replied the chase pilot. "Hold onto your hats. We'll be over your position in a couple of minutes. You should have us in visual contact, over."

McShane rose and peeked around the elephant grass, straining to see the little brown bugs that would take them safely back to civilization.

"One-six, I can just see you now. Hope you brought plenty of friends. We've got a bunch of bad guys on our tails."

"Relax, Dynamic. We'll take care of 'em for you."

He returned the handset to Wormington. "Let's move closer to the LZ, Dave. We'll have to pop smoke."

They moved more quietly through the elephant grass until they were just on the outskirts of the small clearing. By now, the Huey slick and its gunship escort were clearly audible as they bore down on the LZ.

McShane grabbed the handset once again. "Going to pop smoke." He threw a yellow smoke grenade out into the clearing and waited for the pilot to identify its color.

"Dynamic, I see yellow smoke."

"Roger. Yellow smoke," the team leader confirmed calmly. "We're five meters east..." Suddenly, the sound of automatic weapons interrupted McShane as the NVA opened fire from a tree line thirty meters northwest of their position. "We've got contact, one-six."

"Guess those bad guys don't want you boys to leave," the pilot radioed. "Think they're goin' to wish they'd stayed in bed by the time we finish with 'em."

The two Huey UH-1F Blackbird gunships broke from the slick and dove towards the tree line. The team watched in amazement as the gunships fired their twin, four thousand-round-a-minute G.E. mini guns at the trees, splintering branches and blasting holes the size of acorns in the trunks. Moments after the guns started, the small arms fire ceased. The gunships circled, stalking the LZ.

McShane waved the team out onto the LZ as the UH-1B slick descended to pick up the dirty and exhausted men. The chopper hovered a half dozen feet off the ground. One by one the team members threw their weapons onto the floor of the Huey and then pulled themselves up on the skids and into the slick. Wormington helped the trembling prisoner into the chopper.

McShane handed his CAR to the chase medic, Sergeant Williams, who sat dangling his feet over the side, lending a helpful hand to the team members. He grabbed the team leader's arm and yanked him into the chopper. Sitting down in the middle of the floor, McShane smiled. The slick rose slowly until it was above the trees, then nosed forward, picking up speed as it moved away from the LZ. They had actually pulled it off, McShane mused, and without a single casualty.

They observed two Air Force A1E Skyraiders from the 56th SOW (Special Operations Wing) unleash their payload of five hundred pound bombs on the tree line. McShane would suggest an immediate Arclight B-52 bombing mission on the little green valley and the surrounding area to the S-3 when he returned. It would probably necessitate the insertion of another team for a BDA in the next day or so.

* * *

"Sergeant Harper!" shouted the young, red-haired Warrant Officer who was sitting behind the controls of the Huey. "Just heard from the slick pilot."

Harper lay with his head on his pack and his feet propped up on a discarded wooden ammo box. "Good news, I hope."

"They're bringin' in the team. Should be here in about thirty minutes."

"Everybody okay?" Hamilton asked.

"Had a little trouble with a NVA patrol, but the gunships and Skyraiders took care of 'em."

Harper sighed, and closed his eyes against the intense afternoon sun. He could relax, at least for the time being, now that his buddy's team was returning safely from their operation. But he knew that the day after Christmas, RT Rhode Island was scheduled for a mission. Harper couldn't shake the feeling of dreaded anticipation. He didn't look forward to the operations as he once did. And particularly, the day after Christmas.

The half hour had seemed like only minutes to Harper when he awoke to the sounds of the approaching helicopters. He sat up on the grass, trying to focus on the blurry, brown objects. Hamilton crouched in the shade of the backup chopper, talking to the two pilots, while the Indig dozed on the canvas seats inside the Huey. The slick carrying McShane and his team moved swiftly, nose down, towards the small FOB airfield. It circled around the chopper on the ground, then landed. Harper's Indig, now awake, jumped from the Huey and ran over to greet the tired men jumping out of the chopper.

McShane guided the still blindfolded prisoner over to Harper and Hamilton. "Brought you guys a little Christmas present from you Uncle Ho. I want you to meet Sergeant Khai, late of the 5th Battalion, 95th Infantry, North Vietnamese Army."

Seeing the AK's hanging from each team member's shoulder and the three strapped to Khai, Harper asked, "Christ, you guys sellin' guns to the enemy now?"

"Only if I don't get promoted next month," Wormington returned dryly.

"Hey, I almost forgot," Harper said. He pulled his canteen from the canvas cover and offered it to McShane. "Merry Christmas, Steve."

"No, thanks. I've had my fill of canteen water. I'll wait and have a beer at the club."

"Take a drink, you dumb shit. This ain't no ordinary canteen water."

He reluctantly took the canteen, unscrewed the cap, hesitated and took a sip. Smacking his lips, he then took a long drink from the plastic canteen. He handed it to Wormington.

"No," he agreed, wiping his lips with the back of his hand. "That ain't no ordinary canteen water. Merry Christmas, you son-of-a-bitch." And he reached out and hugged Harper.

"Welcome back, Steve."

X

As it turned out, Sergeant Khai proved to be far more of an intelligence coup for MACV and the FOB than the weapons. None of the AK-47's captured by RT Illinois bore the serial number prefixes they wanted. Fortunately, the Sergeant turned out to be more valuable. Over the course of the next several days, Lieutenant Anderson and his team of intelligence experts slowly unfolded his story.

Born in Hua Lac, thirty kilometers east of Hanoi, in 1922, Khai joined the Doc Lap Long Minh, or as it was shortened to later, the Viet Minh, in 1942 and fought against the Japanese who had invaded Indochina in 1941. He fought under Vo Nguyen Giap until August 1945, when the Japanese surrendered.

He returned to Hua Lac and his father's small poultry farm and worked there with his wife until September 1950. Then he was called back into the services of the Viet Minh, again serving under Giap who was readying two infantry divisions to use against the French. On 16 September 1950, Khai, just a Private, was part of an invasion force that attacked a small French outpost at Dong Khe, manned by two companies of French legionnaires on the northeast border of Vietnam and China.

Outnumbered some eight-to-one, the surviving Legionnaires managed to escape the fierce hand-to-hand fighting by stealing away through the enemy troops at night. Private Khai was promoted to Corporal when, during the engagement, his platoon Sergeant was torn in half by a rocket from a French bazooka and Khai took command of the relatively inexperienced platoon, leading them in an assault on a French machine gun emplacement.

Throughout the early fifties, he continued to fight under Giap against the French, until 13 March, 1954. Khai, now a Sergeant with the Viet Minh 308th Division, was part of the some 50,000 troops gathered to attack the 16,000 French soldiers garrisoned at Dien Bien Phu. After a 55-day siege, the 308th began to overrun the French's outer defensive outposts - Gabrielle, Beatrice, Isabelle, and Anne Marie. It was Khai's platoon that first broke through the inner outpost of Elain, which included the village of Dien Bien Phu, on 7 May 1954, and along with the rest of the division thrashed the French defenses, bringing the French to their knees by nightfall when 11,000 troops surrendered.

While the French lost decisively, the Battle of Dien Bien Phu proved to be very costly to Giap's Viet Minh. Some 8,000 of his men were killed and 15,000 wounded. The French garrison lost 2,200 killed and 11,000 captured, which included 5,100 wounded. Many of the captured died on their way to prison camps.

Sergeant Khai was seriously wounded in the battle when a Legionnaire thrust his bayonet into Khai's stomach during heavy hand-to-hand combat. Knocked unconscious by an empty 105mm shell casing when he fell to the ground, the Sergeant was presumed dead by the Legionnaire and survived the ensuing fierce fighting. Later, after the French had surrendered, he was found alive under a stack of dead Viet Minh and French by his platoon medic who was searching for survivors. He was patched up and trucked to a military hospital in Hanoi, 275 km to the east. After three months in the hospital, he returned to the quiet of his farm and there spent the next ten years happily raising chickens.

During the late fifties and early sixties, fighting was renewed in the South. Some 1,000 Viet Minh, who had remained in the South after the Partition of Vietnam on 21 July 1954, joined forces with roughly 2,000 North Vietnamese infiltrators and formed the core of the Viet Cong in 1960. They began recruiting followers from various dissident groups, including the hills tribesman of the Central Highlands.

In addition to training guerrillas, the Viet Cong launched a campaign of terrorism in the South, assassinating local government officials. The acts of terrorism expanded from mere bombings and kidnappings to small scale attacks on South Vietnamese Army patrols.

Beginning in 1961, the United States began sending helicopters and American maintenance personnel. Soon, more Americans arrived to train South Vietnamese pilots and to fly combat missions for Special Forces Advisors and their often ragtag CIDG (Civilian Irregular Defense Group) troops. By the end of 1964 U. S. manpower reached 23,000.

On 4 March 1965, two days after the start of "Operation Rolling Thunder," the bombing of North Vietnam, Khai's wife and two children were killed along with his parents. A bomb intended for a bridge a few kilometers from their farm landed on the chicken coop where they were gathering eggs for a customer.

Khai had been aware of the fighting in the South, but had wanted to stay out of it. Two wars had been enough. But now it seemed that there would be a third. He joined the 33rd North Vietnamese Army Regiment on 7 March after the funeral of his family. He spent four weeks at an NVA training camp near Hanoi, then set out with the 33rd down the Ho Chi Minh Trail.

Ten weeks later they arrived in southeastern Laos, near the village of Ban Pakha, 100 km east of the town of Attopeu and 20 km from the Vietnamese border. Throughout the summer and early fall, the division set up a massive base camp in the thick, mountainous jungle and surrounding caves. Khai, because of his prior combat experience, had been made a platoon sergeant and was responsible for training the new recruits within the company.

In October '65, three regiments from the 33rd totaling some 6,000 men crossed the border into Vietnam, massing in force amidst the tall elephant grass and dense jungle near a Special Forces outpost at Plei Me, 45 km southwest of Pleiku in the Central Highlands. Their objective was to eliminate Plei Me and two other Special Forces camps in the area, capture Pleiku and march to the coast, thus dividing the country in two.

The NVA didn't count on the stubbornness of the twelve American advisors and their 400 Montagnard and South Vietnamese irregulars. Nor had they planned on the two brigades — the 1st and 3rd — of the 1st Cavalry Division (Airmobile) that aided the camp.

The defenders, with the aid of the massive air support, including the first use of B-52 in support of group troops, were able to beat back the NVA. But this was only a temporary setback. They had simply withdrawn into the Ia Drang Valley where the North Vietnamese commander was preparing another attack on Plei Me.

During late October and early November the 1st Cav's 1st Brigade searched the jungle around the outpost for the enemy. Later, when it was believed that the NVA were readying for another assault, the 3rd Brigade was brought in.

When part of the brigade, the 1st Battalion, 7th Cavalry Regiment, landed by helicopter into a LZ located in the back yard of two of the North Vietnamese regiments, the NVA temporarily gave up their plans for an attack on the Special Forces camp and instead pounced on the battalion, inflicting heavy casualties. They then moved on to the little camp.

In hellish fighting and with the aid of the rest of the 3rd Brigade, the Americans pushed back the North Vietnamese attack. The battle raged on and off for six days — 14 November through 19 November — until, burdened with heavy losses from the fighting and the B-52 raids, the NVA retreated into Cambodia, leaving some 1300 dead to rot in the heat.

It was on the sixth day of the fighting that Sergeant Khai's platoon assaulted a squad of Americans pinned down by machine gun fire and snipers hidden in the trees and elephant grass. The platoon rushed through the grass, firing their AK's from the hip and lobbing grenades at the frightened Americans. So intense was the firing that when Khai's platoon reached the Americans, they had expended their ammunition. The Americans, too, had emptied their magazines and both sides had little choice but to turn their weapons around and use them for clubs.

Khai jumped into a foxhole manned by two Privates of Bravo Company, 1st Battalion, 7th Cavalry Regiment, 3rd Brigade, bashing in the head of one soldier with the wooden stock of his assault rifle. The other G.I., a radio operator, swung around in time to ward off another blow from the little Sergeant and shot Khai in the right shoulder, chest, and left thigh with his .45 automatic. The RTO left Khai for dead when he retreated with the remnants of his squad.

Two members of Khai's platoon found him unconscious and bleeding profusely next to the dead American. With help from two other comrades they carried him back safely to their staging area in the elephant grass and then on orders from their company commander, the platoon pulled out of the Plei Me area and made a hasty retreat towards Cambodia with the remaining units of the 33rd. It was the first decisive victory, on a large scale, for the American Infantry in Vietnam.

The 33rd moved under the cover of darkness, avoiding contact with roving units of the 1st Cavalry on search and destroy operations, into Cambodia. After a two week forced march they reached the village of Ba Lev in northeastern Cambodia, 40 km from Vietnam. It was there that Khai, who had partially recovered from his wounds, received proper medical treatment in a small Cambodian hospital set up by the NVA.

It was decided by Khai's commanding officer that when the Sergeant was well enough to travel on his own, he would return to the jungle base camp in Laos and work only as an instructor in the training of new recruits. The C.O. felt Khai was too valuable and experienced a soldier to have killed in a firefight. So far, he had been lucky.

After a month at the little hospital, Sergeant Khai led a detachment of former patients through northern Cambodia to the base camp in Laos and there spent the remaining two-and-a-half years training young recruits. And it was just four kilometers from his base camp that two of his recruits were shot and he was taken prisoner.

* * *

Sergeant Steve McShane sat in front of his room on the rickety wooden steps that were desperately in need of repair, reading some of the half dozen or so Christmas cards he had received the day after New Year's. One was from an old high school buddy he had played football with in Crescent City. The friend had gone to work at Bubba's Texaco right after graduation and had been there ever since. He had written to tell him that he had finally saved enough money to buy the service station from "old man Roberts" who was finally retiring after forty years and going fishing in Oregon. He had thought maybe, when McShane decided to get out of that "awful war, we could be partners or something."

McShane smiled as he read the card. The only way he would go back to Crescent City was underneath an American flag, and even then he wasn't so sure. He slipped the card back into the envelope and then looked up when he heard boots crunching on the gravel walk. It was Owens. Grinning, he said, "Good morning, McShane. Reading old Christmas cards?"

He nodded, "Good morning, Owens. Got these today. You know how the mail gets screwed up over here sometimes."

"Know exactly what you mean." He sat down in an aluminum folding chair. "We just heard from Harper's team. They've made a thorough BDA of the valley and surrounding area. Apparently the B-52's did one hell of a job. The team found a complex of bunkers, a couple of bodies the NVA had forgotten to police and lots of documents. Choppers are pullin' 'em out right now."

"That's good news. Better get over to the club, get some beer, and meet him at the chopper pad. I know that's what he's been thinkin' about the last five days."

"That and a few other things," Owens chuckled. "One other thing. The old Sergeant you brought back last week has kept the boys over at S-2 busy as whores on Saturday night."

"How's that?" asked McShane. This was the first he had heard of their captive since bringing him in on Christmas Eve.

"It seems he was the equivalent of one of our drill instructors in basic training while he was with the 33rd Division. In fact, he was with a company on maneuvers when two VC recruits became separated. He had returned to find 'em and was bringin' 'em back when they walked into your little ambush. They certainly paid for that mistake."

McShane looked puzzled, "So what's the 33rd doin' training VC recruits, practically in our back door?"

"He says they're preparing for a large offensive against this area on Tet. The intel we've received from MACV and the other FOB's indicate the same things. Only the offensive will be countrywide, not just in Kontum. MACV wants the FOB's to step up their operations along the Ho Chi Minh Trail this month. Tet's only four weeks away, on the 30th."

McShane stuffed the cards into the top pocket of his faded green jungle fatigue shirt. "Why's he tellin' S-2 so much? Seems a tough old fart like him wouldn't have much to say."

"Actually," Owens said, propping his feet on the corner of a step, "he's volunteering the information. Says he's sick and tired of humpin' the hills, sleepin' in the dirt month after month, havin' bombs dropped on him and training green VC recruits. He wants to Chieu Hoi ("Open Arms" - the amnesty program) and become a Kit Carson scout."

McShane leaned forward, "How's he know about Chieu Hoi and Kit Carson scouts?"

"Guess he found one of our propaganda leaflets. They have ways of findin' out. Hell, Nha Trang's one of the biggest VC and NVA R & R Centers in South Vietnam.

There's not much those gooks don't know."

"We goin' to keep him? Be a real shame to lose this guy to the ARVN grunts."

Owens rocked back in his chair until it leaned against the building, "S-2 wants to interrogate him a little while longer. Wants to make sure he's not pullin' their leg. But they're takin' good care of the Sergeant. Think he's already gained five pounds from eatin' our mess hall chow. This is probably the best he's been treated in a long time."

"Yeah," said McShane as he stood up, brushing the dirt from the bottoms of his fatigue pants. "Harper's goin' to be landin' any minute. I best get over to the club for those beers or John will never speak to me again. Want to come along?"

"No, I've got to get back to S-3. I'll be seein' Harper at the debriefing. Don't let him drink too much."

McShane grinned. "I wouldn't do anything like that, Sergeant."

*   *   *

Harper and Hamilton went over the events of each day of their BDA operation with Owens at the debriefing. They had found plenty of damage but little sign of the enemy. McShane's once little green valley had been churned by the bombing into a blackened lunar desert. The tiny creek now meandered aimlessly, filling bomb craters until they overflowed. The trail only existed in the memories of RT Illinois and Sergeant Khai.

On their fourth and last day, Harper told the S-3 Sergeant, the team had stumbled onto the remnants of an underground bunker beneath a stack of fallen trees.

Harper's interpreter, Lam, was leading the RT over a tree that bridged a crater when he suddenly disappeared with a yelp after stepping off the end of a large branch onto what he thought was solid ground. Hamilton, a few feet behind Lam, rushed to the end of the tree and was startled to see him standing next to a broken table, ten feet below.

The team huddled around the hole and stared down at him as he brushed the dirt from his face. Posting Tu, the M-79 man and Cao, a boyish Vietnamese whose father had been an Italian mercenary with the French, as sentries, Harper and the remainder of the team leaped into the hole.

Once inside, the hole broadened into a large underground room, apparently a briefing room judging by the blackboard Hamilton found underneath a pile of earth near the table with unintelligible white chalk marks drawn on its surface. They also found, scattered about and half-buried, an unusual amount of maps, charts, and other documents that they gathered up and stuck into Harper's rucksack. Not so unusual, however, as Harper had seen the same phenomena on other BDA's, was the absence of bodies. The NVA and VC always managed to drag their dead from a battlefield in an attempt to baffle their enemies and mislead them into thinking they had failed at killing any of them.

Researching the end of the room that extended some thirty meters into the side of a hill, the team discovered, half covered by dirt, an opening leading into another room. The RT hurriedly began scooping the earth away from the doorway with their hands until it was large enough for them to crawl through. Even in the dim light, Harper had no trouble in identifying the remnants of what once had been an operating table, now covered with dirt and bits of broken glass from a surgical cabinet that had been knocked across the table during the bombing.

They had found the remains of the 33rd NVA Division's hospital. Passing through the ward, the team poked among the debris, finding little of interest, until Hamilton tripped over a partially buried foot next to an overturned cot. He brushed away the dirt, revealing a gaunt, open-eyed, NVA patient dressed in a faded blue hospital gown. He had apparently been buried alive as the team found no obvious wounds.

Satisfied with their inspection, they returned to the room with the blackboard and climbed up through the hole with the aid of a chair placed on top of the table. Tu and Cao helped pull the team members to the surface.

Feeling reasonably pleased with the outcome of the mission, Harper radioed for an extraction, hoping the stack of official-looking documents would prove useful to S-3. He was a little disappointed that the body count for MACV and the Air Force would be so low. They always liked to be reassured of a job well done.

XI

Every American in the FOB looked forward to the Saturday night steak barbecue held on the enclosed patio between the mess hall and the club. It was a convenient spot to have it. One could cook his steak to his own specifications over the split 55-gallon drums and at the same time order a drink from one of the cocktail waitresses standing by with their trays and note pads. When the steak was done, he simply threw it on a plate, took it and his drink inside the mess hall and waited for a server to bring the french fries, baked beans, and garlic bread.

Harper and Hamilton arrived at the barbecue just as the last two steaks were being thrown on the grill.

"Damn that Owens!" Harper shouted. "He had us sittin' in that debriefing room for five hours. He knew it was Saturday! And dammit, Charlie, there go the last two steaks!"

Sergeant Carnes, the massive ex-pro tackle turned Mess Sergeant, pushed open the mess hall's screen door with his enormous ass, and walked over to the two men who were now seated at a table on the patio and ordering a drink from Baby San, a cute, Vietnamese cocktail waitress. Carnes smiled as he plopped into a chair at their table. "Hear you guys had a good week."

"Until now," replied Harper, obviously pissed. "What happened to all the steaks? Some of those KP's in the back sellin' 'em downtown?"

He laughed, "Naw, not any of my KP's. Don't worry, John, I saved you boys the two best steaks in the FOB. Got 'em marinatin' in Carne's special barbecue sauce. They should cook up nice and tender."

Hamilton and Harper grinned at one another. "Well, Sarge, I'm sorry I jumped to conclusions, but you know how it is to eat lurps all week, plan on an FOB barbecue, and then have the last steak snatched up in front of you."

"Damn," interrupted Hamilton as he looked over his shoulder to see who had let the screened patio door slam. "Owens is back to back to squeeze out another pint of blood."

The Mess Sergeant rose from the table. "When you guys are ready to eat, let me know." He turned and trudged towards the mess hall.

"Hell, I'm ready to eat now," Hamilton said to Harper. But before they had a chance to leave, Owens grabbed a chair from another table and pulled it over.

"Wait 'til I tell you what S-2 found in some of those documents," he said, easing himself into the chair.

"Can't it wait until after we eat?" asked Harper.

"Oh yeah, sure, go ahead. I'll go get some beer."

"Good idea," said Hamilton.

Fifteen minutes later, just as they were flipping their rare T-bones onto plates heaped with french fries, Owens returned from the bar with three San Miguels. The men sat down. Owens passed out the beer.

"Okay, Owens, I can hardly wait to hear what S-2 found in those documents," Harper said, stuffing a hand full of crispy french fries into his mouth.

"They pretty much back up what Sergeant Khai told us last week. The NVA and VC are planning one hell of a party for us and South Vietnam on Tet." He stopped to sip his beer. "Those documents you picked up mapped out their plan of attack for the Central Highlands."

"So what kind of surprise do they have planned for us?" Hamilton demanded.

"Well," replied the S-3 Sergeant, "S-2 has just started translating the papers, but they did read where they're planning a heavy offensive in Pleiku province. They're also planning assaults on the major highland cities of Dak To, Kontum, and Ban Me Thuot. I can tell you this," he said, taking another sip, "when MACV reads our report, they're goin' to want us to increase our crossborder insertions into Prairie Fire. They're goin' to want minute by minute reports on all enemy activity. The RT's have a lot of work ahead of 'em. At least until after the 30th."

Pushing his plate to the side, Harper wadded up his napkin, tossed it onto the half eaten T-bone and abruptly left the table to intercept Baby-San.

* * *

Sergeant Owens had been correct in his prediction. After MACV received the S-2 and S-3 report from the FOB, they immediately called upon all the FOB's in the Central Highlands to step up recons of their particular AO's. The teams met with the heaviest resistance of the war, further substantiating what Kontum and MACV had already known.

So heavy was some of the ground fire from NVA

emplacements that many RT's were never allowed to be inserted, or if they were, they instantly made contact and were extracted. However, these contacts led to increased South Vietnamese and U.S. air attacks on the enemy strongholds, which proved to be effective, if in no other way than to psychologically harrass them with the bombing.

During the four weeks preceding the Lunar New Year, RT Illinois and Rhode Island made numerous attempts at finding a weak spot in the enemy's defenses. RT Rhode Island managed an insertion but was hastily extracted on their second day when they made contact with an NVA weapons platoon carrying RPG-7 portable rocket launchers, 82mm mortars and 75mm recoiless rifles.

Fortunately, few of the platoon were carrying light weapons and Harper and his team were able quickly to break contact, killing six of the platoon and wounding several others with only one casualty to the team when Loc was hit in the left thigh by a grenade fragment. The area was recommended to the Air Force as a target for an Arc Light.

McShane's team also had their share of problems. Twice they had been shot out of an LZ. Once they managed to stay on the ground for forty-five minutes before being discovered by an NVA recon patrol. On another occasion, the chopper carrying his team was so severely damaged by anti-aircraft and automatic weapons fire that it was barely able to limp back to Dak To and safety. That was another area brought to the attention of the Air Force.

Meanwhile, the FOB was making its own preparations for Tet. Using Sergeant Khai, who had now pledged his loyalty to President Thieu and President Johnson, and his knowledge of NVA battle techniques, the compound increased their defenses. Sergeant Drake and his team of engineers bulldozed a six-foot-deep-by-eight-foot-wide trench around the outer perimeter and filled it with sharpened bamboo poles. They also tripled the number of claymore mines.

In addition to the combat engineers' task, the teams, when not out on an operation, were assigned various duties to strengthen the compound's defensive perimeter. Plastic sandbags were filled and stacked, replacing the older cloth types. Additional .30 and .50 calibre machine guns were added to the perimeter as well as 60mm and 81mm mortars. It was exhausting work heightened by the torrid sun that never seemed to set.

* * *

A week before Tet, the men of the FOB were awakened by a steady burst from the compound's southwest .50 caliber machine gun emplacement. Only thirty meters from McShane's and Harper's barracks, the gun sounded thunderous in the quiet of the early morning.

McShane rolled off his bunk onto the cold concrete floor and crawled on all fours to the corner of his room where he kept his web gear and CAR-15. Wormington was in Nha Trang, straightening out his pay records with Finance. McShane slipped his arms through the harness of the web gear and buckled the pistol belt securely around his waist. Taking his weapon from the hook on the wall, he crawled to the door and opened it. The .50 caliber had not let up.

Cautiously, he eased along the side of the building to Harper's room. As he reached the steps, Hamilton kicked open the door, swearing quietly, "Goddamn dinks! Wait till a guy's drunk and passed out and then decide to make a probe."

Harper followed his cursing one-one. The three men continued together along the edge of the barracks towards the .50 caliber.

Other team members began to emerge from their rooms and head to their bunkers. Somebody fired an 81mm flare. In the eerie red glow, McShane saw a familiar silhouette standing atop the tower, swinging the machine gun slowly from left to right and then back again. He nudged Harper with his elbow. "Do you see who I see behind that gun?"

Harper squinted in the dwindling light of the flare. Another exploded above, illuminating the tower once again. "Damn," said Harper. "That drunken asshole woke us up so we could play his little game."

They moved closer to the silhouette. McShane shouted, "Sir! What is it? An enemy probe?"

The figure turned from the gun and looked down at the three men bathed in the harsh light. "We have met the enemy and he is ours!"

He returned to the gun and fired another long burst. More flares burst overhead. The three men scanned the concertina-wired terrain. There was nothing.

"Everytime that son-of-a-bitch gets drunk," Harper said, "he pulls off some crap like this. Maybe we oughta shoot the bastard so he won't drink so much of the club's booze."

"I don't know," chuckled McShane. "But, we've got one crazy C.O. Let's get back to bed. My team's got a lot of sandbags to fill tomorrow."

The next evening, during the nightly movie, a gruff voice roared through the room, interrupting the film. A figure moved in front of the screen and raised his arms, "I want all my staff officers to meet me back at my room ASAP!"

No one budged from his seat. Jane Fonda was taking

off her space suit in Barbarella. McShane, sitting in the back of the room by the projector, asked Harper, "What's the ol' man up to now?"

Still standing in front of the screen, censoring the scene behind him, he yelled again, "Mac, Dave, Bob, Chip. Where the hell is everybody?"

No one answered.

"Goddammit! There'll be hell to pay if my staff's not in my quarters in five minutes." And with that, the C.O. staggered through the door and out into the night.

"I think he must be gettin' the pre-Tet jitters," Harper whispered.

* * *

RT Illinois spent the morning of the 28th cleaning their weapons, loading additional magazines, and distributing grenades among the team members. An attack was imminent in the next day or so as RT Nevada had made contact with a VC company in the hills west of the FOB, taking one prisoner.

The prisoner told Sergeant Khai, now an interrogator with S-2, that several hundred VC were massing in the hills and would attack the city and the FOB on the morning of the thirtieth. His own company, four platoons of sappers, was responsible for blowing up the air terminal and destroying as many of the helicopters and planes as possible. When Khai asked him how many men would be involved in the assault on the FOB, the prisoner shrugged and said he thought he had overheard an officer say something about a battalion or two — four hundred to eight hundred men.

With his new information, S-2 immediately informed

the C.O. A hasty meeting was called to discuss the intel with his staff. It was agreed that the FOB would be placed on full alert, effective at once, with fifty percent of the compound on line after dark. A company of infantry from the 4th Infantry Division, 4km to the north, would be requested as support for the compound's three companies of Montagnard CIDG, one hundred Indig team members and sixty Special Forces advisors. The request for the infantry company was turned down by their brigade commander.

As another precaution, the club began serving only soft drinks to the thirsty men and quite understandably, even in the face of major attack, they complained bitterly, particularly John Harper. On the first night of the liquor ban, he sat at the rear of the club, with his dusty jungle boots planted on the edge of the circular table, sipping a club soda with a twist of lime. McShane and Hamilton shared the table.

"This is the shits," Harper said disgustedly. "We're about to be attacked, maybe overrun and wiped off the face of the earth and the ol' man decides to sober up. Doesn't he realize that now is the time we most need the club and all it has to offer?"

McShane looked up from his coke and frowned. "Hey, John, why don't you try and relax? You're as nervous as the C.O. Anyway, maybe it's better this way. We'll certainly be alert when the gooks try and storm our little bastion."

"Aw, bullshit!" Harper shouted. Then, lowering his voice, he said, "Those bastards ain't got a chance. Even drunk, we're twice the fighters they are. Besides, they'll never make it through the mines, the concertina wire, and the pit Drake dug."

"Yeah, John, you're right," said McShane, "but you know they'll rocket the hell out of us first. They probably have the club zeroed-in to go first."

"Hell, what difference does it make?" Hamilton mused, stirring the ice in his grapefruit juice, sans Vodka. "Might as well blow the damn building up. Ain't any use to us anyway."

"It's eight o'clock," yawned McShane as he stood up. "I've got guard duty at midnight. Think I'll try and get a little sleep. See you in the morning."

"Yeah, see you," Harper growled.

Outside, it was a beautifully cool and clear night. McShane strolled along the walk and gazed up at the stars. Lost in thought, he narrowly missed colliding with Deros, who tore across his path in hot pursuit of a Vietnamese delight, a rat the size of a small cat. Deros must have already wounded the rodent, for he ran with quite a noticeable limp. As the rat ran across the road towards the gate of the west compound, McShane realized the limp was a result of a nearly amputated right hind leg.

Deros was toying with the rat, as he ran just fast enough to let the rodent know he wasn't out of trouble, yet. The rat must have sensed his impending fate, for he was losing blood fast and beginning to slow down.

The rat scampered through the gate and across the parade field the best he could under the circumstances. Deros barked excitedly, inches from his prey's tail. They disappeared around the Indig barracks. McShane smiled at the guards who had been busily watching the spectacle. They shrugged and went about their business of searching some late night employees on their way home.

Walking up the path to his room, he was suddenly greeted by a proud and panting Deros who promptly licked his hand. As he stooped down to scratch behind the dog's ear, he caught a glimpse, in the light shining from his window, of the rat's nose and flattened tongue protruding from the side of Deros's mouth. McShane

abruptly stood up and walked to the latrine to wash his
hands.

* * *

The Tet Offensive began ten days early for the Marines
at the Khe Sanh Combat Base and their surrounding hill
outposts, 25km south of the DMZ, when on 21 January
1968, North Vietnamese infantry made an unsuccessful
attack on one of the outposts. This was followed up by
a heavy artillery barrage that destroyed sections of the
Khe Sanh runway, blasted their ammunition dump, and
killed eighteen Marines. The following afternoon, the
Marines were resupplied by air with additional ammunition and were reinforced with the 1st Battalion, 9th
Marines. The 77-day siege of Khe Sanh by some 20,000
men of the 304th and 325th NVA Divisions had begun.

A little over a week later, early on the morning of the
thirtieth, enemy gunners fired on Nha Trang and then
launched a ground attack. Two battalions of communist
soldiers assaulted Ban Me Thuot. An enemy battalion attacked Tan Canh, a district capitol next to Dak To. Then,
three VC battalions hit the Highlands capitol of Kontum
City. The Tet Offensive was now in full swing.

* * *

The first six 122mm rockets landed north of the FOB,
one hundred meters short of Sergeant Drake's bamboo
spiked trench, signaling the beginning of the Kontum Tet
Offensive.

McShane had played it safe. He had gone to bed wearing his fatigues and boots. His web gear hung on the frame of his bunk while his CAR stood leaning against the chest of drawers, an arm's-length away. He had tried to stay awake, but had fallen asleep sometime after 0200. Sometime after 0300 he was jolted upright by the sound of the half dozen exploding rockets.

After three hours, it was automatic. He grabbed the web gear off the frame, shoved his arms through the harness, and buckled the belt securely around his waist. He picked up the CAR with its two 20-round magazines taped together with adhesive tape and sprinted for the door.

"Shit," he mumbled to no one as he ran for the bunker behind his room. "Dave's goin' to miss all the fun."

He could hear the cries of the Montagnard children, as they were herded into bunkers at the west end of the FOB, along with their parents. They had sought the safety of the FOB earlier in the day.

Five of the next six rockets landed only a few meters short of the north perimeter. The sixth fell among a group of seven frightened Montagnards who had panicked and become separated from the others. McShane grimaced as he saw them picked up by the blast and hurtled through the chill morning air like bowling pins at the Crescent City Bowl on Wednesday nights.

He heard two of them screaming, "Bac si! Bac si!" (doctor, doctor) over and over. A CIDG medic hurried to comfort them.

The next salvo landed in the center of the compound, on the parade field and in between the motor pool and the Indig barracks, destroying S-1's jeep. So far, thought McShane, the VC's F.O. (Forward Observer) was doing a lousy job of calling the shots. Thank God.

By now, the mortar crews were firing a steady supply

of flares above the FOB in anticipation of a ground assault. Rather than sit crammed into the team's bunker, waiting for the inevitable, McShane chose to take his chances crouched outside behind the sandbag wall that provided him with a better over-all view of the compound; it was a lot easier to see the enemy sneaking about in the dark from outside the bunker. And this way, he would act as a rear guard for the team huddled inside against a possible sapper attack from within the FOB.

The VC stepped up their rocket attack. They began coming in groups of ten. A rocket splintered the guard shack at the entrance to the west compound. Another blasted a hole in the roof of the latrine. So far the rockets were doing little more than churning up the soil and doing light damage to a few structures.

Suddenly, it seemed that the rocket team had gone for broke, firing everything they had. For five minutes they pounded the FOB. No one doubted now; a ground assault was imminent. And for once, the rockets were doing their job. Two struck between a pair of armed gunships in the east compound, just as the pilots and crew were lifting off. The choppers exploded, instantly killing both crews and touching off secondary explosions that severely damaged three ARVN choppers.

The ARVN chopper crews crawled reluctantly out of their bunkers and tried frantically to prevent the fire from spreading with CO_2 fire extinguishers. But the flames were too intense and the men became frightened when the ammunition aboard the choppers began going off. They turned their attention instead to the two undamaged choppers. The ARVN pilots quickly turned over the engines, while crew chiefs and door gunners scrambled aboard.

Only one chopper made it. The other crashed when the pilot, in his haste, maneuvered the chopper too quickly to the right, clipping the leading edge of the rotor blades in the tangled wreckage of the gunship. The Huey flipped over on top of the still burning chopper. The entire crew was lost when the ruptured fuel tanks were ignited and the chopper exploded.

Rockets hit the Indig Club, the covered porch between the mess hall and the club, the barber shop, RT's Hawaii, Tennessee, Alabama and Arkansas barracks. While damage to the FOB increased, the casualty rate remained relatively low, primarily confined to the ARVN chopper crews and Montagnard villagers. Then, as suddenly as it had started, the rockets stopped. But now, the VC ground assault the men had been expecting was launched from the tree line to the north, a hundred meters from the trench.

The initial VC elements carried wood planks to bridge the eight foot trench. The gunners manning the .50 and .30 calibre machine guns opened fire on the two dozen or so guerrillas as they raced for the trench, raking the ground and the VC with hot copper-jacketed lead. Four of the original group reached the trench and quickly flung their planks across. The four were ripped apart by the intense stream of bullets as they signalled the main assault group to attack.

A few moments after the signal to attack, rockets smashed into the bunkers along the north perimeter, knocking out two of the machine gun emplacements and wounding several of the Indig and two Americans. Under the cover of the renewed rocket attacks and the resultant confusion, scores of VC dashed across the makeshift bridges. Others picked up their fallen comrades' planks and threw them across the trench. The rockets continued to slam into the perimeter. The men in the bunkers laid down a heavy base of automatic weapons fire. The 81mm mortars lobbed HE rounds on the ant-like hordes scrambling across the fields.

When the VC reached the first row of concertina wire, still over two hundred meters from the bunkers, they tossed their dead onto the corkscrewed barb wire and used them as human stepping stones. But what lay waiting on the other side of the wire was far more deadly than anything they had encountered so far. Twenty cinemascope shaped claymore anti-personnel mines, each packed with one and a half pounds of plastic explosives and seven hundred steel balls, were stuck in the ground ten meters apart and tilted slightly upwards.

As the screaming communists approached, an American in each of the bunkers grasped a M57 firing device wired to a claymore. One by one, the mines were detonated. The numbers of running VC were reduced sharply. The blast from McShane's claymore caught more than a dozen men within its deadly killing zone. The little balls shredded flesh, smashed teeth, snapped bones, disemboweled, and tore out eyes. Only two VC moved on after the explosion.

More and more VC poured out of the woods and crossed over the narrow wooden bridges. They knew that the claymores were good only once. Speed was of the essence now, if they wanted their mission to be successful.

With well over two hundred assaulting from the north, the VC launched another attack from the Montagnard village on the west perimeter. It followed the same pattern as the earlier assault. But this time, all but one of the bridge team members was killed or disabled, drastically reducing their chances of success. Undaunted, a new group of comrades rushed to pick up the planks and push forward. With six planks in place, and under another heavy barrage of rockets, stage two of the western siege began with men streaming from out of the village.

The crews on the eight 81mm mortars were hard pressed to keep up their barrage. One mortar had been designated to fire nothing but flares, while the others fired a combination of HE and WP (white phosphorus) rounds, inflicting heavy casualties.

The lone surviving Huey made low passes over the enemy troops, while the door gunners utilized their M-60 machine guns to rake the charging VC with 7.62mm rounds. It was a hell of a morale booster to the men below to see the chopper flying up and down the battlefield, reducing the odds.

Several flares floated lazily overhead. McShane peered over the sandbagged wall. He could see the stubborn enemy slowly making their way towards the perimeter. They were approaching the second row of claymore mines, a hundred meters from the bunkers. He fired a rhythmic pattern of three-round bursts until he emptied the magazine. For every VC shot, there appeared to McShane to be two more to take his place. It was endless.

He rejoined his team in time to see several VC nearing his claymore. He took the second M-57 from the wooden shelf and readied the firing device that would complete the electrical circuit and with it bring death.

Wiser the second time around, the VC sent a suicide team ahead to dive on the mines and in a last-ditch effort try to yank the wires from the back of the claymores. None were successful at disconnecting the wires but most all were victorious in preventing the mines from destroying their comrades.

McShane watched in awe as one of the VC kamikazes dashed for a claymore in a desperate attempt to save the squad of men following him. The squad stopped and let the skinny little soldier do his dirty work. Ngo was also following the VC's movements with his M-16. A couple of steps from the mine, Ngo fired a short burst. The man's head popped back and his lifeless body crumpled to the ground. The squad had little choice but to move on or be cut down by the continuous hail of bullets. A volunteer sprinted to the side of the dead VC. He propped him up in a sitting position, and, using the body as a shield, he began pushing it over to the mine.

RT Illinois opened fire on the human shield. The four M-16's, firing on full automatic, literally disintegrated the body's chest, exposing a faceless volunteer who had been crouching with his head pressed against the body's back. The Indig turned their attention and weapons on the remaining squad members, killing all of them.

Another group of VC charged toward the claymore, completely unaware that the mine hadn't been detonated. McShane grinned as he squeezed the firing device. The team cheered as they observed the enemy smashed backwards by the force of the blast. In the last sixty seconds RT Illinois had personally killed eighteen of the enemy.

Now with the VC only a stone's throw from the perimeter, a third wave of men rushed from the trees, followed by another heavy barrage of rockets. And then what McShane had feared earlier became reality. Three VC infiltrators, hired months ago as CIDG "strikers," began running along the west perimeter, tossing grenades into the open doorways of the bunkers.

The explosions were indistinguishable from the noise of the rockets and went undetected for several seconds until an alert gunner reloading his .50 calibre noticed a bright red flash from within one of the bunkers and saw three men dressed as "strikers" sprinting away. As they came to the next bunker, the gunner swung the big machine gun around and fired a short burst just as one of the men was about to toss a grenade.

The .50 calibre slugs slammed hard into his buttocks and legs. He dropped the grenade. His two accomplices were killed in midstride as they tried to escape the blast.

But not before the infiltràtor's grenades had killed three Americans and five Indig. It became a busy night for the medics of the FOB.

McShane had missed the whole incident. He and his team had been occupied with a Russian-made 7.62mm RPD light machine gun set up by its crew in a shell crater less than a hundred meters from their bunker. Its rapid fusilage of bullets kept him and his men pinned down, unable to return fire. Under the machine gun's protection the enemy edged forward. Another crew, also taking cover in a crater, hurried to assemble the tripod on a 75mm recoilless rifle capable of blowing large holes in the bunkers. The deadly weapons had to be silenced immediately. McShane tapped Trang on the shoulder and motioned for him and the rest of the team to move outside.

The crew turned their machine gun on another bunker when they ceased to receive return fire from McShane's bunker. The RT took up position just outside and to the left of the entrance. Billy crawled up the plastic sandbag walls to the flat roof of their bunker. He put a WP round in his M-79, flicked the sights up and aimed carefully. He squeezed the trigger. The overgrown bullet spun slowly through the air. The gunner had time to fire a short burst before the 40mm round exploded in his lap. A shower of glowing, white hot phosphorus spewed from the hole.

McShane crawled up to Billy. Lying side by side, he pointed out the recoilless rifle to his M-79 man. The VC were loading an HE shell into the breach. Billy acted quickly. He loaded another WP into the grenade launcher, aimed and fired. The round glanced off the barrel of the recoilless and exploded twenty meters away. The crew fired. The three inch shell blasted a two foot hole in Harper's bunker. McShane heard the screams of wounded men. Billy fired again. The recoilless rifle and its crew vanished in a fiery explosion.

McShane leaped from the top of the roof. Grabbing Trang and Loc by the arms, he sprinted to the smoking bunker. Harper was pulling out two of his wounded Indig, Cao and Tu. Tu's arm hung bloody and limp across his stomach. A large gash split Cao's cheek open, disclosing gold teeth. Harper and the others suffered superficial frag wounds.

Mac Stevenson, a FOB medic, came running hard from the west perimeter, where he had finished patching up a couple of "strikers." Cao was lying motionless, staring blankly up at the flares. Tu was screaming. The nasty wound was bleeding profusely.

Stevenson tied a tourniquet around the arm while Trang and Loc held him still. With the tourniquet in place, the medic jammed a quarter grain of morphine above the wound in his arm. He then turned to Cao. His eyes were closed. Stevenson grabbed his wrist and felt for a pulse. The young Indig was dead.

Trang and Loc carried Tu, who had quieted from the morphine, to their bunker. With the threat of the machine gun and recoilless rifle taken care of, it was as safe a place as any.

Just as they approached the bunker, McShane saw two figures slither over the wall and onto the ground. They crept slowly to the doorway. Billy and Ngo were inside. The figures stood erect and lifted their AK's. McShane raised his CAR and emptied half a magazine into the two VC, the bullets driving them hard against the sandbags. Billy and Ngo turned around in time to see the two crumple to the dirt.

Three more VC jumped from atop the roof. McShane finished the magazine before they hit the ground. Looking around the compound, he could see other small groups of enemy scaling the bunkers and walls. But they were quickly taken care of by the "strikers" and gunners. Except for these small band of VC, the siege had suddenly slowed. The rocket attack had stopped. The assault on the west perimeter had been turned back after the infiltrators were killed. And now, the 155mm and 175mm guns from a 4th Division artillery company were heard firing, 4km to the north. Moments later the huge shells began exploding on the battlefield. The VC scattered, trying to escape the shells' wrath.

The VC gave up the attack on the north perimeter and returned across the wooden planks and disappeared into the trees and village. Thanks to a good FO, the artillery rounds followed them. A few huts were damaged but they could easily be repaired by the Montagnards and FOB engineers with materials from S-4.

The Tet siege had ended as quickly as it had begun. Its failure to overrun the Special Forces compound was no doubt a severe psychological blow to the VC battalions. They had prepared for the battle for many months and had been told time after time by their officers that it would be successful. Now the battlefield was strewn with several hundred dead. Two VC battalions ceased to exist as effective fighting units. In fact, it would not be until the Easter Offensive of 1972 that they would be able to successfully launch another attack.

* * *

Despite the victory over the VC battalions, the men of the FOB remained on a one hundred percent alert until daylight. Then the teams and CIDG companies combed the battlefield for survivors and weapons. Deuce-and-a-halfs were brought in and a detail of men were assigned to remove the bodies from the field and stack them in the trucks. The detail went about the task with a great sense of urgency. By mid-morning it would be hot and by noon it would be unbearably hot, and the bodies would begin to bloat and stink under the treacherous sun.

Fortunately for McShane's team, they had been detailed to pick up enemy weapons and sort them into piles. By lunch, they amassed a stack of some two hundred AK-47's, a hundred older SKS rifles, five RPD machine guns and the one recoilless rifle. A hundred or so Chinese and homemade grenades were taken off the bodies and carefully placed in a 175mm shell crater, several hundred meters from the FOB. They were later destroyed by a 4th Division combat engineer platoon.

The body detail's final tally came to two hundred and eighteen dead. As expected, the VC left no survivors. The trucks drove the bodies to an open field several kilometers to the north where the bulldozer had been digging a large pit for the mass burial. One at a time the trucks backed to the hole and the detail threw in the dead. Between truckloads a layer of lye was spread over the bodies to facilitate decomposition. The nasty job was finished shortly after noon, and none too soon for the men assigned to the detail. The Americans in charge skipped lunch and headed straight to the club, which had escaped serious damage. The ban on beer and liquor had been lifted.

The FOB's own casualties were light when compared to the VC's. Four Americans were killed and ten were wounded. The Indig suffered fifteen killed and a like number wounded, while the strikers had twenty killed and thirty-five wounded. Except for the more seriously wounded who were flown by chopper to the 5th Evacuation hospital in Pleiku, the Americans were treated in the FOB dispensary with the Indig and strikers. The bodies of the Americans were stripped and washed in the dispensary's morgue and then placed in body bags and flown to Graves and Registration in Da Nang for processing and embalming before being shipped to relatives in the States. CIDG and Indig dead were turned over to relatives in Kontum.

Now came the long and arduous chore of putting the FOB back together. RT's Hawaii, Alabama, Tennessee, and Arkansas moved temporarily into the building previously occupied by the "Yard" Villagers until their barracks could be rebuilt. The next morning Vietnamese carpenters and brickmasons hired by the FOB engineers began working on the damaged buildings. There was the problem of all the holes dug up by the rockets. Another crew of men rode around in a five ton dump truck, throwing dirt into each of the holes.

RT Illinois and Rhode Island joined some of the other teams and began rebuilding the RT's barracks. However, with McShane due to leave for Cam Ranh Bay the following day for his R & R processing, he was much too excited to provide little more than supervisory help. And then when Dave Wormington came in on a chopper from the Kontum air field, McShane had to take time off from his important position to fill him in on the details of the siege.

They sat on top of a bunker. Strikers unraveled rows of concertina wire, replacing the wire damaged in the fight.

Rubbing his eyes, McShane said to Wormington, "You missed a doozy, Dave. They must've wanted to overrun the FOB awful bad. I've never been in as intense a rocket attack as the one they threw at us. It went on during most of the attack. Damn, it made it hard to think. They counted over two hundred dead yesterday morning. 'Bout a dozen of the VC made it inside the compound."

He paused, staring out over the charred battlefield. "Probably the worst thing to happen was when three strikers hired several months ago turned out to be VC infiltrators. Half way through the battle they began throwing grenades into the bunkers. I think that's where we received the majority of our casualties. At least, I know that's when the Americans were killed. Harper lost Cao. He'll have a hard time replacing him."

McShane let out a deep sigh. "Well, it's over. Doubt if we'll see an attack like that one again." He turned to his one-one. "How did your week in Nha Trang go?"

Wormington leaned back onto his elbows and followed a formation of 4th Division choppers flying west. "It went okay. At first they couldn't figure out the problem at Finance. So they had me come back a few days later and as if by magic my pay records had been squared away and all my back pay was waitin' for me. Never explained what the problem was. Hell, I didn't really care long as I got my bucks. It was actually a little incountry R & R for me. Went to the beach every day. Went downtown every night and got laid. Seven different whorehouses in seven days."

McShane laughed.

"Except for last night," Wormington added.

"Hit Group Headquarters hard?" McShane asked.

"Few rockets, few mortar rounds. Recon school got some probes. I think Charlie wanted to harrass us. Keep us from gettin' our beauty sleep. After all, Nha Trang's one of their favorite R & R spots; they didn't want to screw it up too much. But damn," he sighed, looking over his shoulder at the pockmarked chopper pad and the blackened barracks. "They sure put the hurt on the FOB."

Then, facing McShane, he asked, "You leavin' for Cam Ranh in the morning?"

He smiled. "You bet."

"Still goin' to Tokyo?"

"Yep. Meetin' Chris Dean in Cam Ranh and then we're goin' on together."

"One thing for sure, you won't need to worry 'bout catchin' a social disease with Chris along."

XII

Three dark green Mitsubishi buses jerked to a stop in front of a three-story white wood framed building just before 0600 hours. A large sign above the double-doored entrance read, "R & R Center - Camp Zama, Japan." The one hundred and fifty men in the buses cheered.

The passengers, clutching their suitcases, filed off the buses and pushed their way through the swinging glass doors. A black Sergeant in freshly starched fatigues directed the men to a large room at the end of the hall, where they were to be briefed on their stay in Japan. McShane and Dean fell into chairs in the front row. They had only slept a handful of hours during the last day and a half. When all the men had found a seat, the Sergeant stepped forward to the podium and smiled.

"Welcome to Camp Zama and the R & R Center." His audience burst into applause and cat calls.

"I'll make this briefing as brief as possible because I know y'all are hot to trot. First, however, I want everyone to fill out one of the cards being passed out by my two assistants."

Two young Privates, walking up the aisles, handed the

first soldier in each row enough cards for the men sitting in his row. McShane glanced at his card. Last name first, first name second and middle name last. Makes sense, he thought. Then Rank, Serial Number, Unit in Vietnam, Blood type. There was also a box to check if you were planning to stay in the R & R Center Hotel, located upstairs, for a paltry two dollars a day, including meals.

McShane and Dean both checked the box that said "NO." They had other plans, like staying at the New Atami in Tokyo. After all, this was R & R, not basic training. Who in their right minds would want to live with a bunch of horny, wise-cracking G.I.'s for a week? They could do that in Vietnam.

"Okay," said the Sergeant. "If everyone's filled out the cards, pass them toward the center aisle and we'll move along. For those of you who've chosen our hotel, we have buses leaving for Tokyo every morning at 0800. They'll drop you off at the American Embassy at 1000 hours. From there you can grab a cab, which is very reasonable, or walk to your destination. For those of you who're more adventurous, there are the subways and trains. We have maps and schedules at the front desk that may be of some help. I'd suggest you stick to the cabs or walking. The buses depart in front of the Embassy for Camp Zama at midnight. We'll also have bus tours on the bulletin board to your right."

Automatically, the men looked to their right.

"I'd like to stress the fact that you are guests in Japan, representing the United States and the U.S. Army, and that your behavior should be conducted as such. Now, this isn't to say you can't have a good time and let off a little steam. But we want you to keep in mind that you're not grunts in the Delta or Highlands, nor are you back home in your favorite corner bar. The Japanese are a conservative people with customs that are unfamiliar to most of you. They're friendly, helpful and are slowly westernizing, but at the same time they follow strong and ancient traditions. Respect these customs and traditions. So if you see a pretty girl downtown, don't just run up to her and throw your arm around her like you would a girl back home on the block. Use a little tact. Introduce yourself and maybe try and get to know her.

"Now, for those of you interested in sidestepping formalities, or who feel that time is too short for a proper courtship, then you'll find plenty of professional women walking the streets of Ginza or Akasaka. There's a Trojan dispenser in the downstairs men's room. We don't want any of the medics in 'Nam pissed off at our R & R Center."

The room erupted with laughter. The Sergeant, glancing at his watch, waited for the men to quiet. "Okay. Now that that's understood, there's a bus leavin' in an hour for the Embassy. I'm sure it's enough time for you boys to shower and change into your civvies."

The men stampeded the registration desk to sign in and get a room. All except McShane and Dean who ambled down the hall until they found the door marked MEN. They pushed it open. Several urinals lined the freshly painted green wall on the left. The vinyl floor had recently been waxed and buffed. At the far end of the room were four individual shower stalls. A bench and locker separated each of the stalls. They each chose a shower, placing their single suitcase on the bench, and began undressing.

Yanking off his red dust covered jungle boots, Dean asked, "Do you think we'll be able to wash off the 'Nam stink?"

McShane, smiling, replied, "I've got almost an hour to try."

* * *

Two and a half hours later, the same three buses dropped off their passengers in front of the U.S. Embassy. Walking a short way down the sidewalk to escape the crowd of G.I.'s, McShane and Dean stopped on the edge of the curb and waited for a vacant cab.

A small, blue 100 Yen Subaru skidded to a halt, running up on the curb and nearly crushing Dean's suitcase. A young, grinning cabbie hit the automatic door opener, allowing the rear door to swing open. Throwing his suitcase onto the back seat, McShane opened the front door and sat down next to the driver. Reluctantly, Dean slid across the cramped rear seat, forcing his long legs into a half comfortable position. He prayed their hotel wasn't far.

Grinning back at the driver, McShane said in his best Japanese, "Hotel New Atami, kudasai." The driver nodded and without bothering to look for oncoming traffic, cranked the steering wheel hard to the right and pulled out into the stream of honking madness.

The driver was an expert, maneuvering his little bug of a taxi through the traffic, darting in and out and around the other taxis, buses, and motorcycles. With his left hand glued to the horn, he headed north on the Expressway. Still not accustomed to driving on the lefthand side of the road, Dean clung tightly to the front edge of his seat as the tiny motorcycle powered Subaru shot in front of a commuter bus.

He leaned forward. "Hey, Steve, does everybody drive like this?"

Chuckling, McShane replied, "They have to. It's what keeps the country goin'."

Leaning back in his seat, Dean tried to relax by looking out the window and thinking he was high up in the hotel bar having a beer with a geisha girl.

The cab sped through a yellow light and then made a sharp left turn, narrowly sideswiping a larger, green Toyota cab, onto Sotobori Street. Dean strained to see the Tokyo Hilton next to the Hie Shrine as their cab became entangled in a traffic jam, but instead became involved in watching several college girls dressed in blue sweaters and blue skirts, holding leather briefcases as they stood waiting at a bus stop. Rolling down the taxi window, he stuck his head out into the frigid February air and waved. The girls covered their mouths and giggled bashfully. They didn't return the greeting, thinking, it's just another crazy American.

Choosing the New Atami as a base of operations during their R & R had been McShane's idea. Somewhere he had picked up a 1968 Fodor's guide to "Japan and East Asia."

In looking over the chapter on western-style luxury hotels, he had come across the description of the New Atami — a 17 story hotel, with over 1,000 rooms on ten acres of Japanese gardens. Rotating atop the hotel was the Blue Sky Lounge which took an hour to make a single rotation enabling guests to gaze out across the Tokyo skyline while sipping their drinks. It sounded like an ideal place to while away six days. The hotel also had an indoor pool and spa where a hangover could be painlessly worked off. He had reserved two double rooms on the 17th floor.

Dean tipped the cab driver with a new 1000 yen note. It was worth it. Not even in New York had he experienced such driving skill. And with one hand on the horn.

Still grinning, the driver said, "Goodbye, see you rater," and sped off, leaving his passengers staring up at the enormous hotel, trying to catch a glimpse of the revolving bar through the infamously thick Tokyo smog.

Nudging his friend in the ribs with his elbow, McShane suggested, "We don't have to stand out here freezing our nuts off. We're stayin' here. This is our home. Let's check in. and get a better look at that contraption."

The large plush lounge was crammed with guests checking in and out. Some sat in overstuffed sofas reading any of a half dozen English language newspapers, writing postcards to friends and relatives back home, or waiting in front of one of the elevators.

McShane and Dean confidently strolled over to the registration desk and squeezed in between a German businessman and his pretty wife and an American with a thick midwest accent. Dean was carefully checking out the German's wife, when an attractive, smiling Japanese clerk asked McShane in halting English if she could help him.

He tried to think clean thoughts as he smiled back and replied, "Yes, you can," speaking slowly and deliberately. "We have reservations for two rooms under the names of Steve McShane and Chris Dean."

Feeling a little embarrassed by his undressing stares, she looked down at the counter and said, "One moment, prease," and shuffled over to a stack of cards behind a divider marked "Reservations." Thumbing quickly through the cards, she first found Dean's reservation card and an instant later, McShane's.

While they waited for the clerk to return, the two S.F. Sergeants surveyed the huge lobby. A group of stewardesses carrying overnight bags sashayed through the lobby towards an open elevator.

"I can't stand it," whispered Dean. "All those good lookin' women. How soon before we meet a couple of 'em."

Chuckling, McShane said, "Don't worry buddy, I'm goin' to take care of you."

They signed the guest register, took their keys from the clerk and headed for an elevator, just missing the one carrying the stewardesses. Another arrived and they herded aboard. It was cramped and stuffy. A grossly overweight American conventioner with a red, white and blue name tag pinned to his maroon sports coat was chewing on the end of a smoldering cigar. McShane hoped he would get off at the next floor. But as luck would have it, he stepped out of the elevator with Dean and McShane on the 17th floor.

By then, with the elevator making a stop at each floor, they had learned everything there was to know about the man. He owned a twenty-thousand acre cattle ranch in the San Joaquin Valley. Married three times and had four "gorgeous" daughters.

"Did you bring then along?" Dean had inquired.

"Nope. They're in school."

Too bad, McShane had thought. His name was Harry Barnwald. And would they like to have lunch and drinks with him in the "twirling" lounge?

"Sure," they replied. His room was across the hall from Dean's.

They met him a half hour later in the Blue Sky Lounge. He was sitting at the bar, guzzling his second martini. Laying on the edge of the counter was the same soggy cigar.

"Hey, boys," he bellowed. "Glad you could make it. Bartender," he shouted to the Japanese bartender, "Bring my friends something to drink."

Turning to McShane he asked, "What are you boys drinkin'?" His breath smelled of Japanese gin, stale cigars, and dirty dentures. A piece of the tobacco wrapping from the cigar, caught in the bottom row of the dentures, flapped up and down each time he spoke.

"We'll take beer. Large Sapparos."

The bartender nodded. Rummaging through the cooler underneath the countertop, he pulled out two 500ml bottles and set them in front of the men. Barnwald handed the bartender a crisp 10,000 yen bill.

"You boys here on some sort of business?" he asked, sucking his glass dry. He ordered another martini, "very dry."

"We're here on a six day R & R," Dean replied. "Just got in this morning."

"Well, son-of-a-bitch," Harry hooted, taking the martini from the bartender. "You boys fightin' in 'Nam. Hot shit!" He was clearly excited. "Barkeep, bring two more of those Texas sized Jap beers."

"Hell, I'm honored to be sittin' with you boys. Damn right." He slammed his fist down hard on the bar top.

"With all those faggot hippies runnin' up and down the streets burning their draft cards and throwing rocks at the police, I'm downright pleased to meet somebody who's actually out there fightin' and kickin' those skinny, little, commie, slope asses to keep our great country free."

McShane was finding it increasingly difficult to keep a straight face. It was Dean who finally broke him up. "Who said anything about fightin', Harry? Steve and I are lifeguards in Cam Ranh Bay."

As he broke out in uncontrolled laughter, McShane lost half the beer in his glass up through his nose and spilled the rest on Barnwald's cigar.

"Hate to disappoint you, Harry," Dean smiled, slapping him on the back. "Steve, let's go downstairs and check out the indoor pool."

They left Harry Barnwald, open-mouthed, staring at the spilled beer and his soggy cigar. It was the last time they were to see the cattle rancher during their stay at the hotel, but then they were to spend very little time in the hotel.

Harper needed to see now more than any other time in his life. Swiping at the blood, he tried desperately to clear it from his eyes as it trickled from the cut above his right brow. An AK round snapped overhead, clipping a branch from the large mango tree to his rear. Harper slammed another magazine into his CAR-15. Huong writhed in pain from the deep frag wound an inch below his navel. Half a dozen more bullets chipped away at the bark. Huong moaned softly, holding the field dressing firmly to his gut.

"Relay, relay this is Generous," shouted Harper into the PRC-25 handset. "Contact, contact. One Indig wounded. Need extraction at alternate Lima Zulu!"

"Roger, Generous. Have choppers on their way."

Harper scooted over to Huong. "Damn," he muttered as he replaced the soggy field dressing with a clean one from his first-aid kit. "Our shit's weak. We've got to get our asses back to the LZ."

The Cambode stared up at the one-zero's reassuring smile and listened to his soothing words. "You're going to be okay. We'll get you back to the FOB even if I have to carry you back."

He didn't understand, but he knew everything would be fine.

RT Rhode Island had been inserted two days earlier into Romeo-3, an operational area some 30km inside Laos. Their mission was to investigate reports of an underground POW camp allegedly holding a half dozen Americans and an undetermined number of South Vietnamese. Sergeant Khai had provided S-2 with the information, based on a story he had been told by an Officer in Ban Pakha, six months before he was captured.

But instead of a POW camp, Harper's team had found a deserted camp with a few run down hootches, a rusty Swiss Army knife, an AK-47 magazine, a 1966 Playboy calendar and some empty C-ration cans strewn around an old campfire.

The operation had been running smoothly, until the RT began humping up a narrow wash at the north end of a small camp. Harper had been traveling point with Huong, several meters ahead of the team, when they spotted two NVA soldiers approaching from the west on a trail that passed right across the wash they were walking on.

The enemy soldiers were startled to see the tall, lanky Caucasian standing before them. Fortunately, not suspecting any trouble this far into Laos, the NVA were carrying their weapons by the leather straps as if they were handbags. Always on the alert for the unsuspected while on a mission, it was not as surprising to Harper when the two soldiers practically stumbled into his arms.

The NVA, eyes bulging with unknown fear, fumbled to raise their AK's. But they were already as good as dead. Firing from the hip, Harper and Huong blasted the men before they had even so much as lifted their weapons above their waists.

Knowing they were in trouble, they had started to return back down the wash towards the team. A Chinese grenade, hurling through the jungle, exploded less than ten meters in front of Huong. The concussion and a plum-sized chunk of frag slammed him back into Harper. The one-zero quickly grabbed him by the collar and dragged him over the side of the embankment. A small sliver of pig iron stuck out above Harper's right eye. He had unbuckled the rucksack from Huong's back and kicked it into the brush.

"Okay, sport, time to move out," he said, tightening

the ends of a cravat over his eye. He could hear the rest of the team engaged in a fire fight below.

He popped his CAR over the embankment one last time and fired until the magazine was empty, then threw two grenades. Ducking back down, he took the Cambodian by the arm and led him through the thick underbrush. Scores of deadly AK rounds whistled overhead.

At one point the scrub brush became so dense, they were forced to crawl on their hands and knees. This intensified the pain in Huong's gut and it was all Harper could do to keep the young Cambode from crying out and giving away their position. He finally turned him over onto his back. Grasping underneath his shoulders, he pulled him a foot at a time until they cleared the thicket.

Resting briefly, Harper removed a cravat from around his neck and moistened it with water from his canteen. The cool damp cloth brought a strained smile to the dirt-caked lips of the wounded mercenary. He sucked on the end of the cravat, moistening his dry mouth. Harper took a swig of water from the canteen before returning it to his belt.

He glanced at his Presidential Rolex. The choppers were due in twenty minutes. He could hear Hamilton below, shouting a command to the team. Only a few dozen meters to go. Now that they were out of the thick brush, Harper lifted Huong up and threw him up over his shoulder. He was light and they could cover the distance to the team easily and quickly. He moaned quietly as Harper thrashed through the jungle.

A few meters before reaching the team, he stopped and shouted to his one-one, "Charlie, I've got Huong. He's hit. Don't shoot us." That would be the last thing he'd want; to have his own team mistakenly blow him away.

What a relief it was to Hamilton who had thought the

worst of his team leader and the Indig! He had felt helpless, pinned down by the intense automatic weapons fire and unable to move to help. But he couldn't withdraw the team until the fate of his two team members was known.

Harper found the team tucked behind a downed tree exchanging fire with the NVA. Hurriedly, he lowered Huong to the ground, next to Lam, and crouched beside Hamilton. "The choppers are on the way," he said, looking at his watch once again. "They'll be at the alternate LZ in fifteen minutes. We've got to move."

*   *   *

"Where we goin' tonight?" Dean asked, brushing a spot of dried mud from the toe of his left shoe. McShane helf off answering until he pulled on the Irish fisherman's sweater his wife had knitted for a trip to Yosemite.

"There's a little restaurant a few blocks from here in the Ginza, called Izui. They have great tempura. A Japanese broad I met while in the hospital at Camp Zama showed me the place. Ate there a couple of times when I was able to get away. After dinner, we'll check out one of the hottest night clubs in Tokyo."

"Yeah, what's that?" Dean asked, trying not to sound excited.

"The Mugen. It's a new psychedelic night club in Akasaka. There's a rock group called 'The Lead' that plays at night. They've got a hot singer named Phil. Sounds like Jimi Hendrix, Jack Bruce, and Mick Jagger all rolled into one."

"We ain't left?" Dean queried wryly.

A long line of small, brightly colored taxis parked along

the curb in front of the New Atami, patiently waited their turn for a fare from the stream of guests pouring from the hotel to do up the town. The wind chill factor was below zero as McShane and Dean hopped up and down to warm themselves, waiting for the next empty, warm cab to pull ahead and whisk them away.

The driver of an older model Datsun motioned frantically for the two cold men to hurry up and get inside his cab. Without hesitation, they jumped inside.

Looking at the deeply lined face of the unconcerned driver as he expertly and less than lovingly maneuvered the cab through the evening traffic, McShane sensed he and Dean weren't really welcome in his country. Much older than any of the other taxi drivers they had seen, he was part of that traditional Japanese way of life the R & R Sergeant had briefly discussed that morning. It was no doubt a painful way to make a living; driving American and European tourists who spent more money in a night drinking and eating than he was able to make in a month driving twelve hours a day.

He dropped them off in front of the Izui, pocketing the 1000 yen tip McShane had folded around the 500 yen fare, without even so much as a smile, let alone a thank you. They walked briskly across the sidewalk anxious to escape the bitter wind and to fill their stomachs with something other than mess hall chow or airline TV dinners.

A pert little woman met them inside with a pair of menus. She had them exchange their leather street shoes for throw away paper slippers she pulled from a box behind the cash register. Dean, noting the restaurant was hotter than Cam Ranh the day they left, immediately shed his sports coat and handed it to the hostess. She led him to a small room and slid back the rice paper door, revealing a low Japanese style table with a pillow and folding wicker backrest at either end. When the hostess was assured they were comfortable, she glided through the door, quietly closing it behind her, leaving the men alone with a ceramic pot of tea and cups.

Dean, reaching for his menu commented, "This is real livin', Steve. I wonder what those poor slobs at the FOB are havin' for chow tonight?"

* * *

"Gladiator one, this is Generous. Over." Harper released the handset push-to-talk button and waited for the chopper pilot's reassuring voice.

The team lay in a semi-circle behind a stand of elephant grass, eyes searching for enemy movement, fingers loosely wrapped around the triggers of their CAR's. A company of ants marched quietly over a rotting tree limb underneath Hamilton's forearm. Upon a silent signal, the commanding officer motioned for the company to attack. Bravely, the ants raced across the limb, assaulting the forearm. Hamilton dropped his CAR and fought back ferociously with the palm of his hand, inflicting heavy casualties. The commander called for a retreat and the ants hastily withdrew into the cover of the leaves, abandoning their dead and wounded. The victor grinned and picked up his weapon.

"Generous, this is Gladiator One. Have you reached designated Lima Zulu? Over."

"Negative," whispered the one-zero. "I have one wounded Indig. Enemy movement 360⁰ our position. Can't reach the Lima Zulu before dawn. Can you pick us up then?"

"Roger, Generous. See you in the morning with a cold one. Good luck."

There was movement in the jungle beyond the elephant grass as he replaced the handset on his pack strap. The team tried to melt into the earth. Voices chattered back and forth among the soldiers in the NVA search party. Some of the troops were laughing. What a lackadaisical bunch of soldiers, thought Harper, peering into the tall grass. The talking and laughter grew fainter as the squad moved north. The RT relaxed a bit.

It had been quiet for over a half hour. Lam slowly pushed himself up from the sweat dampened bed of leaves and stood. He performed a couple of deep knee bends, removing some of the stiffness from his too long idle legs. Huong gazed expressionlessly at a lizard crawling along a vine hanging from a tree. The wound in his stomach had stopped bleeding. Lam unsnapped the cover on the first-aid pouch hooked to his pistol belt and unraveled a clean field dressing. A piece of small intestine protruded from the three inch gash. Lam carefully washed the dirt and dried blood from around the wound with some of the water from his last full canteen. He moistened the fresh bandage and gently tied it around the wound. Huong grimaced with pain.

Crawling over to his team leader, Lam spoke quietly, "Huong, maybe he fini soon. Maybe team fini soon. When chopper come, Trung si?"

Harper placed a reassuring hand on his interpreter's shoulder and replied, "No fini RT. We stay here tonight. Choppers come in morning."

The little Vietnamese frowned and rightly so. No team relished the thought of spending a night in a jungle crawling with the enemy, particularly with a gravely wounded team member who may not be alive in the morning. But there was no other choice. It would be dark in another hour, improving their chances of survival.

Lam squatted next to Tran, and Vanh, who had replaced the still hospitalized Tu. They were kneeling beside Huong. Tran was dabbing a water soaked cravat on the wounded Indig's forehead. Lam began to speak. Listening attentively, they displayed little emotion as he informed them of their deteriorating situation. They accepted it without question. In fact, they rather looked as though they enjoyed the prospect of spending a night practically under the noses of their hunters. Their only immediate concern was for Huong. He had to be evacuated soon, before infection set in.

Foremost on Harper's mind now was surviving the night. He sent Lam and Vanh out to find a suitable RON (rest over night) sight for his team. He knew they had broken a cardinal rule: to break contact immediately and escape and evade the enemy. Too much time had already been spent in one spot.

The two Indig returned twenty-five minutes later. They were smiling excitedly. Lam told his team leader of a massive clump of snarled, twisting wait-a-minute vines that afforded excellent cover and concealment. It was the first good news Harper had heard all day.

The Indig hurriedly constructed a makeshift stretcher utilizing two stout branches from a silk cotton tree and Harper's poncho liner. They carefully lifted Huong onto the liner. Vanh and Tran lifted the stretcher and followed Lam and Harper to the clump of wait-a-minute vines. Hamilton took over Huong's job providing rear security.

They arrived shortly before dusk. Lam led the RT through the narrow opening in the thicket of vines. The team quickly settled down within their wooden cocoon and ate a hasty meal of cold lurps.

Leaning back against a decomposing log, Harper watched the Indig shovel the food eagerly into their mouths as if they were eating a filet mignon. He only toyed with the little orange chunks of chili con carne with the edge of his plastic spoon, occasionally placing a bite in between his teeth and chewing slowly, lost in thought.

S-2 had told him to investigate a purported underground NVA POW camp believed by Sergeant Khai to be located near where the team had discovered the enemy hootches and the two NVA earlier in the day. But as the team had found out, locating the underground prison was proving to be difficult, if not entirely impossible.

Rubbing his tired eyes with the palms of his dirty hands, Harper slid down onto his back and rested his head on the edge of the log. He gazed up at a cluster of stars shining dimly through the tiny opening in the vines. They would either have to send in another team or forget the camp, he mused, closing his eyes. A mosquito fat with the blood of North Vietnamese soldiers buzzed around his ear, finally zeroing in on a tender spot on his neck. A hand crushed the insect before it was able to add the blood of an American to its obese body.

* * *

Prying their way through hordes of hot, sticky bodies, gyrating recklessly around the dance floor to "The Leads" hard driving rock music, the two Americans, out of place with their tanned faces and short, bristly hair, found an unoccupied table near a far corner of the club and sat down.

"Hey, man, didn't I tell you this was a great place?" yelled McShane into Dean's ear, trying to be heard above the thunderous music blaring from tall speakers mounted on the walls throughout the club.

No matter where one sat, he could hear every note and every word from the rock group performing on the postage stamp-sized raised platform that served as Mugen's stage. A bank of flickering strobe lights hung from the ceiling while two synchronized 16mm projectors showed the rollercoaster ride from a 1953 3-D movie over and over again on a large screen behind the band. The dance floor was awash in twirling, multi-colored lights operated by club employees from platforms positioned around the club.

Phil was singing "Louie, Louie," leaving nothing to the imagination in his own rendition of the infamous lyrics. Only a handful of American students and tourists fully appreciated the unslurred words.

A pretty Japanese cocktail waitress wearing a crotch length brown suede mini-skirt with a maroon, tasseled blouse and white vinyl boots cruised up to the table and asked in halting English, "You like something to dlink? Club have three dlink minimum."

"Sounds like we don't have much choice," Dean said as he glared at the waitress' exposed navel. "You can get me a large Sapporo. How 'bout you, Steve?"

McShane, resting his chin in the palms of his hands and gazing up at the girl's beautiful almond eyes, thought for a moment and then replied, "Yeah, I'll have one." And then in Japanese that equalled the quality of the cocktail waitress's English, he ordered, "Nippon Sapporo, kudasai."

She nodded, writing the order on a cocktail napkin, then scurried off to take another order at the next table before she had to push her way through the crowds to the bar.

Leaning across the table, Dean shouted above the music, "Steve, this place is crazy. Let's grab a couple of broads, get a bottle of Chevis at the Embassy and go back to our rooms."

"Hang on, Chris. Besides, who were you figurin' on grabbin'? We haven't met anyone yet."

"Who cares?" replied Dean, obviously high on the dozen urns of sake he had guzzled down with his tempura. "The waitress is in love with me, so I'll take her. I've heard about these Japanese girls. They take real good care of their men." He scanned the room. "Hey, take a look at that one over there."

Turning in his chair, McShane looked in the direction Dean was pointing. Two girls sat watching the band. The one facing McShane smiled a little self-consciously at the gawking G.I.'s. At least she was good looking, he thought.

"What do you think?" Dean finally asked. "She smiled at you, didn't she?"

"What else could she do with two half-crazed, drooling drunk Americans ogling at 'em? She was just being kind. What the hell do you know? I mean, take a look at us. Take a look at those people out there killing each other with their hips and arms. Shit, our hair looks like someone cut it with a pair of sheep shears. We probably look like a couple of freaks to that girl."

"Well, she must like freaks. She's still smiling at you."

McShane caught the tail end of a sly smile as she raised a drink to her lips. She lowered her eyes and sucked at the red straw in the glass. Two American students sauntered to the table and asked the girl and her friend to dance. As she rose, she brushed her long dark hair over her shoulder, then winked at McShane.

Dean gave his friend a shove, nearly knocking him out of his chair and cried, "See there, I told ya. Man, she digs you. When those two cub scouts bring 'em back, we'll ask 'em to dance."

"Hell, we don't know how to dance like that."

"What's there to know?" Dean said. "Just swing your

184

ass around and pretend you're screwin'. Nothin' to it. Keep your eye on me.''

But Dean's chance as a dance instructor was long in coming. The girls danced the next several numbers with the students while Dean sulked, guzzling beer. McShane sat quietly, amusing himself by watching the throng of sweaty bodies whirling to "The Lead.''

Finally, the music stopped. Phil announced that the band would take a break and return in twenty minutes to "play more of your favorite hits.''

Sitting up in his chair, Dean waited eagerly for the girls to return to the table. He whispered across the table, slurring his words, "Okay, buddy, let's make our move.''

But McShane grabbed his arm, keeping him from getting up. The students had sat down at the table with the girls.

"The hell with them,'' Dean raged. "I'll clean the dance floor with their skinny little college asses.''

McShane laughed, "Settle down, ol' buddy. There're easier ways to meet broads. I didn't fly to Japan to spend my R & R fightin' civilians. I'll handle your college friends. Let's finish our beer and then we'll make our move.''

The members of the band, each clutching a voluptuous Japanese girl, roamed through the club, stopping from time to time to chat with friends and fans and to hand out promotional copies of their new single. McShane sipped his beer, waiting patiently for them to return to the stage. Dean, he felt, was getting too drunk. Another beer or two and he would have to carry him back to the hotel without ever meeting the young beauty, who continued to smile seductively whenever he glanced her way.

The band began to take their places just as the cocktail waitress brought two more Sapporos to their table. But Dean had passed out and lay snoring with his head resting on his forearms. The waitress, snickering, placed a beer in front of each of them.

McShane rose, handed the waitress a wrinkled 1000 yen bill and ambled, a bit uneasily, to the girls' table, going over in his mind what he would say in Japanese. He wanted to really impress the girl. However, once he stood in front of the table, staring into her luring brown eyes, he forgot everything he had rehearsed. He waited frantically for his lips to mouth the prepared speech. But they wouldn't move. He just gazed dumbly, wishing like hell his brain would transmit a signal to his feet and legs that would send him back to his table. After a millenium of silence, she spoke first.

"Yes? Is there something I can do for you?" she asked in flawless English.

His mind raced. She's speaking perfect English, he thought. What now? "Well, yes, there is," he replied in something less than perfect English. "But I can't get over your English. I've been standing here like a dumb ass trying to remember what I was goin' to say to you in Japanese."

"I'm only half Japanese," she chuckled. "My father's Greek, but he was raised in New York. I was born in New York and went to school there."

Feeling more at ease listening to her soft voice, he pulled an empty chair from another table and sat down next to her. The two students exchanged puzzled looks and then glared at the intruder, waiting to see what he was going to do or say next.

"So then you're just a tourist like myself?" McShane asked.

"Oh, no. My dad works for Singer here in Tokyo. I'm going to Sophia University in Yotsuya."

"You mean you live in Tokyo?" he asked, surprised.

"Well, in Sagamihara. It's about forty-five minutes by train."

The lovely sound of her words was suddenly drowned by the band as they began playing "Psychotic Reaction." McShane attempted to learn more of the Eurasian beauty but found it impossible to carry on any sort of audible conversation. One of the students abruptly stood up and asked the girl to dance. Before he got an answer, McShane took her hand and led her out to the dance floor.

"Hey," he shouted above the music, shuffling his feet in an attempt to appear to be dancing. "What's your name?"

"Ellen Strathos. What's yours?" she yelled back.

"Steve McShane."

XIII

The night was cool and crisp. A few stars still flickered through the vines overhead. Unable to sleep, Harper crawled out from under his poncho liner and sat up. He rested his back against his rucksack and stared at his wrist. The luminous dials on his watch showed there was still more than five hours to twilight.

Lam stood guard near a narrow opening in the vines and heavy brush that was the only easy way into the tiny clearing within the wait-a-minute vines. He watched his team leader slowly stand and limp over with his CAR tucked under his right armpit.

Whispering to his interpreter, Harper said, "Lam, go sleep. I take watch." He obediently returned to his own poncho liner and instantly fell fast asleep. Harper sat down beside the tall grass and rested the weapon in his lap.

Going over in his mind what Owens and the S-3 officer had told him at the briefing the day before their insertion, he couldn't help but think that his team had been sent out on another one of the recent senseless Prairie Fire missions. Not that he really cared. He wanted the missions. FOB life quickly became boring without them.

S-3 had wanted him to check out Sergeant Khai's story of the underground POW camp. Now they were surrounded by an undetermined number of angry NVA who would love nothing better than to string the whole team up by their balls and leave them in the jungle to rot.

During the briefing, Harper had been introduced to a Lieutenant Colonel from MACV and an Air Force Colonel from the 20th TASS. They had proposed a plan, complete with maps and charts, involving an NVA divisional headquarters near Ban Pakha, whereby the Air Force would supply a squadron of Sikorsky CH-53 helicopters — Jolly Green Giants — for use in a massive brigade-sized operation utilizing a battalion of strikers from each of the FOB's. Two RT's from Kontum would be inserted several days before the operation to set up communications and reconnoiter the AO. The objective of the operation, they said, was to liberate the POW camp and inflict as heavy a damage as possible on the divisional headquarters.

At the time, Harper had thought the operation was preposterous. But the Colonels, referring often with their pointers to the charts, made assurances that the operation was entirely feasible and practical. The battalions would be provided air support by a Strike Group of Air Force F-4 Phantom jets, Huey gunships from the 20th and a C-47 "Puff the Magic Dragon." The operation had been code named "Ground Hog."

Well, he thought, surveying the dark jungle, the whole future of Ground Hog depended on his team and what they found on this mission. It looked like the Colonels would have to scrap the operation, at least the POW phase, because his team had found no evidence of any such underground camp. And now that their mission had been compromised, with a team member seriously wounded and an extraction at first light, it was unlikely that they would come across any signs of the camp.

His legs cramping, Harper rolled onto his right side, resting his head in his hand, and stretched out his legs. He finally felt sleepy. He would carry on the vigil for another hour, then turn the guard over to Hamilton, whom he could hear breathing soundly, wrapped comfortably a few feet away in his poncho liner.

Turning his thoughts away from Ground Hog, Harper wondered how McShane and Dean were doing on their R & R. Probably drunk in a bar somewhere in Tokyo, he mused, chuckling quietly. Hell, they had better enjoy themselves, because there would be a real shit storm to face when they returned to the FOB.

* * *

She came out of the bathroom wearing only a pair of sheer bikini underpants. Standing at the wet bar with his back to her, McShane carefully poured Jack Daniels into a shot glass. She crept slowly behind him, catching him totally by surprise as she threw her arms around his neck, and pulled him tightly against her bare breasts. He spilled his carefully measured drink on the formica bar top. Dripping over the edge, the brown liquid puddled on the beige wool carpet.

"Dammit, Ellen!" he cried, turning to face her. "You scared me. Not to mention spilling my drink all over your big bucks carpet."

She nestled closer to him, burying her head into the fold of his wool sweater. His skin was warm as she reached up underneath his sweater and began rubbing his chest with her soft hands. It had been a long time since he had been with a woman other than a whore, or his wife. He felt uncomfortable and pulled away to make another drink.

"Slow down, honey," he said, taking hold of the four-sided Jack Daniels bottle. "We've got all night. And right now, I need a drink. Want one?"

She sat down on the edge of her kingsized bed and replied, "I don't think so, Steve. I had enough to drink at the club." She slipped her fingers into the panties and pulled them down along her thighs and over her knees. "How do you suppose your friend Chris is doing?" she asked, kicking them under the bed.

"Maybe I'm wrong, but he's probably passed out. Unless, maybe your friend's experienced enough to keep a drunk awake. But judging by the condition Chris was in when we hauled him out of The Mugen, I doubt that there's little more goin' on next door than some heavy sleepin'."

McShane stood leaning against the wall next to the wet bar. He took a sip from his drink, observing what lay spread out before him on the biggest bed he had seen in six months. He gulped down the rest and walked over to the side of the bed.

"You're not wasting much time, Ellen."

"I don't have much time. I'm flying to California at eight tomorrow morning and it's already nearly midnight. I haven't even packed."

"So this will be nothing more than a Saigon quickie?" he asked, taking her hand.

"That's up to you. We still have several hours before I have to think about getting ready."

She fell back onto the blue comforter, pulling him to her. McShane rested his head on her silky smooth belly. He felt her heartbeat quicken, as she lay there running her long fingers through his hair. He also felt himself grow stiff. He smiled. He hoped he wasn't too drunk to get a good hard on. It had happened a couple of times back in Nha Trang, but the whores were always good sports and had refunded his money.

Uninterested in just a quickie, he lay on her tummy for a long while, tracing his fingers through the dark brown hair between her thighs. Her breath shortened as the tips of his fingers found their way inside the moist warmth beneath the hair. He began kissing her stomach, allowing his fingers to move deeper and deeper. She cried out, bending forward and taking his head into her delicate hands. Her long, lithe legs locked around the back of his neck and drew him to her sweet scent.

Finally, fearing he would tear a hole in the crotch of his slacks, he eased out from between her legs and rose to rather wobbly legs. He hurriedly unzipped his pants and kicked his loafers out into the middle of the bedroom floor. He stepped out of his pants and then his baggy O.D. underwear and stood at the foot of the bed grinning.

"Are you going to take off your sweater and socks?" a dreamy voice asked.

McShane rubbed his hands down along the front of the sweater, then looked down at his feet and answered, "Will they be in the way?"

She grabbed his hands and laughed, "Come here, you big hunk." He knelt down on the carpet and drew her close, kissing her parted lips tenderly. Without remembering how or when, he found himself straddled atop the Eurasian beauty. He wanted to scream, as he penetrated deeper. It felt so good. Never before had he been in such a position with anyone as comely or sensuous as Ellen Strathos and he was going to savor every moment.

* * *

Shortly before dawn, a hand rested gently on the back of his shoulder as he lay asleep on his side. Startled, Hamilton whipped his head around, right hand on the handle of his CAR, instinctively reacting to the rustling leaves somewhere out in the darkness.

"Shhh," Harper said, almost inaudibly, pressing his index finger to his lips. "It's Lam and Tran. I sent them ahead to check out the LZ. It's less than four hundred meters away. Want to make sure the LZ's not crawlin' with dinks before I confirm the extraction."

Hamilton relaxed, easing his grip on the CAR. It had been largely a sleepless night for him. This was the first operation where the team had been unable to be extracted. And now he wondered, rubbing the sleep from his eyes, if they would make it out as a complete team. He searched for some sign of reassurance in his team leader's otherwise expressionless face. His one-zero looked tired, gaunt from too many sleepless nights in the jungle, wondering whether there would be another. This was Harper's third year with the special projects and it showed.

"Think the gooks will sleep in for us this morning?" Hamilton jokingly asked.

"Not likely. But hopefully we'll be at the LZ before they've had time for their morning shit. Now get your ass out of the sack. We're movin' out the minute Lam and Tran return."

Harper stooped down beside his pack, stuffed with the team's only source of communication with the outside. He switched the PRC-25 radio to "ON" and picked up the handset, pressing the transmit bar.

"Relay, Relay, this is Generous. Over." He waited nervously for a reply, then repeated the procedure.

"Relay, Relay," he said, raising his voice slightly. "This is Generous. Do you copy? Over."

After an eternity of static a sleepy voice replied,

193

"Roger, Generous. Read you five-by. How the hell are ya?"

Grimacing, he answered, "Just dandy. Have the choppers left yet? Over."

"Negative. We're waitin' to hear from you first. Over."

"Dammit. Now you've heard from me. Send them now."

"Roger that, Generous. Out."

"Waitin' to hear from you first," mimicked Harper under his breath. He refastened the handset to the strap of his rucksack.

Growing impatient with the slowness of the Indig's return, he sidled up next to Hamilton who had just stuffed his poncho liner deep into his rucksack. He looked up from the ruck and studied his leader's deep frown. It worried him. "Get that damn pack on your back. It's startin' to get light. We're movin' out."

"What about Lam and Tran?" Hamilton asked.

"They know their way. Probably run into 'em. The choppers will be arrivin' in less than thirty minutes. It's goin' to take us every bit that long to carry Huong to the LZ. I don't want to hang around here any longer than we have to."

"Okay. I'll help Vanh carry Huong."

Huong had spent a sleepless night too, only for much different reasons than Harper. Even with the one-quarter grain shots of morphine, one at sunrise and another a midnight, the pain in his gut had been excruciating. The Indig had found it necessary to sleep closely to their wounded buddy since he frequently woke during the night and wanted to cry out. They had removed the cravat from around his neck and tied it around his mouth to muffle his cries. Taking turns, the men had calmed him, washing away the sweat from his forehead with a cool, moistened field dressing. They greatly feared the oozing hole below his navel, for stomach wounds were the most painful and often the most lethal.

Huong appeared to be sleeping as the two Americans solemnly walked over to him. Vanh had just given him another quarter grain syrette of morphine. Hamilton reached down, firmly grasping the end of the poles. Vanh likewise took his end and the two men slowly and gently raised the stretcher. Harper adjusted the gag around Huong's mouth. The procession passed through the narrow opening in the vines with Harper leading the way.

The first hundred meters progressed smoothly. The jungle was relatively open and dawn's first light helped illuminate their way. But then the jungle thickened and quickly became dark once again. The men began losing their footing, tripping over vines and stumbling over exposed roots. Fortunately, Huong was out cold. But their movement towards the LZ slowed to a crawl.

Suddenly, Harper spotted a slight movement through the thicket ahead. He motioned for Vanh and Hamilton to stop. They froze and eased slowly to a crouch, allowing the stretcher to rest on the ground. Kneeling behind a vine-entangled tree, Harper raised his CAR to his shoulder. He flicked the safety to full/auto. They waited nervously, peering into the dark jungle with the hope that the movement was only Lam and Tran returning from the LZ.

The thicket suddenly erupted into a shattering fusilade of automatic weapons fire. Hamilton and Vanh, laying next to Huong, searched fruitlessly for a target. Holding his fire, Harper scanned the darkness for a clue to the whereabouts of the gunshots as they appeared to be directed somewhere other than at their position.

But then, as abruptly as it started, it ceased. Harper's frown faded as he glanced over at Hamilton who looked just as puzzled. Unexpectedly, Vanh hopped to his feet and dashed through the trees. The two Americans watched him until he disappeared into the jungle. Finally, they understood.

They joined Vanh as he embraced Lam and Tran. Lam was pressing a field dressing to a wound in his left shoulder in an effort to stop the heavy flow of blood. They stood over four dead NVA. Lam explained the NVA were the point element for a large search party traveling a few hundred meters to the northwest. In the points' careless haste, they had nearly collided with the two Indig, necessitating their immediate disposal. Harper nodded approvingly, motioning for the Indig to hurry back and pick up their wounded teammate. He knew it was only a matter of minutes before the search party would be on its way.

Vanh and Tran took over the duties as stretcher bearers. Harper and Hamilton led the RT in a zigzag route through the dense foliage. Lam had told them that the LZ was only another two hundred meters to the southwest, much closer than Harper had figured. If the choppers were on time, they would be over the area in ten minutes. They were going to have to hustle.

The route Harper had been following got a lot tougher as they turned off from the relative ease of the level thicket and headed up a steep slope, leading to the top of a ridge and the site chosen for the alternative LZ. The team stopped about a third of the way up the hill to allow Vanh and Hamilton to take over the stretcher. The crisp morning chill faded as the men began to steep in their own perspiration as they continued trudging up the incline. Huong moaned softly as he bobbed around on the poncho liner.

Vanh and Lam made it to the top first. They could already hear the magical popping sound of the Huey rotors far off in the distance. It looked as if the team had made it through another mission, Harper thought.

He hunkered down behind a bamboo thicket and unhooked the handset. Hamilton and Vanh lowered the stretcher, sat down and listened while Lam scanned the jungle for the NVA.

"Gladiator One, Gladiator One, this is Generous. Do you copy?"

There was an almost instant reply. "Roger, Generous. Good to hear from you," replied a thick New England accent. "How did you sleep last night?"

"Never mind. Just get my ass off this mountain."

"Roger, Generous. Out."

The Huey slick dropped through a funnel-like opening in the thick, triple canopy and hovered over the dry grassy LZ. The team darted from the thicket. Hamilton and Vanh stumbled over fallen limbs and half submerged rocks as they strained to keep Huong from flipping out of the stretcher. Harper, Lam and Tran held back to provide covering fire.

They slid the stretcher across the chopper floor and leaped aboard. Harper and the two Indig quickly followed. The pilot pulled back on the control stick and the Huey angled upward.

From the treeline, there was a futile attempt to fire on the ascending slick by three members of the search party who had arrived ahead of the others. But the helicopter was already several hundred meters above the LZ and banking sharply towards the border and safety.

*　*　*

"Ohhh, I like that," she murmured. McShane slowly and rhythmically worked himself around, concentrating

197

on making each single little movement pleasurable for the woman beneath him. They had made love more times than he could remember and now this was their last. It would be dawn soon and she had a plane to catch. He began to quicken his pace as he felt himself building up inside. Sensing his urgency and ready herself to explode, Ellen moved her sensuous body to meet his. They became totally lost in one another, unable to think beyond their one goal. Release. And then in a blinding moment of bliss, it was over.

They held each other tightly for what seemed only a short time to McShane. The first rays of light began to pour through the large sliding glass door of the bedroom, forcing Ellen to reality.

"Steve," she whispered tenderly. "I've got to get ready, my plane leaves in a couple of hours."

"I know," he sighed, rolling onto his back. "Just thought I'd drag this out to the last minute."

"Don't look so gloomy, honey." She swung her legs over the edge of the bed and sat up. "You can help me pack. Come on," she said cheerfully and slapped him lovingly on the butt.

"Yeah, sure. But let's take a quick shower together."

"Wouldn't miss it. But let's hurry."

He tried his best at one last fling in the shower, but she gently pushed him aside, placing a bar of soap in his hands with instructions to wash her back. Submitting finally to defeat, he dutifully took the soap and a wash cloth hanging from the shower door and scrubbed her back. It had been a one night stand he would never forget.

An icy drizzle began to fall over the city as McShane descended the apartment steps, carrying two of the largest Samsonite suitcases he had ever come across, to the waiting taxi idling on the narrow street below. Bounding out of the cab, the driver hurried around to the trunk and with a smile so cheerful that it seemed to cut through the dreariness, opened the trunk door. McShane lifted the bags into the trunk and returned the driver's smile. As he closed the trunk door, McShane turned and faced Ellen who was struggling to open her umbrella. Finally, she freed the catch and the canopy snapped open.

Not very adept at good-byes, he stood numbly in the rain thinking of what to say. Understanding, she spoke first. "Steve," she said softly, taking his hands, "this has been a beautiful night that neither of us will ever forget. And I want you to think of me, as I will you. Please write when you can at the address I gave you. I promise I'll write back."

She softly touched his wet cheek and tenderly kissed his quivering lips for the last time. He started to reach for her, but she swiftly moved away, stooping low as she slid into the back seat. The driver quickly closed the door and sped away.

McShane stood on the street corner for a long time, staring blankly down the street as the drizzle turned to a downpour. He knew he would never see her again. And then suddenly, he wished like hell he didn't have to go back to Kontum or Vietnam. His blue eyes began filling with tears.

* * *

He found Harper and Hamilton sitting at their favorite table in the far corner of the club, animatedly chatting with Owens and Wormington. He strode towards the table, swiping a beer from the tray of a passing bar maid. They were so wrapped up in their conversation that they didn't notice him until he pulled up a chair.

Harper said, "Look who's back! And not a minute too soon. How was Tokyo? Come on, sit down and tell us all about it."

He sat back in the chair and lifted the can of beer to his mouth, draining half the can in a few quick swallows. The men at the table waited patiently for him to finish.

"Well," he said, bringing the can down hard on the cigarette burn scarred tabletop. "There's really not much to tell."

"Bullshit!" laughed Harper. "Out with it. Tokyo's crawlin' with women. You can tell us. How did you do?"

"Oh," he replied timidly. "Well enough." Then, trying to change the subject he asked, "What were you guys talkin' about when I walked up? It looked pretty involved. Anything I need to know?"

"You're damn right you have a need to know," Harper said, pounding his fist on the table.

McShane, pleased that his question had gotten his buddy onto another subject, leaned forward to listen to what he had to say.

"This crazy asshole," Harper continued, pointing to Owens, "wants my team and yours, Steve..."

"Okay, John," interrupted Owens. "Keep your voice down. This is classified information. Most of the men in the FOB don't even know anything about the operation yet. And we surely don't want the waitresses to overhear you or every gook in II Corps will know about the operation."

"Yeah, all right," he said, lowering his voice to just above a whisper. "S-2 and S-3," he went on, "want you and me to take our teams into Prairie Fire as an advance recon party to set up communications and LZ's for a larger invading force. A brigade of strikers," he emphasized. "Each of the FOB's in II Corp are goin' to supply a battalion. In addition, Kontum is to provide the two recon teams. Us! It's part of a scheme concocted by the wizards down at MACV. A squadron of Air Force Jolly Green Giants will be movin' in with us."

"Where are they puttin' 'em and the people needed to make 'em run?" McShane asked.

"That was the first thing I thought of when the Air Force Colonel briefed me and Hamilton last week. It seems they're goin' to convert some of those old buildings in the east compound, behind the Indig Club, into barracks for the fly boys. It's goin' to be some big deal around here in the next couple of weeks."

Wheeling around in his chair, McShane grabbed Baby San, one of the cocktail waitresses, by the arm and pulled her gently to the table.

"Be nice, Steve," she said.

"I'll show you how to be nice," Harper said sweetly. "Meet me in my room after work."

Baby San stuck her tongue out at the drunk Sergeant and then focused her attention on McShane.

"Never mind that numba ten Harper, Baby San. Just bring me another beer, please." He quickly glanced around the table. "Anybody else want one?"

They nodded.

"Okay, bring beer for everyone. Except Harper."

She winked at McShane and then scurried off toward the bar.

"Shit, Steve. You've always had a way with the broads. Now tell me about the ones you and Dean had in Tokyo."

"I'll get to it later. But right now I want to hear more about this little incursion into Prairie Fire," McShane insisted, speaking once again in hushed tones.

"Well, first of all," Owens began, "the operation is called Ground Hog. MACV came up with the cute name and general concept several months ago. At least that's when I first heard about it. They were lookin' for a way to halt the heavy traffic along the Ho Chi Minh Trail and at the same time chalk up larger casualties."

"Whose casualties?" asked a smirking McShane.

"Well," replied Owens, showing only the slightest hint of a smile. "Naturally the NVA."

"Somehow," McShane said, "it's hard for me to visualize fifteen hundred or more strikers being flown in and dropped off into an AO they know nothing about. I mean, what the hell's their objective? Shoot up some dinks? Inflict a few casualties for the MACV scoreboard in Saigon? Bullshit!

"Actually, Steve," continued Owens, "there is a specific objective."

"And what's that?" he snapped.

"Sergeant Khai has told us the whereabouts of the 325th NVA Divisional Headquarters in Prairie Fire and alleged site of an underground POW camp."

"Yeah, well we certainly disproved that part of the plan." Harper chimed in. "Right, Sarge?"

"Not necessarily, John," Owens quickly responded. "Sergeant Khai thinks you were maybe a klick or so too far east. And the troops you bumped into were nothing more than a routine patrol. Not guards, as originally thought."

"Routine patrol, my ass!" Harper cried. "Those slimy little bastards knew we were there. They were lookin' for us. And found us!"

Everyone at the table laughed heartily.

* * *

Three days later, precisely at 0900 hours, the four engine Air Force C-130 landed at the Kontum airport and rolled to a stop. A group of officers and NCO's hurriedly drove their fleet of recently washed jeeps to meet the contingent of Air Force personnel disembarking from the rear of the plane. McShane and Harper each drove a jeep.

As they skidded to a stop alongside the C-130, Harper recognized one of the Air Force officers standing in the crowd of waiting men. It was the same Colonel, along with the Lieutenant Colonel from MACV, who had given him the briefing on Ground Hog. He was to be the Commander of the squadron assigned to the FOB in Kontum. Harper didn't like the man, nor did he care for the MACV Colonel, either. Guys like those two, he thought, adjusting his beret, could shorten your life span.

As the Colonel approached his jeep, Harper leaped over the door and presented him with his best salute. The Air Force commander, returning a less than snappy greeting, pulled open the door on the passenger side of the jeep and settled down into the seat.

It was a miserably hot and stifling humid morning. Two Air Force Sergeants sat down in the back of Harper's jeep. Their starched fatigue shirts, sopping wet with Mennen spray-scented perspiration, stuck to the hot canvas seat.

Harper popped the clutch, jerking the Colonel and his Sergeants back hard against their seats. Feeling the hard stares of his passengers, he accelerated, pretending his driving was perfectly okay. Looking into the rear view mirror, he could see McShane following close behind, driving at a breakneck speed to keep up. His passenger was the Lieutenant Colonel from MACV.

"Sir," Harper shouted above the whine of the noisy four cylinder engine. "When do your pilots get here with the Jolly Green Giants?"

The Colonel waited for Harper to negotiate a sharp s-turn on the narrow, one lane road leading into Kontum. He held tightly to the top edge of the rattling metal door.

"They'll be arriving sometime next week," he replied nervously, afraid to take his eyes off the road. "It all depends on how soon the FOB completes the facilities for the flight crews. Naturally, the sooner, the better. We're anxious to get this operation off the ground."

"Right, Sir," Harper said, hoping he didn't sound too sarcastic.

They drove in silence the remainder of the trip to the isolated Special Forces compound. The Colonel appeared to be totally disinterested in the new countryside as he stared straight ahead through the dusty windshield the whole way. It was something Harper couldn't understand, for each time he drove along the narrow two lane dirt road into town he could always count on seeing something different: the water buffalo boldly sloshing through the murky rice fields, paralleling both sides of the road, the giggling groups of Montagnard women walking into town under brightly colored umbrellas. Then there were always the mossy green Highlands themselves, jutting majestically above the fields and patties of Kontum.

Major Fernwood was standing underneath the broad wood awning of the headquarters building with his staff as the convoy of jeeps drove past the small cluster of civilian houses, and through the main gate. They waited until the jeeps stopped in front of the building, then strode out into the harsh light to greet their visitors.

Executing another one of his marginal salutes for the approaching FOB commander, the Air Force Colonel quickly got out of the jeep and ducked into the shade of the porch. His entourage of officers and NCO's followed closely behind. He fell into one of the several lounge chairs set up for the momentous occasion and helped himself to a beer from the ice chest. Wiping dust and sweat from his forehead with a clean, neatly folded white handkerchief, the Colonel surveyed the compound.

"Nice little camp you have here, Major Fernwood," he observed, swallowing several gulps of beer. "Damn nice. Looks better than it did during my last visit."

"Well, Colonel Spencer," replied the C.O. proudly, "the men have been working hard preparing the FOB for your boys."

"You've done one damn nice job," he said, taking a last look around before turning his attention to the icy beer he held in his right hand.

McShane and Harper drove their jeeps back to the motor pool, quickly hosing off the morning dust, then walked towards the Headquarters. Throwing his arm around McShane's shoulder, Harper told him, "Sergeant, you've done one damn nice job of fixing up the FOB. It's something you can be damn proud of. Now how 'bout a beer back at my room?"

"Not yet," replied McShane. "We've got that briefing in a half hour."

"Half hour's plenty of time for a couple of beers. Besides, I've heard the Colonel's briefing."

"I'm afraid you're goin' to have to hear it again. Let's go over to the mess hall. I'll buy you an iced tea."

As they passed by Headquarters, everyone was still huddled under the porch, listening to Major Fernwood brag about how his FOB was the best and how his men would score the highest kill ratio during Ground Hog. McShane turned to Harper and grimaced.

The weeks to come for the men at the FOB were the busiest since its conception in 1965. Far busier than the preparations they had made for Tet. For now they had to ready the FOB for an additional population of one hundred men.

The team of camp engineers, once again led by the wiry and tireless Sergeant Drake, worked long hours on the little section of uninhabited east compound real estate set aside for the Air Force. In addition to remodeling an abandoned building that would become home for thirty of the men, Drake's engineers built three new barracks alongside it. A new latrine was constructed to accomodate the extra waste the men would bring. A much larger building was built as a maintenance shop for the huge Sikorskys.

Papa-San, the stoop-shouldered foreman for the Vietnamese laborers, worked his men relentlessly in the hot, shadeless sun mixing concrete in an ancient, gas powered mixer borrowed from AID (Agency for Internal Development). The concrete was used to repair and enlarge an old chopper pad to accommodate ten of the larger Jolly Green Giants. The wet concrete was also poured into dozens of wood forms, making concrete blocks for the construction of the buildings.

Directly behind Headquarters, a huge pit was dug by one of Drake's men in a Case-back-hoe. A group of Vietnamese masons from Kontum then began laying some of the hundreds of concrete blocks manufactured by Papa-san and his men. A mystery at first, the Americans learned later that the hole was to become an underground communications center for Ground Hog.

This made little sense to McShane and Harper as they stood at the edge of the hole one day, mesmerized by the score of Vietnamese masons and laborers scurrying about like uprooted ants.

Looking up from what could have been an archeological dig to an uninformed passerby, McShane faced Harper and said, "John, I'm havin' a hard time believin' they're, — MACV, I suppose — spending all this time and money on an underground commo shack just to direct this one operation. I think Ground Hog is just the beginning. If it's successful, there will be other large Air Force supported cross border operations into Prairie Fire."

Harper sighed, and without looking up from the hole replied, "You may be right, Steve. Higgins, Drake's back hoe operator, told me in the club last night that he's got two more pits to dig over there."

He pointed to a vast field of vacant dust, spreading a hundred meters west of the hole. "And I agree. I don't think the FOB would go through all the trouble to build new barracks and latrines and helicopter pad for just one mission. Hell, if that's all it was, the Jolly Green Giants could fly from Da Nang or Tuy Hoi and pick us up. We wouldn't need to go through all this trouble."

"They'd better keep this thing ultra-secret," added McShane. "Or our long-haired, bearded friends back home will kick up such a stink that the country may never hear the end of it."

Shortly after their conversation by the pit, McShane and Harper were called into S-3's office by Owens. Colonel Spencer and Colonel Evans, the MACV officer, who had been commuting regularly between Saigon and the FOB, stood by the large map on the wall of the office. Lieutenant Anderson, the S-2 officer, motioned for the two Sergeants to be seated in the chairs set up for an apparent briefing.

As soon as they were seated, Colonel Evans began. "Sergeant McShane and Sergeant Harper." It was more like a question than a greeting.

"You two know more about Ground Hog than any other enlisted man assigned to the FOB, other than Owens, who's been in on our little secret for several months. What we need from you is more hard core intelligence before we launch the operation next month."

Turning to the map, he tapped a red circled area with his wooden pointer. The men had become all too familiar with the MACV engraved pointer and the red circle.

"To get right to the point," continued the Colonel.

Ohhh, shit, thought McShane, here it comes. "We're pulling Wormington and Hamilton off the construction detail and sending both your teams in day after tomorrow. Sergeant Khai will accompany your team, McShane."

He nodded.

"Hopefully, he'll be able to lead you to the POW camp. Harper, your team will be inserted three kilometers to the north."

He rubbed the tip of the pointer on a little spot within the circle. "Your objective is to gather information on the strength of the NVA in the area. We need to know the density of the jungle as well as any anti-aircraft guns they may have set up."

He stopped momentarily to take a few swallows from a glass of iced tea. McShane took the opportunity to steal a quick glance at Harper, who sat slumped in his chair, obviously unimpressed by the briefing. Returning to the map, Evans went on, "Both teams are to be on the lookout for possible LZ's and alternate LZ's large enough to accommodate the Jolly Green Giants."

"Sir?" interrupted Harper, now sitting up straight in his chair. "Is this to mean LZ's for the other FOB's as well as ours?"

"I was about to come to that, Sergeant Harper," Evans replied. "The other FOB's aren't goin' to be in on this particular operation, which we are now referring to as Ground Hog I. The Kontum FOB, you might say, is to be the guinea pig. If they're successful, then MACV and the Air Force will commit the necessary resources to expand Ground Hog into a major, devastating force that'll help bring this war to a swift end."

Clearing his throat, he took another drink from the glass of tea. "Are there any questions?"

"I don't think I have any. Sounds pretty routine," Harper lied.

"I've got one," McShane broke in, still mulling over the Colonel's phrase 'a major, devastating force.' "Harper's RT spent the better part of a week searching the jungle for that POW camp. They never found a thing. Does Sergeant Khai really think he can locate the place?"

"Khai," Evans replied, "figures Harper was in the wrong area. You'll be inserted a little further east. He says he's positive he can find it. Let's hope he's right."

"Yes, Sir," agreed McShane, thinking of the possible consequences if he wasn't.

"By the way," Evans added. "A company of strikers with their American advisors will be on an emergency stand-by at Dak To in the event you need help."

"Great, Sir," said Harper as he winked at McShane.

XIV

It was cooler than usual as he carefully made his way through the darkness to the RT's latrine. In a little more than an hour RT Illinois and RT Rhode Island were to report to the chopper pad. And McShane always enjoyed a last shower before a mission. It relaxed him; gave him a few private moments to clear his thoughts and psych up for the insertion. He figured he would need an extra long shower before this mission.

A bare 40 watt bulb shone dimly inside the doorway. Pushing open the screened door, he reached around the doorjamb and flicked the main light switch. Several more bulbs blinked on, spreading an even glow throughout the large bathroom. Seemingly, from out of nowhere, June bugs began beating themselves against the hot bulbs.

McShane placed his black leather toilet kit on a narrow wood shelf above one of the sinks. He kicked his white boxer shorts onto one of the benches outside the individual shower stalls. The room smelled of Lysol and mold. Scratching his crotch, he stepped into the stall and turned on the water. The cool spray hit him full on the face. Already he felt more at ease. Yes, he thought, I'll make this shower a long one.

Feeling refreshed at last, McShane stepped from the shower and walked over to the towel hanging on the hook next to his toilet kit. Quickly, he dried off, thinking as he looked into the mirror that he should shave. No reason for that, he concluded and pulled on a clean pair of underwear. As he was about to leave, his old buddy Deros playfully bounded across the floor and licked the tops of his bare feet. He bent down and scratched his chin.

"Hello, boy. Been out catchin' rats?" His tail whipped back and forth. "I want you to take care of yourself while I'm gone. Make sure Sergeant Carnes keeps you well fed. You tell me personally if he holds out on you. Okay?"

The dog began to whimper.

"That's enough of that. You're a big boy."

Deros sat down and offered him a paw.

"Come on. Walk me back to my room." McShane gave him one last scratch and stood up. Deros followed him out through the door and down the path, happily wagging his skinny black tail.

As they arrived in front of his building, McShane leaned over and gave Deros a quick pat on the head and said, "See you later, boy." The dog answered with a short yelp, then disappeared into the darkness.

Wormington was sitting on his bunk with his back pressed against the block wall. He was midway through the last chapter of the tattered copy of THE NEW LEGIONS McShane had loaned him. Looking up from the book, he asked, "What's Deros barkin' at?"

"He was just tellin' me goodbye," McShane answered, closing the door. "He always hates to see me go away. It means less bones and steak scraps. But I always make up for it when I come back."

Noticing his book clutched in Wormington's hands, he asked, "You 'bout ready to put that crap down and go on a real operation?"

Wormington chuckled, "Yeah, I'm ready." Then, glancing down at McShane's shower shoes and his white skivvies, he inquired, "But are you?"

Both men laughed. "Won't take me but a second," replied McShane.

Hamilton and Harper sat in the middle of their room and stuffed last minute supplies into their rucksacks. They were adding an extra one hundred and twenty rounds to their usual four hundred and fifty. S-3 told them to expect trouble, so they were preparing for it. Just to be on the safe side, Harper added four more grenades to his web gear. Even the Indig were taking along additional magazines and grenades. Tran added extra M79 canisters to his pack.

Both teams, however, were still a little leary of Sergeant Khai, particularly since Huong's unfortunate accident on the last hunt for the POW camp. Some of the team members felt he had purposely misinformed S-2 and S-3 as to the whereabouts of the camp, realizing full well they would run into trouble. But this time, knowing he was going along seemed to ease at least some of their minds.

Picking up his rucksack, McShane guided his arms through the straps until it rested comfortably on his back. At least as comfortable as possible. He helped Wormington with his ruck, as it was weighted down with the additional load of the PRC-25 radio as well as extra magazines, grenades and rations.

"Christ," McShane groaned, struggling to lift the pack. "You've got enough crap in here to take on the NVA by yourself. Why don't I stay here and you can take the team in?"

Ignoring the question, Wormington remarked, "Well, I didn't want to get caught short."

"Don't worry. At least I know where to come when I need something."

They were abruptly interrupted by the slamming of the screen door. "You pussies finished helpin' each other with your rucksacks?" Harper demanded. "Anytime you're ready, there's a couple of nice, clean choppers waitin' to take us for a little early morning ride."

McShane cinched Wormington's pack straps snuggly against his shoulders. "Yeah, I'm ready. Just helpin' out my Supply Sergeant here. He's single-handedly trying to carry S-4 on his back."

"Well, don't complain," Harper chimed. "He'll be a good man to have around when the fireworks start."

Jerking his thumb over his shoulder towards Hamilton, who sat slumped in a chair, he added, "I think Charlie and Dave must've packed theirs together. Charlie's is the same way."

"Then we're both in luck, right John?" asked McShane. Harper shrugged. Then, looking around the room to see if he had forgotten anything, McShane said, "Let's move out."

He flipped the light switch off as he walked out the door. Standing in front of the screened door, McShane twisted the black dial on the combination lock several times until the U-shaped bar swung open. With the door closed securely, he hooked the bar through the latch and snapped it closed. Just in case, the supply officer kept a written record of the combination.

The tips of the eastern mountain range were just beginning to lighten, turning a pastel orange as the four Americans walked a little unsteadily under the heavy loads towards the parked helicopters. Trang and Lam's men, squatting in between the two Huey slicks, spoke in hushed tones. Over by the command and control chopper, Sergeant Khai sat on his overstuffed pack, staring intently at the changing hues of the Highlands.

As McShane and Wormington approached, Trang and

the Indig stood and followed the Americans to the slick on their right. Lam's men joined Harper and Hamilton as they climbed aboard the other Huey. They sat down as comfortably as possible on the hard metal floors of the helicopters, and waited for the engines to come to life.

Suddenly, the serenity of the early morning silence was disturbed by the high pitched whine of turbine engines. The rotors slowly picked up speed. Poking his head out the chopper door, McShane flashed his buddy a last smile as he felt the shimmying helicopter lift off the concrete. Harper returned a thumbs-up.

Passing over the cluster of Montagnard huts in the Village below, McShane couldn't help but notice the expressions that spread across the youthful faces of the mercenaries. Expressions of excitement as a new mission began. Expressions he had seen on the way to every insertion. It reminded him of an elementary school class he had seen riding in a bus on a field trip to a zoo. For some reason he wished now he was on that bus.

Over Dak To, the two slicks and the command and control ship were joined by an escort of four Huey gunships loaded for bear. Besides their 7.62mm rapid fire General Electric Gatling guns, the ships carried a pair of 40mm rocket pods mounted on either side of the chopper's belly. They were an impressive sight, flying in formation in front of the slicks and C & C ship. Not to mention one hell of a morale booster to the men riding inside the helicopters.

Thirty minutes into the flight, the co-pilot swiveled in his seat, leaned over and tapped McShane, sitting with his back against the seat, on the shoulder.

As he lifted his head, the co-pilot shouted above the turbines, "We've just crossed into Prairie Fire. Be over the LZ in ten."

Straightening his head, McShane nodded. His gut churned, and he wished now only to be out of the noisy helicopter and on the ground. The Indig squirmed restlessly.

He got a brief glimpse of Harper as his slick broke away from the formation with two of the gunships. His LZ was located three kilometers farther north.

Nearing their LZ, McShane's team moved to the edge of the open chopper door. They slammed twenty round magazines into their CAR-15's. Flying down low the gunships separated, one flanking left of the LZ, the other to the right. The slick and C & C ship circled slowly above. Upon an "all clear" radioed from the gunships, McShane's Huey dropped quickly to the postage stamp landing zone. From above, the C & C ship directed the pilot to the LZ, as he was unable to see clearly the tiny LZ looming directly below him.

The slick hovered a couple of meters above the sloped terrain, while the door gunners nervously pivoted their bi-pod mounted M-60 machine guns, anxiously searching the tree line and brush for the enemy. Quickly, one by one, each man moved to the edge of the chopper, rested his feet momentarily on the landing skids, then jumped to the ground. In less than thirty seconds, RT Illinois was on the ground. The slick pulled back and joined the gunships, circling above the little clearing.

McShane moved the team to the tree line. Taking the handset from Hamilton, he radioed, "Hard Charger, this is Dynamic. Looks good down here. See ya in a week."

"Roger, Dynamic."

The team remained crouched for several minutes, silently surveying the surrounding trees and underbrush. Wormington was suddenly aware of a voice coming from the handset. He pressed it to his ear.

"Dynamic, this is Generous. Do you copy?"

Wormington handed it to McShane. "Roger, copy you five-by. What's your position?"

The handset crackled once again. Harper replied, "We're a few meters from the Lima Zulu, heading towards objective. Check with you at lunch. Out."

Returning the handset to his radio operator, McShane stared at his watch. It was several hours yet to noon and a hell of a lot of walking, if they wanted to reach the site of the purported POW camp by tomorrow. It would also take Harper roughly a day to reach the area near the little village of Ban Pakha.

It was Sergeant Khai who finally stood up first. So far he had kept a low profile, suspecting the Indigs' dislike for him. Nevertheless, he was anxious for the team to get going. He motioned to the Indig to rise and with some reluctance, they complied. The two Americans lazily pushed themselves up. It was all too easy to become lax sitting in the shade of the trees. McShane felt like taking off his pack, stretching out his legs and spending a quiet morning contemplating his bellybutton. He quickly shook the thought from his mind and concentrated on the task at hand.

With Khai taking the lead, they headed northwest. It was still cool and the team was able to make good time as they traveled over a long unused trail, partially overgrown with small ferns and scrub brush. Khai had remembered the trail from several years before when he trained recruits. A feeling of calm swept through McShane as he followed the old Sergeant, just knowing he was in the hands of such an experienced professional. He looked back over his shoulder, quickly studying his one-one and the rest of the team. They too seemed to walk with a sense of ease.

* * *

He swore at the beads of sweat that dripped at one second intervals from some invisible eye dropper hanging over his head. Signaling for the team to stop and rest, Harper untied the cravat from around his forehead and wrung out the perspiration. Squatting against a tree, he gulped down long swallows of tepid water from his plastic canteen. He peered into the jungle, wishing he could see beyond its dark entanglement of vines and limbs. It was some of the densest he had encountered in a long time. But then that's why S-3 sent us out here, he reflected: to recon the terrain and locate a suitable LZ large enough to land a Jolly Green Giant. He grimaced.

As he tried massaging away some of the soreness from his left thigh, where he had slept on a rock during the night, Harper studied his new men. With Huong in the hospital, he had been forced to take on another replacement, Duc. This was Duc's first mission and he was as yet untested in battle. Harper was a little apprehensive at having him along. He felt fortunate, however, that he still had his trusted interpreter, Lam, as his zero-one and Tran, who had taked over the M-79.

Through the jungle, Harper spotted Lam, who had been picking his way ahead of the RT in search of an easier route. He came up to Hamilton, his usual ear to ear grin replaced with a concerned frown. Lam crouched next to Harper.

He was clearly distressed as he said, pointing to the trees, "Beaucoup NVA. Maybe five hundred meters."

"How many NVA?" Harper asked.

"Not know. But many soldiers in big camp."

Turning to face his radio operator, Harper pulled the small folded map from his pocket. He tapped the fading green map and said, "The camp must be right here. Call in the coordinates, Charlie. Then we'll get a closer look. This might be what MACV's lookin' for."

While Hamilton radioed the relay station the map coordinates, Harper asked the interpreter, "How close can we get to the camp?"

The little Vietnamese, looking down at the ground, scratched the back of his neck.

When he looked up his frown had deepened. "Maybe I think we not want to see camp. Beaucoup NVA. Maybe call for Arc-light." His right hand flattened, becoming a B-52, as he passed it back and forth in front of his team leader's face.

Just then, Hamilton interrupted. "John, relay's waiting for an answer from the FOB. I think they may want us to check out the camp."

Lam winced.

"Well, Lam," said Harper. "It looks like maybe we go." They waited in silence for an answer. Duc, Vanh, and Tran, confused by the delay, stood idle, anxiously hoping for some word from Lam.

A few moments later, Hamilton raised the handset to his ear. He nodded to Harper and grinned. The Indig exchanged uneasy glances.

"Okay," smiled Harper. "The FOB wants us to go in. Tell the men, Lam, we'll take a break for lunch."

Lam left the two Americans and solemnly walked over to his team. They could tell from his idle stride that something was wrong. Huddling around him, Lam explained. They began to smile. The three mercenaries didn't share the interpreter's disdain for the mission. But then they were young and eager for the excitement such an operation would bring. Helpless, Lam sat down with his team and ate lunch.

Harper had acquired a taste for the Indig's squid and rice ration during his first tour in Vietnam. Realizing they contained less salt than the American lurps, he had begun trading the beef hash or chili-con-carne or beef stew rations for their squid. And with water so often at a premium on an operation, the lower salt content cut down on his desire to drink.

Curling the top of the foil package closed, Harper stuck it in the baggy pocket on the left side of his jungle pants, ready for a quick snack. With his thumbnail he worked diligently at dislodging a sliver of tenacle wedged in the space between his front teeth. He flicked the piece of squid into the underbrush and glanced over at his one-one. Deep in thought, Hamilton sat comfortably leaning against his rucksack, staring up at the trees.

Harper's question was barely audible. "Ready to go, Charlie?"

Tilting his head to the side, he replied, "Suppose so."

Harper rose to his feet, "Call Steve and tell him we're checkin' out the NVA camp. If we get into trouble we may need his help."

Hamilton nodded and made the call while Harper stood off to the side and pissed on an anthill. Buttoning his pants, Harper lifted his pack to his shoulders, once again keenly aware of the simmering heat. Visions of cold cans of beer lined up along a hundred foot bar momentarily took his mind off the heat, only to be suddenly wiped clear by the high pitched sound of Lam's broken English. He peered down at the pencil thin interpreter, trying his best to conjure up even half of the vision.

"I take point, Trung si," he interrupted. "You follow to big numba one mango tree. Not far from camp. Can see okay."

Nodding in agreement, Harper waved his arm forward. The RT fell in behind Lam as he pushed his way into the jungle. A beam of light eerily found its way through an opening in the thick canopy above. A reminder that a sun still existed.

* * *

Stumbling on what he thought was a vine, McShane spun around angrily, cursing silently both at the obstacle and himself. He had been daydreaming. A dangerous pastime. But as he looked back up the wash he saw nothing. Puzzled, he motioned for the team to stop. Backtracking a few steps, he bent down to where he thought he had tripped. He ran his hands over a clump of brush growing at the edge of the wash. About to admit his stupidity and give up the search, his thumb caught on something.

Wormington and Trang were standing over him, exchanging quizzical glances. They stooped down low to get a better look at their team leader crawling on all fours.

Entwined around McShane's thumb was a dull black rubber-coated cable, a quarter-inch in diameter. He laughed to himself, as he lifted the cable. It ran perpendicular to the wash for a few meters, then twisted north, following the general direction of the wash. Trang and Khai followed the cable while the rest of the team walked along the wash, eyeing the men's progress.

After several hundred meters, the cable turned east and the RT stopped as Trang and Khai pursued its course.

McShane took the opportunity to pull the team off the wash and rest behind a grove of trees.

Losing visual contact with their team, Trang and Khai proceeded cautiously. The jungle thickened. The men dodged and weaved their way around stands of elephant grass and gnarled vines that hung from the trees like executioner's ropes. But all the while, they kept the black cable in sight as it meandered ahead.

Unraveling his sweat soaked cravat, Wormington poured a little water from his canteen over the cloth. He wrung it out and repeated the process. He twisted the cravat into a tight roll and tied it around his forehead. Easing back against the trunk of the tree, he poured some of the water into his cottony mouth. Closing his eyes, he swished the water around with his tongue, swallowing some of it and spitting out the rest. He wanted to take a nap and forget all about POW camps, NVA headquarters and Ground Hog. But a tug at his sleeve forced him back to reality as his eyes opened to see McShane kneeling next to him.

"Don't fall asleep on me, Dave," he said. "I know it's real tempting. It's this damn heat."

"Nah, I wasn't goin' to sleep," Wormington replied. "Just thinkin'."

"About the operation, I hope." McShane gave his one-one a sly wink and then gazed off into the jungle searching for the two mercenaries.

* * *

Khai held up his left arm, abruptly bringing Trang to a halt. The former NVA Sergeant twitched his nose as he surveyed the clearing from behind the elephant grass.

A familiar and unmistakable smell penetrated his nostrils. A smell he had all but forgotten. The aroma of highly seasoned vegetables boiling in fish broth. Wrinkling up his nose, Trang too smelled the repugnant cooking odors. They looked around curiously for a campfire or a hootch. But they saw nothing.

Carefully, Khai circumvented the clearing, keeping to the shadows of the jungle. Trang stayed behind, covering the Sergeant with his M-16.

Something was peculiar about the little clearing that had suddenly appeared in the middle of the Laotian jungle. At first Khai was perplexed by what he saw. But, circling around the other side, he realized the clearing lacked any sort of vegetation except for a half-dozen evenly spaced clumps of elephant grass. And as he neared one of the clumps, the fish stink intensified.

The shock of the strong odors forced him to stop and study the grass. It paid off. For amidst the elephant grass, he noticed a plume of smoke rising from the backside of the grass. He eased down to his hands and knees and then to his belly, low crawling with the M-16 cradled across his forearms towards the smoke.

Reaching the grass, he paused. The air around the grass was foul with the cooking odors. Parting the grass with the muzzle of his rifle, he peeked inside. More grass. He crawled a little closer, the M-16 probing. Suddenly, the tip of the muzzle clanked against a metallic object. He stretched his arms inside and spread the grass apart. In front of him, a little cockeyed, stood a green six-inch metal pipe with a crudely made conical hood. Smoke was drifting slowly upward from the air shaft. Through another small pipe to the left disappeared the black communications cable.

Back pedalling his short legs, Khai moved away from the pipe and crawled quickly to another stand of elephant grass several meters to the left. He peeled back the grass. Another air shaft. Satisfied, he stood up and dashed back to the edge of the tree line. He made his way back to Trang.

Trang smiled with delight as Khai told of his findings. Khai then led Trang across the clearing, passing the smoking elephant grass, and into the jungle. He knew that somewhere, there had to be an entrance to the underground camp.

Less than fifty meters north of the clearing, the two men came upon another open area. And another surprise. Standing before them like two mammoth tombstones were a pair of recently constructed concrete bunkers. From an opening in each of the bunkers, poised in waiting, protruded twin, radar operated 37mm anti-aircraft guns. They were an awesome site from so close a distance. Khai and Trang crept up to the monoliths, concealed from the air by a canopy of camouflaged netting. They studied the doorways for the enemy. Cautiously, Khai peeked inside the first door. It was empty. They moved to the second bunker. Trang held the butt of the M-16 firmly to his shoulder as he sighted down the barrel at the entrance. Again, Khai eased around through the opening. In the corner, stacked to the ceiling, were scores of wooden crates. He stepped over to one of the boxes and began prying open the lid.

Trang flinched as he heard the top squeak open. Nervously, his eyes darted from the doorway. He thought he saw movement in the brush. Someone must have heard Khai. But there was nothing. He was beginning to imagine things. Once again, he turned his attention to the bunker. He wanted to get away from there in the worst way.

Closing the lid on the box of 37mm ammo, Khai retreated from the bunker. He double-timed across the opening with Trang hot on his heels. He breathed more easily as they entered the protection of the jungle.

McShane was beginning to worry about the two Vietnamese when he heard a twig crack on the other side of the wash. The team tensed as they slowly swung their weapons toward the noise. Slipping down behind the trees, they waited for the sound to show itself.

Trang swore at himself for being so noisy. He was getting too old, he thought. The jewelry store his brother wanted him to buy was looking more and more appealing. He made a promise he would look into it when he got back to Kontum.

Wormington eased his finger away from the trigger, relieved to see Khai and Trang emerge from the jungle. They hurried anxiously over to the men huddled behind the grove of trees. Flanking McShane, they sat down. Trang began to tell him what they had found.

Folding his hands in his lap, Trang waited for his team leader's reaction. McShane thought for a short time, then told Wormington to call in the position of the guns and possible POW camp Khai and Trang had found. He told Trang to have the team ready to move in five minutes.

XV

Leaving the security of his home built in the tiny hole at the base of the limb, the little yellow spider, suspended by a silver thread, swung out into the open. Had he known what lay ahead, the spider might never have left the comfort of his hole. As he spun the near invisible line out farther and farther, a large green object loomed up from below.

Mosquitoes swarmed unmercifully around Harper's head, repeatedly diving and sucking the exposed flesh. He swatted at a group of three as they burrowed deep into his neck. Another taxied up his forearm, zeroing in on a tender spot near his elbow. Harper reached down with his hand and flipped him into oblivion.

He tried to concentrate on the line of hootches some sixty meters from his position behind an outcropping of basketball-sized rocks. Laotian insects, he believed, must be the biggest in the whole damn world. Suddenly, something scampered down the side of his cheek. He swung upward with his dirty right hand and rubbed his jaw. A yellow streak stained his palm. Wondering what the hell it could have been, Harper once again continued his surveillance of the bamboo constructed shacks.

His team had been observing the hootches for over an hour. They all appeared to be deserted. He couldn't figure out what had become of the "beaucoup NVA" Lam had talked about. Unless he had been exaggerating about their numbers, if they existed at all. Well, he wanted to be damn sure the camp was deserted before sending in the RT. They could hang on for another few minutes. It had to be safe.

Lam crawled over to Harper from his vantage point several meters away. His team leader was involved in another dogfight with a buzzing enemy.

Lam tugged at his shoulder and asked, "What we do? NVA di di. Men want to go to village."

His heart wasn't in it, but he looked over at his interpreter and told him, "Okay, Lam, we go now." He quickly crept back and informed the team.

Harper patted Hamilton on the shoulder and motioned for him to get up. The Indig were instantly on their feet. The team fanned out and moved cautiously toward the first cluster of hootches.

Splitting the Indig into two fire teams with Hamilton leading one and Harper the other, the RT was carefully able to search the two rows of hootches that extended the length of the camp.   Harper couldn't help but think as he poked his head into a short doorway that some sort of evil was lurking about in the camp. An evil that would reach out and chew up the team and spit them back out into the jungle. Finding the room empty, he massaged the bridge of his nose, easing the tension.

The camp appeared only large enough to house a couple of companies. Not the large divisional headquarters MACV had briefed them on. Unless, of course, this was the headquarters, intentionally kept small to avoid detection. Or maybe it was one of several smaller camps comprising the division. Harper decided it was the latter.

They took a short break on the steps of what seemed to be the camp infirmary. Hamilton radioed in a brief message describing the empty camp, while Harper stared at the unfolded map balanced on his left knee. Now what, he mumbled. He speculated that the NVA had probably heard the choppers and moved to safer ground. He wanted to grab the receiver from Hamilton and tell the FOB he wanted to do the same with RT. But he knew better. He would have to continue the operation for a least another three days.

Rested, the two fire teams continued their exploration. The dim, diffused light filtering through the thick protective layer of triple canopy jungle overhead, added to the tension of the search. As Harper checked out the last hootch on the left side of the camp, he still couldn't shake the feeling of an evil intruder from his mind.

Discovering the hootch empty, like all the others, except for a woven straw mat and a captured U.S. Army wool blanket, Harper breathed easier. The little camp would be destroyed by an Arc-light at the end of the week and so would the intruder.

The two fire teams joined forces, once again becoming RT Rhode Island. They hurriedly retraced their steps back through the compound. It was almost a day's walk back to the primary LZ. They would start now. Spend the night somewhere in between and arrive the next morning. Once at the LZ, the team would wait for RT Illinois.

As the RT reentered the jungle, leaving the headquarters and its shanty town behind, Harper's ghostly intruder suddenly became reality. And bringing with it, all the fear and hell it could muster.

As Harper stepped around a small burrow, a searing, white hot pain rammed through his left shoulder, driving him hard against a tree. He looked down at a red hole torn in his fatigue shirt. Spurting blood soaked his shirt and ran down his pants legs. His eyes became transfixed on the warm, pulsating liquid. Somewhere, he could hear the sounds of automatic weapons fire. Lam would have to be informed. For now, he just wanted to sit down and sleep.

A hand tugged at his pants leg, then pulled him down behind a tree. The hand quickly slapped a field dressing over the wound. He tried to raise his head, but the hand shoved him back down. Why, he wondered, doesn't all the shooting stop?

Forcing open his eyes, a familiar face smiled down at him. A reassuring voice quietly said, "Hang loose, John. We bumped into a couple of NVA. It's okay, the Indig took care of 'em. But we've got to get out of here. I've called for an extraction. Can you stand up?"

No, he wanted to say, just give me my pillow. "I don't know," he finally whispered. "Give me a hand."

Hamilton freed the cumbersome rucksack from Harper's back and gently wrapped his left arm around the wounded team leader's good shoulder. Ever so carefully, he helped Harper to his feet. Blood oozed from around the edges of the bandage.

"We're going to try and make it to the alternate LZ. It's a lot closer," said Hamilton. But Harper never heard a word. He fell limp and unconscious into the radio operator's arms.

Throwing him up over his shoulder, Hamilton trotted over to Lam. He was going through the pockets of the dead soldiers.

"Lam, Harper's hit bad. Beaucoup bleeding. Maybe hit artery." He paused a moment wondering if his interpreter understood the word artery. "We di di, choppers be at LZ."

Lam took a look at his ashen faced team leader slumped over Hamilton's shoulder and grimaced. What he had feared earlier about the operation was now bitter reality.

* * *

Sitting up against one of the large roots jutting from the huge, towering mango tree, McShane slowly chewed the last of the beef hash he had saved from breakfast. He thought over the good, as well as the bad news Khai and Trang had brought back with them. MACV would certainly be pleased with the discovery of the underground camp, but on the other hand, quite enraged over the construction of the anti-aircraft bunkers. They were going to have to take another long look at Ground Hog and its chances for success. And he still felt the same about the operation. It was risky and dangerous and from the start, a long shot.

Off in the distance, he thought he could hear gunfire. Putting down the empty ration packet, he looked over at Wormington who was talking into the PRC-25 handset. All color seemed to fade from his normally rosy cheeks. Anxiously, McShane waited for him to finish with the radio.

Wormington got up and moved closer to his one-zero. Solemnly, he sat down and said, "John's been hit. Charlie's called for an extraction. He wants us to meet 'em at the alternate LZ ASAP. He thinks the NVA will be hot on their trail now, and they'll need all the help they can get."

Trang, squatting across from the two Americans, overheard their conversation. He was immediately on his feet, passing along instructions to Khai and the other team members. They rose instantly, eager for a fight.

With Khai once again taking the lead, the RT continued over the wash they had been following since breakfast. It was easy to follow and headed in the direction of the LZ. McShane prayed like hell they would make it in time.

As they rounded a narrow bend in a particularly overgrown spot in the wash, Khai suddenly thrust his arm above his head. The team came to a rapid halt, weapons poised. Palm down, he motioned for the team to get down. They eased to a crouch.

Roughly fifty meters up the wash, an NVA squad was hurriedly moving on a collision course with the RT. As quietly and quickly as possible, they stepped off the wash, finding whatever cover was available. McShane and Wormington took refuge behind a hedgerow paralleling the wash. They knelt down, training their CAR-15's on the oncoming enemy.

The squad, almost at a dead run, noisily passed in front of the hedgerow, erasing the imprint of McShane's jungle boot sole a few inches from his hiding place. He counted ten soldiers through a hole in the brush. Certainly an easy match for his boys, he thought, but not worth the risk of compromise. So far, they were only aware of the existence of Harper's team. He waited until the last man in the squad was safely out of sight, then stood up. The Indig followed suit. They moved back to the wash and continued their trek.

The afternoon heat combined with the breathless humidity made McShane feel as though he had been stuffed inside a pressure cooker. His fatigues, soaked with perspiration, clung tightly to his skin. God, what I wouldn't give for a deuce-and-a-half load of ice and beer, he almost said aloud.

The RT followed the wash as it meandered up a narrow ravine, heavily covered with scrub brush. The team's progress slowed. Concern for Harper and his men increased. But they were now less than three hundred meters from the top of the ridge and the LZ as they carefully searched the steeply wooded walls of the ravine for a simpler route.

McShane stopped the team for a quick break while he and Khai looked over the map. Their exact position was difficult to pinpoint. Their outdated map was based on old French maps drawn up in the '50s by the Legionnaires. The map indicated they were traveling over gently rolling terrain, not up a steep ravine.

Brushing the map aside, Khai abruptly turned to his left and began climbing up the hillside. Knowing full well that the old Sergeant's knowledge of the area was better than an archaic military map, McShane sighed and thrust the map disgustedly into his pocket. Unquestioning, he scrambled up the slope behind him. The team followed.

Near the top, the hill leveled out somewhat. They picked up speed. As it turned out, too much speed. For in their haste to reach the LZ and the crippled RT, they failed to see or hear the NVA platoon traversing the slope from the west.

The enemy platoon, in its haste to intercept Harper's team, failed to notice the little six man RT scrambling up the slope. And it was Khai, concentrating on his handholds in the rocky soil, who happened to look up and survey the hill. The NVA were one hundred meters above and to the left of their position. For the second time that afternoon he swung up his arm to warn the team. But this time he was too late. A tall North Vietnamese spotted Khai partially hidden in the brush, signaling to the RT. He motioned for his platoon to take shelter.

A devastating storm of Russian-made 7.62mm bullets suddenly rained down upon the recon team. McShane's team scrambled for cover. As Khai dived behind a hedgerow, a score of AK rounds slammed into his left thigh and buttocks. The impact twisted his skinny body into a pretzel-like form, throwing him powerlessly back down the hillside. He rolled to a stop between McShane and Wormington. McShane flipped him over as Worm-

231

ingon blindly fired short automatic bursts into the brush above. A gapping pit in Khai's temple told McShane all he needed to know. Together, they quickly turned his lifeless body over, positioning it in front of them, and returned fire.

The NVA platoon leader patted his favorite squad leader on the back and signaled for him and his squad to move down through the brush. With them they carried the platoon's only machine gun.

Pausing to reload, McShane turned to his radio operator and shouted, "We're goin' to end up like Khai if we don't get off this damn hill."

Wormington nodded, then fired off another half-dozen quick rounds.

McShane tugged on his sleeve, "Come on. They're eatin' us up. Let's pull back and get the Indig. Move up the ravine."

Nodding again, Wormington emptied his CAR at the invisible target. He reloaded and followed his one-zero, sliding down the slope.

Trang and Ngo lay about ten meters below the Americans, returning a steady fusilage of bullets. Wedged in a crouch behind a blackened tree stump, Billy methodically and swiftly dropped 40mm HE canisters into his M-79. A sinister grin appeared each time he pulled the trigger. And with every pull, the platoon grew a little smaller. The jungle was soon filled with the cries and screams of teenaged soldiers riddled with .223 caliber slugs and bits and pieces of spring steel bursting from the canisters. McShane and Wormington took refuge behind Billy's stump and returned the NVA's fire.

The NVA squad leader had lost over half his men. He tried maneuvering the survivors into position behind a group of saplings. He himself had taken charge of the machine gun after losing his two gunners to Billy's M-79.

A young Private, with his left arm severed an inch below the elbow, used his right hand to guide the metal belt of ammo through the squad leader's machine gun. He grimaced from a pain he had never known existed. Before his squad leader could praise him, one of Billy's rounds fell between the back of his legs. Their sudden screams were lost in the deadly sounds of battle.

McShane then instructed Billy to fire a tear gas canister into the ranks of the still standing enemy. Under the cover of the gas, the RT pulled back towards the ravine.

The last few enemy soldiers, choking and coughing, fired aimlessly at the retreating team. Holding back, Billy loaded another phosphorus canister into the grenade launcher and fired into the handful of NVA, staggering from the gas.

Billy sprang from his position and hurried to rejoin the RT waiting below in the wash. Sliding down the last couple of meters of the hill, he greeted the team with a broad, gold-capped grin.

Taking over the lead vacated by Khai, Trang skillfully guided the team up the ravine several dozen meters, then headed north once again. Scampering up the slope, McShane followed closely behind, then Billy, Wormington and Ngo, covering their rear. Near the top of the ridge, McShane glanced off to his left at the blackened underbrush where the platoon had gallantly stood its ground.

Charred and mutilated bodies lay scattered about in grotesque forms. A group of soldiers tried desperately to drag off their wounded. Billy raised his M-79 and fired one last round into the crowd of NVA. McShane quickly looked away and hurried to catch up with Trang, standing impatiently at the top of the hill.

Swarms of mosquitoes buzzed their heads, as the team double-timed along the ridge towards the LZ, now less

233

than two hundred meters to the east. Moving up and over a short rise, firing erupted in the vicinity of the LZ. They quickened their pace to a dead run, racing against an imaginary clock ticking away seconds of hope.

As they approached the gently sloping LZ, McShane stopped the team. He signaled for Trang and Billy to cross the log that spanned a narrow gully, and to investigate the firefight. The two mercenaries unsteadily crossed the log and disappeared into the eight foot high elephant grass.

Moments later, the RT heard the unmistakable sounds of exploding HE canisters from Billy's M-79 as he rapidly lobbed three rounds at an unsuspecting enemy. McShane thumbed the selector switch on his CAR while waiting for the Indig to return.

Without warning, Trang's skinny little frame popped from out of the grass. He waved his arm spasmodically, beckoning. McShane was halfway across the log before the interpreter put his hands down. Wormington tried to hurry across the makeshift bridge, but the extra weight of the radio in his rucksack forced him to walk more carefully. Two steps shy of reaching the other side, he slipped. Frantically, he flailed his arms to regain his balance. Ngo, right on the radio operator's heels, reached out with his right arm to steady him. He gave the American a firm shove, thrusting him head on into the elephant grass.

RT Illinois was unable to hear the whop, whop of the Huey rotors — music to any RT's ears — faintly echoing off the sides of the hills. They had taken refuge in two grass-lined bomb craters, evidence of a B-52 strike months before. McShane, Trang, and Billy huddled in the larger of the two and Wormington and Ngo in the crater to the right.

Billy and Trang had caught an enemy force, behind

some trees no more than thirty meters to their front, engaged in a firefight with Harper's team. Now, forced to split their men into two fire teams, the enemy suddenly found themselves in a deadly crossfire between the two teams and unable to return effective fire.

With unrelenting fury the team poured round after round down upon the trapped enemy. McShane caught a brief glimpse of Hamilton as he quickly poked his head around a tree, unleashing .223 caliber hell from his CAR-15. One by one, the NVA were silenced by the two RT's until finally the gunfire ceased.

Exuberant, the men of RT Illinois climbed from out of their craters and dashed across the LZ towards Harper's team. Their high spirits quickly faded as they came upon the remnants of RT Rhode Island.

Out of the six-man recon team, only Hamilton and Vanh were able to stand. Duc's face lay floating in a pond of bright red blood, his glazed eyes fixed upward as if searching for his lost body, which was crumpled in a heap a few feet away. Tran was heaving up blood and chili-con-carne from lunch. Red fluid mixed with bits of torn stomach lining poured from a pair of gaping holes in his gut. As Ngo knelt down to tie a field dressing around his wounds, a horrid, guttural hissing sound emerged from deep in his throat, splattering red mucus on his shirt. He pitched forward and died.

Suddenly, the men were conscious of the choppers, circling above. McShane stooped. "Hear that, John? We're safe," he whispered.

Harper managed a smile. He lay motionless behind a log where Hamilton had laid him before the firefight.

"They're making their descent now," he continued, wiping back a dirty tear. "The pilot told Dave there's a case of beer on board," he lied.

Harper turned his head towards the sound of the rotors.

The first of the two Huey UH-1B slicks swooped down upon the LZ. McShane and Hamilton carefully picked up Harper and carried him out onto the clearing to meet the chopper. Wormington followed a dozen paces to the rear, carrying Lam piggyback, his right foot dangling from a thin strand of tendon. Vanh and McShane's Indig held back, providing covering fire until the Americans and the wounded interpreter could reach the safety of the first slick. As the Huey hovered a couple of feet off the ground, McShane saw a bright flash come from the treeline.

Jumping into another of the craters that pocked the LZ, McShane and Hamilton sheltered their wounded friend. The RPG-7 rocket ripped through the cockpit. They shuddered as a bright explosion tore the half-million dollar craft in two. A storm of blackened green sheet metal and shredded flesh rained down on the three Americans huddled in the hole.

When McShane peered over the top of the crater, four F-model Huey gunships were circling over the treeline. Miniguns hummed their tune of death. The second slick began its descent. Once again they picked up Harper, and stumbling out of the hole, they made for the chopper. McShane jerked to a stop. He looked down in disbelief and horror at the shapeless mass heaped in a pile. Only the broken tubes, scattered metal knobs, and twisted antenna identified the remains of his radio operator. Lam's body, charred from the fiery blast, was nearly indistinguishable from the scorched earth.

A screaming door gunner forced his attention upward. He motioned for the men to hurry. They scrambled towards the chopper, McShane firmly holding Harper by his shoulders and with Hamilton grasping his ankles. Sliding the wounded team leader into the cabin, McShane glanced over his shoulder, searching for the Indig. Dammit, he thought, they must be chasing down the NVA. Grabbing Hamilton's arm, the two men sprinted over to the log where they had last seen their team.

A grizzly site greeted them. Strewn about the area were all that was left of McShane's and Harper's teams. Their Indig had been caught out in the open when the Huey exploded.

As they surveyed the scene for any possible survivors, renewed firing started up from the trees. The men turned and ran to the waiting chopper. Hamilton lunged into the slick and extended his hand to McShane. Taking his hand, with a left foot firmly placed on the skid, the chopper began to lift off. Suddenly, McShane winced and let go of the hand. He fell several feet to the ground. A patch of crimson spread irregularly over his back.

Hamilton screamed to the pilot to set the Huey back down. He leaped from the doorway. A frightened door gunner fired a continuous burst at the treeline. The gunships pounded the trees with rockets.

Staggering to rise, McShane stumbled forward. An AK round had slammed into the back of his right thigh, buckling him to the dirt. Hamilton bent down, wrapped his arm around his waist and hoisted him up onto his left shoulder. As he reached the chopper, the door gunner jerked back, then fell forward, slumping over the smoking M-60. A trickle of blood ran from his mouth.

Flipping McShane up onto the cabin floor next to Harper, Hamilton looked around the LZ one quick last time for survivors, then climbed onto the skids and into the helicopter. The pilot pulled back on the control stick. The chopper lifted up and away from the LZ.

The firing began to fade. Only the whine of the turbine engines disturbed his thoughts as McShane lay next to his buddy. They were safe. More than likely going back to "the world." He blinked open his eyes.

A smiling Dave Stevenson, the chase medic, knelt over him. "I'm going to turn you over, Steve." There was reassurance in the way he spoke. "Want to bandage your thigh."

Stevenson and Hamilton gently rolled him onto his stomach. Turning his head, McShane faced Harper, still on his back. "Well, buddy, we made it out of the shit again. Takes a lot more than a couple of platoons of slopes to put us under, right?" Not waiting for an answer, he continued, "Hey, I'm buying the first round when we get to the FOB."

A voice quietly spoke to him, "It's no use, Steve."

McShane looked up at Stevenson questioningly.

"I'm sorry, man. He didn't make it." Stevenson paused, waiting for some sort of response. Then he continued, "Harper's dead."

McShane closed his eyes, forcing back a cloudburst of tears.

Epilogue

"Dammit! Ain't that a batch of shit?" McShane yelled, waving his hand in front of the typed list thumbtacked to the bulletin board. "That's the third time this week. Those guys at headquarters are killin' us with these mickey mouse details!"

A short, red-haired Buck Sergeant looked down from another list tacked on the corkboard and faced McShane. "What's the matter, Steve? Got another garbage detail?"

"Damn right. It's the third time this week I've been assigned 3rd Group Sergeant-of-the-Guard. I pulled it last Saturday, then Tuesday and now tonight of all nights. Pay day Friday."

The little Sergeant laughed, forcing McShane to smile.

"Come on, Dan, let's get out of here."

They picked their way through the small groups of men eagerly waiting to check one of the several posted lists of details. It was the end of the first week of details for the 3rd Special Forces Group. They were to continue for another twelve weeks.

Outside, it was a bright, clear summer day. The two men hurriedly walked to the comfort of Dan Starks' air-conditioned '62 Impala Super Sport. Even at ten in the morning it was already hot and humid on Smoke Bomb Hill, home of the U.S. Army's Special Forces at Ft. Bragg, North Carolina.

"Where do you want to go before guard tonight?" asked Starks, opening his door.

McShane sat down in the spongy, black bucket seat and stared out the window at the vast, black topped parking lot. He had been out of the hospital at Ft. Bragg for less than two months and already he dreaded the beginning of each day on "The Hill."

It started with a formation and a roll call of "A" company in front of the three story, red brick barracks, housing most of the company's men. After a roll call, the Sergeant-Major read over the day's activities and then the men filed into the day room to check the detail lists for their names. The duties ranged from pulling guard to K.P. to working at the motor pool to painting, to mopping the barrack's floor, to picking up others' cigarette butts in the 3rd Group area. The men lovingly referred to the details as "ash and trash." It was no wonder the three company clerks were swamped in stacks of 1049's requesting assignment or re-assignment to Vietnam.

"Hell, I don't care," McShane replied. "Got seven hours before I report for inspection."

Starks fit his key into the ignition. There was a sudden rumble. The Impala pulsated violently as the massive 427 cubic inch hemi roared. McShane watched the silver needle on the tach climb to 4200 RPM. Suddenly, he was flattened back into the naugahyde seat as Starks popped the clutch, catapulting the hot Chevy into a screech through the parking lot. Grabbing the edge of the seat, he could feel the rear tires losing their grip and the rear end fish-tailing back and forth across the asphalt. McShane prayed that all the M.P.'s were busy drinking coffee or ticketing officers' daughters for jaywalking.

Stopping at the red light at the corner, McShane suggested, "Take me down to the Main PX. I want to call Mrs. Gardner at the puzzle palace in D.C. Maybe she can get me out of Bragg. If anybody can, she can."

"Okay. Hang on." Hell, he'd never let go.

He found an unoccupied phone at the far end of a long row of glass enclosed booths. He inserted a dime, dialed "O" and waited. Shortly, a sexy, southern drawl spoke into his ear, "Operator. May I help you?"

Closing his eyes, McShane tried to visualize what the operator looked like, "Yes, I'd like to place a person to person call to Mrs. Gardner at the Pentagon."

"Do you have the number, sir?" she asked.

"Sorry, I don't."

The sexy drawl replied, "One moment please."

* * *

McShane was careful to touch only the recently polished brass doorknob of the C.O.'s door. A small sign taped to the left read, FRESH PAINT.

The C.O. looked quite comfortable sitting in his overstuffed leather chair. The grey metal desk was neat and tidy. He peered up from the manila folder and gave McShane his best how-are-you smile and said, "Sergeant McShane, good to see you. Please, take a seat. Make yourself at home."

"Yes, Sir," he answered, glancing around the room for a chair. Now all he needed, he thought, to make himself really at home would be a beer and football game on T.V. But he settled on the uncomfortable metal folding chair in the corner.

Tapping the folder, the C.O. continued, "Couple of citations came in for you today. A Silver Star for your POW operation and another oak leaf cluster for your Purple Heart. How many clusters does that make now?"

McShane thought it over a moment, staring out the window at two prettier than usual WAC's wiggling their way to work.

"Well, Sir," he replied, trying to sound modest, "I haven't really kept track."

He struggled to keep the two young girls in view from the corner of his right eye but gave it up, adding, "I think it's my fourth."

"You certainly have an exemplary record, Sergeant. Three tours in Vietnam. You know they're beginning to pull out American troops?" He closed the folder and sighed, "It'll be over in two or three years."

McShane frowned. "Yes, Sir."

"Something else came for you today." He picked up a stack of typed papers stapled together. Leaning over the desk and without standing, he held them out, forcing McShane to leave his chair. He took the papers from the C.O.'s outstretched hand and quickly scanned over the first page. "Got any ideas where you'll be spending your leave?"

"Umm. Maybe Japan, Sir. There's someone in Tokyo I'd like to see again."

The C.O. walked around from behind his desk and stuck out his hand, "Well, Sergeant, good luck. I'm sure you'll have a great time in Tokyo."

McShane squeezed his hand firmly.

"I was there in '59."

"Yes, Sir," McShane said, giving him his best salute. He turned and walked out through the still wet door.

Outside in the hall, he re-read the paragraph that began:
Subject: Sergeant First Class, McShane, Steven A. RA 10 123 055. Individual is to report to Ft. Lewis, Washington, Overseas Replacement Company ASAP for further assignment to Headquarters Co., 5th Special Forces Group, 1st Special Forces, Airborne, APO 96240, Republic of South Vietnam. Individual is authorized 30 days leave and will comply...

Smiling for the first time that day, McShane stepped through the hall door and out into the harsh southern sunshine.

MORE SUSPENSE/THRILLERS FROM BART